8—
10/10
F

ALTERED STATE

OTHER BOOKS AND AUDIO BOOKS
BY GREGG LUKE:

The Survivors

Do No Harm

ALTERED STATE

A NOVEL

GREGG LUKE

Covenant Communications, Inc.

Published by Covenant Communications, Inc.
American Fork, Utah

Printed in Canada
First Printing: June 2009

16 15 14 13 12 11 10 09   10 9 8 7 6 5 4 3 2 1

ISBN 10: 1-59811-832-3
ISBN 13: 978-1-59811-832-2

To my children: Brooke, Erika, and Jacob.
You are my constant joy.

ACKNOWLEDGMENTS

As usual, there are scores of people—dear friends all—who have contributed to the creation of this novel. I would especially like to thank my amazingly patient editors at Covenant Communications (particularly Noelle Perner), my family, David Dickson, Melissa Duce, Dr. Aaron Jones, Shawn Osborne, and Betsy Green. Foremost, I would like to thank fellow author Tracy Winegar, who shared her personal experiences in raising autistic boys, and who allowed me to use her last name.

ONE

Saturday, September 5

Approaching the shaded area, Peter Stokes paused as a feeling of unease slithered up his spine. The grassy nook on the Utah State University campus was usually one of his favorite spots in which to collect his thoughts; a large sycamore provided the perfect backrest, and the location was somewhat secluded and always tranquil. But today it seemed different. Although everything *looked* the same, the area now felt as menacing as a steel trap poised to spring with bone-crushing force. He shook his head at the silly premonition and headed under the tree anyway.

Perhaps if he read some scripture first . . .

Peter opened his French translation of the Book of Mormon, starting at 1 Nephi for the umpteenth time. It was the personalized copy his mission president had given him just before returning home. In it, President Chalmet had written the promise, "If you read from this French Book of Mormon every day, you will retain your language skills and your testimony."

> *Moi, Néphi, étant né de bons parents, je fus, pour cette raison, instruit quelque peu dans toute la science de mon père; . . .*

It had taken Peter most of his mission to learn French. He still considered himself a novice at its pronunciation. It felt like he had to have a mouth full of spit to get it just right. Many of the inflections, syntax, and grammatical idiosyncrasies were still a mystery to him, but he felt the spirit of the language deep within his soul regardless of how he pronounced it.

Peter leaned back against the sycamore and continued reading. He liked the quietude the university grounds offered on the weekends. Fewer distractions, less stress, easier to concentrate—unless, of course, you were being pestered by a bunch of obnoxious birds.

He closed his eyes and grimaced at the magpies squawking at each other in the branches overhead. Although visually exquisite, the birds struck him as more of a nuisance than creatures of beauty, especially when it came to their abrasive calls. The musical background in him preferred birds that actually *sang* songs as opposed to those that seemed to vomit them. Maybe they were the reason he felt so uneasy.

"They give me a headache," a female voice exclaimed.

Peter opened his eyes to see a very attractive girl standing in front of him. She was staring up at the pesky birds with an expression of outright disdain. The clear afternoon sun highlighted her blond hair, giving it a brilliant, halo-like outline. "You wouldn't happen to have a BB gun on you, would you?" she asked without meeting his gaze.

He blinked. "I, um . . . I don't believe they're allowed on campus."

"Too bad," the girl said, finally looking down at him.

Peter's mouth formed a half smile as he gawked at the beautiful stranger. She had purple eyes—or at least eyes so darkly blue they could easily be described as violet. Perhaps she wore designer contact lenses. Or perhaps it was simply the harsh backlighting that altered his perceptions. In either case, her gaze was demure yet hinted at unrestrained mischief.

Suddenly realizing he was staring, Peter glanced up at the birds and quipped, "Why? Are you part of some anti-magpie society intent on wiping out the species?"

The girl laughed. "Heavens, no. I was only going to scare them away so you could study without distraction." She hiked her backpack higher on her shoulder and angled her head for a better look at what Peter was reading. "What *are* you studying, anyway?"

"My Book of Mormon," he said with a shrug.

Still smiling, the girl doffed her backpack and rested it against the tree. She then sat down and scooted unexpectedly close to Peter to peruse the open book. "French?"

"*Oui.*"

"Wow. What a gorgeous language—so mysterious and fluid. I wish I could speak it."

At that moment, Peter couldn't remember much English, let alone French. The girl kept her eyes focused on the open page of scripture, doing her best to mouth some of the words. The hint of perfume teased Peter's sinuses, and the girl's unabashed forwardness had him strangely tongue-tied.

He knew he wasn't the best-looking guy on campus—far from it, in fact. But he wasn't exactly homely either. Peter considered himself worthy of an initial glance but rarely a second look. For whatever reason, this girl didn't seem to care what he looked like. So much for the *birds* distracting him.

Finally finding his voice again, he said, "My name's Peter."

She looked up. Yep, they were purple all right. "Jacqueline."

"Hi."

"Hi."

"*Jacqueline* is French, you know," he said, putting a French *Zjah-* at the beginning of her name, and an *-eene* at the end.

"Is it?"

"Yep."

An awkward silence passed before Peter asked, "Are you wearing contacts or something?"

She frowned playfully. "Come now, Peter. Is that your best pickup line?"

"Hey, whoa," he balked. "Who came up to who here? It's no line; you just have very colorful eyes."

"Oh, that. I put food coloring in them every night. It stings a little, but I like the results. Don't you?" Jacqueline asked, looking at him intently.

Peter gave a confused frown. He wasn't stupid enough to believe she actually dyed her eyes with food coloring, but he decided to play along. "Um, sure. Whatever you say," he answered.

The magpies began chasing each other through the branches of the sycamore, and their squawking increased in volume. Jacqueline looked up and glared. "You sure you don't have a BB gun?"

He laughed. "I'm sure." Closing his Book of Mormon, he continued. "Want to go someplace else?"

She flashed a coy smile. The look was obviously well-practiced. "Are you asking me out on a date, Peter?"

"Whoa," Peter said again, squirming aside an inch or so. "No. I don't even know who you are."

"I told you: I'm Jacqueline."

Peter cocked his head and scrutinized the girl sitting next to him. She was *very* pretty—drop-dead gorgeous, in fact. And she had a swimsuit figure to boot. No doubt she could have her pick of guys on campus. So why was she coming on to him? Or was she? Perhaps she was just being friendly. Overly friendly. Friendly to the point of audacity. And that scared him a little. Well, okay, a lot.

"Sorry, right, Jacqueline. It's just that I'm not used to girls coming up to me and initiating conversations."

She looked truly curious. "Why not? You look like an interesting guy. And you speak French. That's totally cool."

He tried to smile. Perhaps she did come across too strong and even seemed a bit bubble-headed . . . but those eyes!

The magpies screeched again and fluttered closer, causing both students to flinch. "Let's move someplace where we won't risk getting splattered," he suggested.

"Good idea," she said, standing.

Jacqueline walked briskly to a bench across the courtyard. It was in full sun and, being a Saturday, was conspicuously empty. Peter tagged along then sat and glanced back at the sycamore. The magpies still squawked, but it wasn't as bothersome from this distance.

"So, have you been a student here long?" Peter asked, trying to sound more confident than he felt.

"About a year now. I'm studying marketing. How about you?"

"Music and French."

"Where did you learn French?"

Peter raised an eyebrow. Since the majority of students at USU were Mormon, he assumed she would know he had acquired a second language serving an LDS mission. Perhaps she wasn't a member of the Church.

"You're not from around here, are you?"

"No. Is that a problem?" She sounded somewhat put off by his question. Almost defensive.

"No, no. It's just that most people here would assume I learned French on my mission."

"Oh, of course you did." She laughed, punching him playfully in the arm. "That really is so cool, Peter. Music *and* French. You must be way smart."

He shrugged. "Not really."

Jacqueline smiled admiringly. Her amazingly white teeth and a single dimple in her left cheek were the *pièce de résistance* to her model-worthy looks, and the *coup de grâce* to his self-assuredness. He was instantly smitten.

She flashed a quick glace at the sun. "It sure is hot today," she said, teasing her long hair off the back of her neck.

"Yeah. September can get that way in Cache Valley," Peter said.

Jacqueline smiled again and then opened her backpack. "You want an energy drink? I've got an extra one."

"Sure," he said, not wanting to refuse this girl anything at the moment.

She retrieved a can of Tribe, one of the newer energy drinks available on the market. Peter normally didn't drink that kind of stuff. It always made him feel more jittery than energized. He'd heard that the amount of caffeine in one can of Tribe bordered close to overdose concentrations. Besides, his church didn't condone the consumption of such addictive substances. But Tribe was supposed to be different in that it contained no *added* caffeine. It had some guarana and yerba mate—both natural sources of caffeine—but its thermodynamic energy supposedly came from an herbal substance called the candle nut. It was indigenous to the Australian outback and was touted to have been used for centuries by the Aborigines on long hunting excursions. The plant's energy-laced fatty oils provided the stamina needed to chase down animals over vast expanses of open desert. At least that's what Tribe's advertising gurus claimed. Many teenagers who had tried the new product discovered that chugging a can dry led to a wicked buzz they coined "going tribal."

Jacqueline snapped open the pull tab and handed the can to Peter.

"Never tried one of these before," he said while inspecting the container's artwork. The jet-black, sixteen-ounce can was covered with eerie red and purple scrollwork and dark umber caricatures resembling Anasazi figures. The center of the can displayed a repeating chain of feral, doglike creatures with bristling body hair and large, pointed teeth. The product lettering dripped like blood, giving the can an overall feel of danger and foreboding. Perhaps that was why it was rapidly becoming a best seller, especially among young men.

He tipped the can and took a quick sip. It had a peculiar taste: strongly herbal but not bitter, almost fizzy but not carbonated, bracingly sweet but not headache-inducing. Curiously, he felt instantly refreshed. Peter swirled the can and took another sip.

"Good stuff, huh," Jacqueline said. "It's my favorite flavor. It's called 'Dingo's Dance.'"

Peter nodded. "Not bad at all."

"But don't just sip at it. Walk on the wild side, Pete. Go tribal," she said, giving the can a gentle boost toward his mouth. "That's how I like to do it."

It seemed odd that this girl was so anxious to have him drink the entire thing so quickly. But then again, his encounter with Jacqueline had been pretty odd from the get-go.

He finished the entire sixteen ounces in a few loud gulps. It took only a few minutes before he felt a curious buzz tingle through his veins, making him feel not only refreshed but energized to the point of zero fatigue and maximum alertness. A rapid, scintillating euphoria surged through his entire being. He instantly felt limitless, fearless, incapable of failing at anything. And he liked that feeling. He liked it a lot.

"Thanks, Jacqui."

"Jacqueline. I never liked 'Jacqui' or 'Jack.'"

"Sorry."

Jacqueline reached into her backpack again and pulled out a slim MP3 player. Its metallic exterior was colored much like the can of Tribe.

"So are you from Salt Lake or something?" Peter asked, feeling more confident by the second.

Jacqueline shook her head as she worked an earbud into place. "No."

He waited for more, but she seemed strangely reluctant to offer further information.

"So, where *are* you from?" he prodded.

"Santa Barbara," she said, working in the second earbud.

"No kidding—California? Man, that's great," Peter said, suspecting that his chance for further conversation was slipping away. "I'm from Mendon, myself. You know where that is?"

"I think so," Jacqueline answered while tracing her finger across the touch pad to load a specific song.

Peter frowned. The way she'd been flirting with him, he'd assumed she wanted to talk and get to know each other. In fact, he now felt confident enough to ask her to a movie that evening. But she suddenly seemed bent on listening to her music collection instead of engaging in conversation. He shrugged and pulled out a music history study guide. At least they were still sitting together.

Almost fifteen minutes passed in silence before another word was spoken. He saw Jacqueline glance at her watch a few times then finally pause her MP3 player. She removed the earbuds and shook out her long hair. Leaning close and putting her lips to his ear, she whispered, "You wanna hear something totally wicked?"

Peter detected her perfume again along with a pronounced, throaty suggestiveness in her voice. "Okay," he said, praying his voice would not crack as it often did in these situations.

She handed him the earbuds and waited as he wriggled them into place. He nodded when he was ready. She toggled the PLAY command and suggested he close his eyes, which he did.

The song was unfamiliar to Peter and sounded nothing like the music he'd heard on the local pop station. It began with a seductive cadence of low bass notes and percussion; then something that sounded like a panpipe joined the pulsating rhythm, along with some maracas and a plucked stringed instrument. After a sensuous underscore was established, an Australian didgeridoo warbled up and began a deep, buzzing ululation that was both haunting and spellbinding.

Peter felt astonishingly moved. His entire being was tingling, and his mind cleared from all previous thoughts and worries. He was happy—no, more than that. He felt uplifted in body and spirit. Nothing was wrong in the world. Nothing *could* be wrong.

The song ended all too soon, but Peter remained floating in his altered state of euphoric bliss. Then Jacqueline's lips were at his ear again. "The only thing we have to fear . . ."

". . . is fear itself," Peter voiced, finishing the oft-quoted phrase by Franklin Delano Roosevelt. He didn't know why he said it; it simply seemed the right thing to do.

"Remove the earphones," Jacqueline said in a tone that was more of a command than a request.

Peter complied, again not knowing why. Somehow, he felt he was *supposed* to obey—that if he *did* obey, he would be greatly rewarded.

"Stand up," she said.

He did.

"Sit down."

Sure.

"Retrieve your Book of Mormon."

Peter pulled out his Book of Mormon without hesitating.

"Tear it in two," she said flatly.

Peter's mind screamed in revolt. An emotional inner voice begged him not to do it. The book was sacred scripture—he believed that with all his heart. This girl's command went against everything he knew, everything that defined him. He raised the book to his chest. His hands trembled, and his forehead beaded with sweat, yet he calmly adjusted his grip and bore down harshly. He could not believe his eyes as he watched his own hands do the unthinkable. With surprising ease, Peter tore his scriptures in half, right along the spine.

With the despicable task completed, a numbness settled over him. Confusing tears stung his eyes as he stared at the tattered half of sacred writings held loosely in each hand, but he knew he wouldn't actually cry. The act had been reprehensible, and yet there was little true guilt that followed. He had done what was commanded of him. He had obeyed, and for his obedience he was rewarded with an unbelievable feeling of pride and deep, intense satisfaction. He detested what he had done, but not that he had done it. Instead, he experienced an immeasurable sense of . . . *ecstasy;* an overwhelming rush of fierce satiation that swept through his body. A smile pulled at the corners of his mouth. A low sigh escaped his lips. He was absolutely . . . fulfilled.

Jacqueline stood. "Now, go back to your place under the sycamore tree, and wait for the carillon to chime. When it does, you'll return to your former state and not remember anything about our encounter. Understand?"

Peter nodded. "Yes, I do."

Jacqueline smiled, leaned over, and gave Peter a quick peck on the cheek. Then she walked away, taking her MP3 player and the empty can of Tribe with her.

Peter knew exactly what she had said. He knew it sounded like something out of a 1960s spy movie, where an agent is drugged and then forced to do something against his will. It all seemed so absurd. The word *brainwashed* came to mind, but that wasn't quite right. He could stop anytime he wanted to. Only he didn't *want* to. The feeling, the drive, the need was so compelling that nothing else seemed to matter.

He moved to the sycamore, sat down, and began reading from one of the halves of his French Book of Mormon. The fact that his precious book was ruined registered with him, but at that moment, it didn't concern him. He had needed to comply—that had been his primary concern.

In just over five minutes, the carillon chimed its classic Westminster eight-note descending and ascending tune. Peter closed his eyes then opened them and looked around. Nothing had changed. It was as if he had merely fallen asleep and dreamed of . . . something.

He looked down and saw the torn book in his hands. *What the—?* He drew a sharp, anguished breath. When did that happen? He looked around but saw no one nearby. Obviously, something bizarre had just transpired, but what?

The strangeness of the inexplicable event evidenced in the torn book in his hands scared him beyond imagination. His entire body began to tremble. He was mortified, frightened almost to the point of passing out. And then he started to cry.

TWO

"Zimbabwe? Where in the world is Zimbabwe?" Homer Winegar asked with a chuckle, already knowing the answer.

"Africa," his son answered without hesitation.

"Africa? My word, Zachary, you must be the smartest boy in the world."

Sitting on their couch, the nine-year-old responded by playfully bumping against his stepdad's shoulder. "No, you are, Daddy."

As Morgan Winegar sat at the kitchen table working on next week's psychology lessons, she occasionally looked up at her husband, who was doing a word puzzle with her son. Each time she did, heart-felt gratitude welled within her.

Shaking her head, she closed her eyes and inwardly chastened herself. *Our son,* she had to remind herself—even after three years of marriage. She still could not believe how effortlessly Homer had bonded with her Zachary and, perhaps more amazingly, vice versa. At times like these her emotions were so poignant, so overpowering, she could barely stop her chest from tightening or her eyes from misting.

Homer Winegar had loved Zachary almost immediately, showing the kind of intrinsic, father–son bonding she had only read about in conservative child psychology texts and LDS books and magazines. That was the first thing that had attracted her to him.

Homer was an average-looking man: average height, average weight, average build. His pale brown eyes and thinning brown hair were almost boring. His lean face, fair skin, and tenor voice did not conjure images of debonair men of mystery or rugged back-woodsmen. And his first name was anything but dashing or romantic. Yet Homer boasted an inner confidence and an aura of stability that more than made up for any physical shortcomings. Additionally, he was honest—a trait generally lacking in the world. Besides, Morgan knew that outward appearances were often devastatingly misleading. Such was the case with Zachary's biological father.

Morgan had fallen for Bradley Marquis while attending the University of California in San Diego on a full-ride scholarship in psychology. The fast-paced, highbrow lifestyle of southern California was a culture shock for the nineteen-year-old country girl from Brigham City, Utah. Her family was assumed to be from one of the many lines descended from Brigham Young. Brad was from a well-to-do family in Del Mar, California, some twenty-five miles up the coast from San Diego. Brad's father—tanned, handsome, and authoritative—was the head of an elite law firm in downtown San Diego. His mother was the quintessential professional's wife: classy, elegant, and formidably confident.

Morgan had met Brad at the beginning of her second year. Brad had sat next to her the first day of Essential Economics and asked if she wanted to *essentially economize* their efforts by studying together. It was a silly line, but far better than the ones she got from the boys back home: "You got a Band-Aid? I just scraped my knee falling for you." Or, "I've got a mouth full of Skittles. You wanna taste the rainbow?" Or highest on her gag-reflex-o-meter: "Your dad must be a thief because he stole the stars from the heavens and put them in your eyes."

Much to her surprise, Brad's approach wasn't merely a ruse to get her phone number. He seemed honestly fascinated by her and her interest in economics. On top of that, Brad was seriously good-looking: beach-blond locks; a firm, square jaw; piercing, gunmetal-blue eyes; dimples; and a knee-weakening, movie-star smile. His broad shoulders and sculpted body didn't hurt things either.

Their first date was the following weekend. Brad moved a little too fast for Morgan in more ways than one, but she figured it was simply the way things were done in southern California. She certainly did not want to come across as the shy, naïve cowgirl from the sticks, so she went along with just about everything.

She quickly found that she loved the attention she got just from being with Brad—on and off campus. She also found that he was a good kisser. A *very* good kisser. They dated regularly for a year. Morgan was so totally swept away in the rush of her new life that she didn't see the tidal wave coming until it was crashing down on her.

It struck unexpectedly at an all-night, end-of-semester party aboard the Marquis family yacht. Being raised in the LDS faith, Morgan had never consumed alcohol, nor did she have any desire to start. Graciously declining one drink after another, she stuck to the fruit punch, even if it did have a funny aftertaste. Then, late into the party, someone slipped her an ecstasy-laced pineapple-mango smoothie. The next thing she remembered was waking up in the master berth next to Brad, naked, humiliated, and, she found out a few weeks later, pregnant. He offered to pay for an abortion. She was resolutely pro-life. Morgan's parents offered to raise the child back home in Brigham City, but she felt it wasn't right for them to assume responsibility for her error in judgment.

It took a full month, but Brad finally came through for her with a strained marriage proposal. Morgan figured it was either out of a desire not to soil the family name or fear that she might press date-rape charges in an effort to secure her financial future. But her innate sense of pride would never allow her to do that. In the end, Brad claimed his proposal was simply a heartfelt outpouring of moral responsibility. Oh, and the fact that he truly did love her, too. Morgan sensed that neither explanation was completely true.

Although Brad's parents disapproved of Morgan's lack of recognizable social genealogy and her puritanical lifestyle, she *was* an exceptionally pretty young woman: thick, amber-blond hair; vivid blue eyes; a striking face; and flawless skin. *Stunning* was the word Brad's mother had used. And Morgan had a good head on her shoulders. She would make an excellent piece of arm-candy for their up-and-coming son.

The wedding was a whirlwind affair. The Marquis' estate footed the bill—an embarrassing $38,000. A paltry sum. But what could one expect on such short notice?

After the wedding, Morgan became increasingly mistrustful of the way her husband responded to the ogling he received from other girls on campus. Perhaps it was nothing new. Perhaps she only noticed it now because she wore his ring on her left hand and was carrying his child. When she glared at the brazen flirts, they would simply return a guiltless courtesy smile and go back to whatever they had been doing. Morgan soon realized that the smiles were not offerings of apology but, rather, indications of forthcoming competition. It had never occurred to her that her handsome, rich husband would be a constant attraction to other girls, most of whom didn't seem to care whether he was married or not.

For some time after the wedding, Brad continued to be charming, spontaneous, and fun—at least until Morgan's model-perfect figure began to accommodate the rapidly developing fetus. Not surprisingly, Brad's affections diminished in proportion to her enlarging belly. Immediately after she began wearing what he coined "frumpy maternity clothes," he began spending more time at his parents' estate or at a friend's house "studying," and less time at their apartment in Chula Vista. That's also when the phone calls started—the ones where Morgan would answer and the other end of the line would disconnect. Morgan might have been naïve, but she was not stupid.

Finally, when Morgan was just over seven months along, a young woman left Brad a blatantly suggestive message on their answering machine. She went on and on about their "silly accident" at the campus coffee shop, and offered to make it up to him "any way he'd like," then left her number and a saccharine, "Call me soon, Bradley-bear. Kissies."

Morgan immediately called back, identified herself as a deputy from the San Diego police department, notified the girl that young Mr. Marquis had been arrested for fraternizing with some skanky sleaze suspected of prostitution on campus, and informed her that *Bradley-bear* would be unavailable for continued fraternization for a very long time.

"Oh, that's terrible. I guess you never can tell about some people. He seemed so sweet, too," was her obtuse reply. Obviously, Morgan's pejorative had gone right over the top of the airhead on the other end of the line.

When Morgan slammed the receiver down and tried to stand too quickly, her water broke. She called Brad's cell phone, but he didn't answer. She next dialed her mother-in-law. The woman simply could not break away from her luncheon at the country club, but she wished Morgan the best of luck. Morgan then dialed 911.

Early childbirth brought with it preeclampsia and other complications: low birth weight, fetal anemia, and low oxygen saturation—whatever that meant. Brad showed up long after the delivery. Their son, a three-and-a-half-pound preemie, spent the first two months of his life in the hospital. While he appeared to develop well physically, emotionally he exhibited several early warning signs of autism: he had no interest in people's faces or voices or even in bright colors or sounds, he rarely cried, and he was well into his sixth month before he made any gurgling or cooing sounds.

By then Brad had all but moved out. There had been a brief argument over the child's name. The Marquis had a tradition of naming the first son after the grandfather on the mother's side. But Morgan didn't care for the name Ignatius. The thought of her son growing up as Iggy gave her a migraine. One of her best friends in high school was named Zachary. He was fun-loving, thoughtful, strong in the Church, and had a sense of humor that kept her in stitches. When she informed Brad she was naming their son Zachary, he shrugged with a *whatever* acceptance.

Mr. and Mrs. Marquis would have nothing to do with their grandson or their daughter-in-law. Not only had the impromptu wedding been a disgrace, but now Morgan's inferior offspring was an undeniable discredit to the Marquis family legacy. Brad's mother was convinced Morgan had intentionally done something during gestation to cause this humiliation. It simply could not be Bradley's fault. Was it drug use or simply substandard genes on Morgan's side of the family? Continued loose morals, maybe? Who knew whose baby it really was anyway? There *were* a lot of amorous young men on the yacht that evening. When the hospital offered DNA testing, Brad's parents declined. Even if the test did show *something*, it simply was not going to work out.

Brad's unscrupulous father had the marriage annulled with amazing efficiency. A heretofore unseen prenuptial agreement appeared with

Morgan's signature on it. The subsection entitled ENTRAPMENT was set in bold print. Magnanimously, and to add credit to the Marquis name, Morgan was left with a generous payoff—one that she was loath to accept. At least it would pay the bills until she graduated. What the paperwork didn't bother to mention was her emotional distress and personal slander, or an autistic baby.

Suddenly finding herself with the responsibility of raising a unique child by herself, Morgan was determined to succeed without asking for help. One thing was certain: she wasn't going to give up on her schooling. Not now. Not when she had just one more year to go before starting on her master's program. With almost blind tenacity, she gripped the reins of life, resolute to gallop down whatever path was placed before her.

Fortunately, the Marquis' payoff was generous enough to allow Morgan to hire quality daycare while she completed her schooling. Morgan redoubled her efforts—if only to show Bradley's family the kind of stuff she was made of. Her dissertation on psychosocial behavior patterns was lauded as publishable. She completed her degree six months early, turned down a doctoral extension option, and accepted a teaching position at Utah State University in Logan.

It was in Logan she had met Homer Winegar.

THREE

"The process is really quite simple," Dr. Steven Pendleton explained excitedly.

The scientist wore a wrinkled blue lab coat, randomly stained with who knew what, and gestured wildly with his hands each time he spoke. His boyish eagerness, his sparse, downy goatee, and an occasional pimple did little to exude maturity or scientific expertise. The fact that his name badge read STEVIE didn't help much either. But the twenty-eight-year-old was brilliant. Everyone knew that.

"We've isolated a preconditioned biofeedback response in the limbic system—that's the cerebrum, thalamus, and hypothalamus; some call it our 'primordial brain'—which causes an extraordinary catecholamine release, in this case the neurotransmitters dopamine and norepinephrine. We're now able to synthesize a chemical that artificially activates an identical response by binding to the same receptors."

Gunter Bjorkman, CEO of Scandia Labs, Inc., nodded appreciatively, as if fully comprehending the information presented to him.

To Dr. Ethan Greene, the other scientist in the plush office, the telltale blank look in the CEO's eyes said otherwise. He knew Bjorkman was very intelligent, but the level at which his lab partner spoke about biochemical processes often left the man in a stupor.

"Very simple. Yes, I see. Go on," Bjorkman said.

Pendleton continued: "As you know, these chemicals—dopamine and norepinephrine—cause a concomitant release of natural endorphins that bind to opiate receptors and give the mind and body an overall feeling of joy and well-being. When fully stimulated, our natural, self-restricting chemical thresholds are breached, which then causes a dramatic surge in these neurotransmitters. The effect is overpowering. It's what one experiences during heroin buzz or sexual fulfillment. The chemical we found is structurally identical to THIQ and seems to—"

"Similar to *thick?*" Bjorkman interrupted.

"THIQ," Ethan, explained. "T-H-I-Q is an acronym for the chemical tetrahydroisoquinoline."

"Exactly," Pendleton continued, his voice rising a note or two in his excitement to reveal their findings. "THIQ is an opiate-like molecule produced in the brains of heroin users, which some argue is the cause of heroin's high addiction potential. The same mechanism is thought to exist with other recreational drugs, too—crystal meth, crack cocaine, ecstasy—and perhaps even in non–morphine-based addictions like gambling, alcoholism, pornography, compulsive violence, and the like."

"And you can make this THIQ chemical in the lab?" Bjorkman asked.

"Not THIQ itself, and not in a form that is fully absorbed through the GI tract. But we stumbled onto a prodrug isolate when examining alcoholism."

"A precursor?" the CEO asked.

"No, a prodrug. A precursor is an inactive entity that is metabolized into an active entity," Ethan tried to clarify. "A prodrug is an active entity that is metabolized into a second active entity. It's kind of like two drugs in one."

"Exactly," Pendleton affirmed. "As a rule, THIQ is created only through heroin metabolism, but it's also known to form over time in chronic alcoholics. Normally, alcohol breaks down into a chemical called acetaldehyde and then further into water and carbon dioxide. The process is harmless. That's why not everyone who drinks becomes an alcoholic. But in *chronic* alcoholics this pathway is interrupted when acetaldehyde combines with other neurotransmitters—possibly even our own endorphins—in a way that forms THIQ."

When Ethan saw Bjorkman's blank stare intensify and his brow furrow in puzzlement, he decided to take another tack. "You see, Mr. Bjorkman, because THIQ is chemically similar to opiates, it binds to the same receptors in the body that opiates do, and elicits a similar response to natural endorphins—our 'feel-good' hormones. But THIQ is structurally different enough that it *over*-stimulates the receptors, and what's more, doesn't seem to want to let go."

"Ever?"

"Well, all chemicals eventually go through metabolic processes and are broken down. If they weren't, they would build to toxic levels and kill the host—that is, the person carrying them," Ethan explained. "The thing about THIQ is that not only is it highly addictive, but because it holds on so long, the body thinks it has too many natural endorphins and subsequently stops making them."

"And that's bad?"

"From a physical standpoint, yes and no. But from an emotional and psychological standpoint, it's devastating. If the body can't make its own endorphins, it seeks them out in other ways, usually from outside sources."

"Like alcohol and street drugs," Bjorkman caught on.

"Exactly," Ethan said. "Of course, we've only seen this response in rats thus far, but a rat's chemical system reacts surprisingly a lot like a human's."

Bjorkman nodded again, this time with some degree of actual understanding. Leaning forward and tapping his fingertips together, his elbows rested on his $30,000 Brazilian teak desk, which was inlaid with a tapestry of exotic hardwoods from around the world. The CEO's $6,000 suit was made of virgin wool, expertly tailored to his trim physique by Ede and Ravenscroft of London—the very tailors used by many in the royal family. His tie was made of Taipei silk woven into a seamless pattern of glossy red diamonds amid precisely angled gold stripes. A stylist received $300 a week to keep his full head of silver-gray hair looking distinguished while at the same time potently virile. And his deeply set, sky-blue eyes and tanned face mesmerized onlookers with the magnetism of a Hollywood icon. A subtle Danish accent added the final capstone to his overall omnipotent persona. One minute in Bjorkman's presence told you this was a man of limitless money and power.

"This is fascinating stuff, gentlemen," the CEO said. "But if this chemical is only found in addicts, why are *we* interested in it?"

"Because we've created a drug—well, a prodrug—that is metabolized into something chemically identical to THIQ." Pendleton reentered the conversation in an even higher voice. "What's more, it's colorless, odorless, tastes only mildly bitter, and is orally bioavailable."

"Meaning it's absorbed through the intestinal tract?" Bjorkman asked.

"You got it," Pendleton chimed back.

Ethan slipped his hands into his smock pockets as his eyes wandered to something outside the CEO's twentieth-story window. His unenthusiastic grin betrayed the fact that he did not share Stevie Pendleton's effluence of excitement. At least not for the same reasons.

Often, where Scandia Labs saw unprecedented money-making potential, Ethan thought of more humanitarian ways in which to use their discoveries. He knew where Stevie was heading with this, and he didn't like it. Their test results were preliminary at best, but he recognized the wicked potential of their discovery. In the wrong hands, their breakthrough could be ruinous—even malevolent. Still, they had yet to see the drug's effect on humans. That testing would not be done for a long time, and even then the new chemical might very well end up useless. Maybe.

Then again, maybe not. Ethan knew that his lab partner had presented the information with the intent of fast-tracking the process. He also knew that Gunter Bjorkman had a keen eye for multi-billion-dollar opportunities and, pushing ethics aside, would not hesitate to exploit a groundbreaking discovery.

"Isolating THIQ and how it works may lead us to a way to help cure alcohol addiction or perhaps even prevent it," Ethan explained.

"It could also be used in other ways . . ." Pendleton said, leading.

The CEO continued to tap his fingertips together while holding the two scientists in a steely gaze. After a lengthy pause he asked, "Anyone else know about this?"

Pendleton shook his head. "Our lab techs are always involved in the processes, but they rarely foresee the final outcomes. As far as they know, we're still in the animal testing phase, but . . ." he paused, lowering his voice, "we've had human results already confirmed."

"What?" Ethan unintentionally shouted.

Pendleton hesitated as he cast a quick glance toward his lab partner, then turned back to his boss. "And there's more."

"More what?" Ethan demanded. "When did this take place? Who authorized it?"

Pendleton remained silent, staring at the powerful man behind the desk. A silent message seemed to pass between them.

The CEO gave a curt nod and rose to his feet. Extending his hand, he said, "Dr. Greene, I thank you for your explanations and congratulate you on your contribution in this amazing discovery. Please type up a confidential report and have it on my desk by week's end. Thank you."

Ethan hesitated, clearly understanding that he had been dismissed. Bjorkman wanted him out of the office so he could discuss further aspects of the new chemical with Pendleton. He could only imagine what the two men wanted to talk about, but at that point, he wanted nothing more to do with their would-be plans.

The realization that Stevie Pendleton had gone behind his back irked him considerably. He found the idea of unauthorized human testing grossly unethical, appalling—not to mention downright illegal. The fact that it was a felony offense not only looked bad for the company, but the fact that Ethan's name was listed as chief researcher on the project potentially also made it a career-stopping death sentence.

FOUR

Monday, September 21

Homer Winegar sat at the kitchen table despondently hunched over a pile of bills. A hefty mortgage on their modest River Heights home, a home improvement loan, the payment on the Subaru Forester, a dental bill resulting from a crown-removing caramel, VISA and MasterCard statements, gas and electric bills, and Special Education charges all conspired to spike his blood pressure and cause his stomach acid to churn.

As a numbers analyst at Wasatch BioChemical, Homer brought home a decent income, but it certainly wasn't enough to live on Cliffside with the doctors, lawyers, corporate bigwigs, and the other movers and shakers of Logan, Utah, let alone get ahead of his mounting debts. He regretted the fact that his wife had to work just to stay above water, but she didn't seem to mind. In fact, she claimed she loved teaching, which was undoubtedly true. Morgan had worked hard to obtain her master's in psychology, and Homer wasn't going to let his male vanity stand in the way of her dreams. She loved interacting with the students at Utah State University, and although she often returned home bone weary, Morgan rarely complained about her day. Besides, her studies kept her abreast of their son's special needs.

Homer reorganized the bills in the order in which they came due. He had just deposited his check from Wasatch BioChemical and knew he could meet the deadline on all of them if he made minimum payments. He hated doing that, knowing most of his check would go to interest instead of principal. He was all too familiar with the saying "A wise man earns interest; a foolish man pays it." But he really had no choice. Once Morgan's check came in, things would lighten a bit . . . until next month.

Recently, he had gotten into the habit of working late and some weekends for a few extra dollars, but he hated that too. Like Morgan, Homer loved his job. What he hated was any extra time away from his family.

If only he could go back to his old salary—

"Four-four time. Key of G."

Homer glanced over at Zachary. Being autistic, the boy rarely voluntarily spoke to anyone; but conversations with himself were common occurrences, especially when listening to music. To his parents, Zachary was a young Mozart in the making. He could detect pitch, tempo, meter, and counter rhythms, all within a few seconds of listening to any recording or live performance. It was an enviable, prodigy-like talent. And it always filled Homer with button-bursting pride.

"Whatcha listening to, Zach?"

Zachary held up a CD jacket but said nothing. Because he was playing the recording in the living room, which was open to the kitchen, Homer knew it was the latest from the Mormon Tabernacle Choir, but he wasn't going to let his son get away with a visual answer. Zachary's developmental and behavioral therapist said that his language skills would only improve if he was encouraged to use them.

"I can't read it from way over here, son," Homer claimed, which was only partly false.

"A CD."

"I figured that much. Which one?"

"Mormon Tabernacle Choir. *Celestial Realms*. Mack Wilberg," Zachary answered in a monotone voice.

"Good choice, Zach. That's one of my favorites, too."

As Zachary continued listening, his body swayed slowly to the haunting melody. The arrangement was lush and deeply moving, typical of Wilberg's inimitable style. It was a bit melancholy for

Homer, considering his current state of mind, but he never dissuaded Zachary from listening to anything that piqued his interest. Fortunately, the boy's musical preferences never ventured into such genre as grunge, metal, or rap—the latter of which Homer spelled with a silent C.

"Is that 'O My Father'?" Homer asked, knowing full well it wasn't.

"No."

"Who's the composer?"

"Ralph Vaughan Williams."

"Is it the 'Angel Fly' song?" Another false lead.

He waited for a laugh from his son, but none came. Zachary loved the joke about proof of insects in the afterlife, as confirmed by song fifteen in the LDS hymnal. Presently, the witticism was lost on the boy. At times like these Zachary was so at one with the music that a herd of elephants could pass by without detection.

As the music swelled and grew more intense, Zachary's right hand began directing the choir and orchestra. His tempo and beat were flawless.

"Zachary?"

"Not 'O My Father,'" Zachary said a little louder.

"Then what is it, son?"

"'If You Could Hie to Kolob,'" he said as a perfectly modulated key change brought his other hand into action.

"That's very good, Zach. Do you remember what I told you 'hie' means?"

"Go fast."

"Excellent, Zach. I'm very proud of you. I'm so happy I'm your dad."

And he was. In fact, Morgan and Zachary did more than fill Homer's new life; they completed it. His wife and son made him deeply happy. He knew that the path he'd chosen would likely never bring him notoriety or wealth or even much excitement, but that was okay with him. His little family more than made up for any adventure or profit he might have experienced. He counted himself lucky. No, more than that—he felt *blessed* because of it.

Homer returned his attention to the bills on the table and began writing a check. His wife would be home soon, and he wanted to have dinner ready when she arrived. Mondays were always crazy for her, and he liked to lighten her load whenever possible. Besides, he felt guilty for going into work early that morning to finish up something he hadn't quite completed late last week, so he'd taken off extra early to catch up on household honey-dos and other chores.

As he sealed the last envelope, Zachary approached the table with a thick world atlas in hand. "Show me Kolob," he said.

Homer chuckled. "I don't think it's in here, little man."

"Where is Kolob?"

"It's where Heavenly Father lives."

"In heaven?"

"Yes, that's right."

"With Emily?"

Homer's eyes instantly burned with the painful memory. He reached out and vainly tried to flatten Zachary's stubborn, ubiquitous cowlick. "Yes, son. With your baby sister."

"Is Kolob nice?"

Homer stood and lifted his son onto his arms. "Yes, Zach. It's beautiful there. You'd like it very much."

"Do they have music?"

"Always."

"Good music?"

"The best."

"And ice cream?"

Homer laughed and hugged Zachary. "I don't know, but my guess is that they do." Then, setting his son down, he said, "Now, put the atlas back and then let's make Malt-O-Meal for supper."

"Yucky, noooo," the boy wailed as if Homer had asked him to eat dirt.

"Okay, okay," he said, backing off from teasing. "No Malt-O-Meal. But we need to get some supper ready before Mommy gets home, and then maybe we can go to Charlie's for some ice cream afterward, okay?"

"I get Fudgilla the Hun?" Zachary asked excitedly.

Homer smiled broadly. "You bet."

"Hurray!" Zachary cheered as he ran back to the living room to return the atlas to the bookshelf.

Homer watched his son with a loving yet critical eye. He could not help but analyze the boy's every move. The doctors had explained that Zachary had a form of autism known as Asperger's Syndrome, named after the Austrian physician who first described it in 1944. Asperger's was similar to classic autism except in regard to social inter-action impairment and obsessive compulsive behaviors. The biggest difference was that AS patients usually did not exhibit delays in speech or significant cognitive retardation.

Homer had done a lot of reading on the subject in order to better understand his adopted son. The more he studied, the more enam-ored he became with the boy. On any given day, Zachary could show marked improvement over his regressive characteristics. But the very next day could bring just the reverse. A lot of it came down to repeti-tion. Zachary seemed to have an inner gear-drive synced to daily patterns and familiar habits. Any change in the fixed routine could send him into fits in which he'd scream, lash out, and, in extreme instances, go into an absence seizure where he'd simply regress into a nonresponsive, catatonic state that could last for hours. Homer would never forget the first time he had witnessed it; it nearly scared him to death.

If the change in pattern was something associated with a reward, it was easier for Zachary to accept. Homer quickly learned to tie such occurrences to something he knew his son loved. Zach's favorites were word search puzzles, music, and ice cream.

"What is for dinner?" Zachary asked, returning.

"How about we make some knucklehead sandwiches?"

"Oh, boy!" Zachary exclaimed.

A knucklehead sandwich was nothing more than grilled cheese, but because Homer had told Zachary that they were so easy to make any knucklehead could do it, the name stuck. It was one of many family jokes that never failed to bring them closer together.

FIVE

"THIQ was only the beginning. From it, I was able to synthesize something even more amazing," Stevie Pendleton exclaimed.

"Proceed," Gunter Bjorkman said, leaning back in his plush Italian-leather office chair.

After taking the weekend to review Ethan Greene's prospectus on THIQ, Gunter Bjorkman had asked Greene's lab partner to come to his office to discuss additional, potentially more lucrative aspects of their research. Unbeknownst to the majority of the company, Scandia was not as financially liquid as the internal money-crunchers claimed. The building of a new research complex had all but dried up the company's money pool. Bjorkman had even contributed a significant portion of his personal retirement fund in the hopes of striking it big in the risky but potentially fortune-making biochemical research business.

Pendleton stepped closer. Although the CEO's office was secure, the young scientist nonetheless acted as if the need to keep this information private was of paramount importance. Nevertheless, his boyish eagerness clearly overrode any worries he might have harbored about secrecy. "I call it 'SPAAM.'"

"Cute," was the CEO's unenthusiastic response.

"Thanks. That's S-P-A-A-M. It's an acronym for S-Pentanoic-Adenosyl Apomorphine. It's a prodrug that acts a lot like heroin—which itself is a prodrug to morphine—but it also stimulates gamma amino butyric acid, or GABA, which is the chemical anti-anxiety drugs like Xanax work on. But what's really cool is that SPAAM not only potentiates GABA, it somehow also redirects specific autonomic nerve transmissions—"

"Dr. Pendleton," Bjorkman hedged. "Could you be a bit less obfuscating?"

"Um . . . okay. Sure," the scientist replied, apparently not totally clear on what his boss had just requested. "GABA is the nervous system's primary regulating neurotransmitter. You see, neurotransmitters enable the brain to send impulses from one neuron to another via incredibly fast electrochemical signals. GABA works by telling neurons to slow down; otherwise we'd always be in a state of debilitating anxiety or hopelessly epileptic. That's how anxiety drugs and sedatives work: they stimulate GABA receptors, which in turn slow down hyperactive nerve impulses."

"I understand," Gunter said, patiently tolerating Pendleton's pedantic approach.

"Cool. Almost 50 percent of ten-*billion*-plus neurons in the brain respond to GABA. After we discovered THIQ, I became curious about the brain pathways involved in *all* addictions, like those with anxiety drugs and pain killers. We know that the body synthesizes THIQ from ingested chemicals mixed with our own natural endorphins and certain bio-processing enzymes. I'm still not sure of the exact mechanism or metabolic pathway, but I do know that SPAAM bypasses the normal routes and binds to our opiate receptors, which then elicits a huge catecholamine surge along with oxytocin and—"

Bjorkman held up a hand and favored Pendleton with a disapproving scowl. "As fascinating as this is, can you boil it down to a final result?"

"Yeah. I've created a THIQ SPAAM sandwich." The young scientist burst out with a braying laugh that sounded disturbingly like a donkey.

Bjorkman slowly tapped his fingertips on his desk. He was not smiling. "Is that humor you're attempting?"

"No, sir," Pendleton quickly demurred. "My sense of humor is about the same as the Grim Reaper's—or so I've been told. No, by 'sandwich' I mean the joining of two or more chemicals that utilize the same pathways in our bodies. By *sandwiching* them together, and in the right order, a previously unseen reaction occurs."

"And exactly what reaction is that?" Bjorkman said, rubbing his eyes with one hand while continuing to thrum his desktop with the other.

"A GABA-mediated dopamine surge that enables subconscious manipulation."

Bjorkman's fingers froze mid-tap. He leaned forward slightly. "What was that?"

"We can isolate and control the subconscious mind. To the best of my knowledge, it's never been done on this level before. In fact, it's been considered virtually impossible by many researchers. Some don't believe it even exists."

"The subconscious mind?"

"Yes, sir. You see, our minds are basically split into conscious and subconscious halves. Each half receives and stores information through the five senses: sight, sound, smell, taste, and tactile inputs. However, the subconscious can grasp things that occur too quickly or that are too subtle for the conscious mind to recognize."

"Like?"

"Well, let's take sight, for example. We see thousands of images every day, with tens of thousands of details in each image; perhaps even millions. Our subconscious mind sees and catalogs all of them, but our conscious mind only fixates on a fraction of those images, and even fewer of the details. The same is true with the other four senses. The conscious mind is pathetically limited as far as processing data, but our subconscious accepts data we didn't even know was there."

"You're talking about subliminal input," Bjorkman deduced.

"Exactly. Because the subconscious is the dominant mind, subliminal input is thought to account for almost ninety percent of our mind's perceptions. What's even better, the subconscious *believes* everything it downloads."

"Downloads?"

Pendleton shrugged. "For lack of a better word. The point is the subconscious is the primary controller of the conscious mind, even though it can't distinguish between truth and falsehood."

Bjorkman quickly saw where this was heading, liked it, but had a few questions about its effectiveness. "Can't the conscious mind override the subconscious, especially in instances of social or moral objection?"

"Yes, but it's highly unlikely, because quite often the conscious doesn't know where the objectionable input is coming from and, therefore, cannot directly combat it. That's why addictions like alcoholism and drug abuse are so strong. It's not simply a chemical dependency; it also encompasses a thoroughly conditioned subconscious reminding the body of the immense happiness and comfort it feels when under the influence."

"And you've found a way to control a person's subconscious without them knowing?" Bjorkman asked in an awe-hushed voice.

"Total subconscious control, sir," Pendleton said with malevolent glee.

The Scandia Labs CEO sat in quiet contemplation before he asked, "Is this the same as brainwashing?"

"Sort of, but not in the traditional sense."

"How so?"

"Well, we haven't perfected it yet—rather, *I* haven't. Dr. Greene doesn't know about this. Apparently, the SPAAM stimulation opens a subconscious channel in the primitive brain that responds to specific sensory input, particularly audio input. When we imbed a command in a media source, then play it for a subject at the proper time, the SPAAM-induced primitive brain seems to take control."

"You can't simply give a direct command using a key word or phrase?"

"Oh, sure. An overt command is the most obvious auditory control, but it's also the most easily overridden—it's not embedded deep enough, so the conscious recognizes it. That's why subconscious input is preferred; it's a more dominant way to imbed a command."

"*Imbed* a command?"

"Well, yeah. Whatever message we want can be subliminally encoded inside a recording of music or a podcast or anything else, and repeated thousands of times during the dopamine surge SPAAM triggers. That's when the primitive brain is most susceptible to subliminal input. In reality, this comprises a time span of only a few milliseconds, but the conscious brain never catalogs the input; only the subconscious does. All the conscious mind knows is how incredibly good it will feel once the primer is triggered."

"What primer?"

"A feedback trigger that overrides conscious control; a sequence of words I use to initiate subconscious manipulation. From that point on, whoever has control over the subconscious has total control over all other areas of the brain."

"For how long?"

"I don't know. I'm still testing that part," the scientist admitted. "I'm hoping that once the subliminal trigger is in place, the body will do anything—and I mean *anything*—to receive the biochemical surge again and again."

"Yes, but how long will the trigger stay active in the brain?"

Pendleton shrugged. "No one knows how long the subconscious holds on to any input. My guess is that it depends on how often it's called to action."

CEO Bjorkman pondered silently without diverting his piercing stare. "So . . . what happens when someone takes your 'sandwich' but doesn't receive the correct auditory messaging or triggers?"

"Again, I'm not sure, but I think some other learned, repressed, or dominate behavior takes over."

"You're not sure about a lot of this, are you?" Bjorkman stated with an air of censure.

"Well, no. It's still very early in the testing phase. I've got an assistant doing some preliminary field tests right now."

"Where?"

"A small town up north," Pendleton said cryptically.

Bjorkman nodded.

The scientist continued in a subdued voice: "This is the kind of testing some might consider . . . unethical."

"Unethical or illegal?" Bjorkman asked flatly.

"Yep," Pendleton responded with a wink.

What a geek, the CEO didn't say. Instead he softly asked, "And if you *can* get it to work the way you predict?"

"Then you would have control over anyone you wanted, whenever you wanted," Pendleton crooned.

Bjorkman tried unsuccessfully to hide his excitement. His eyes darted to and fro as a grin stole across his face. Personally, he saw hundreds of ways in which to use the chemical-subliminal control for his personal gain. Without stretching the imagination too much, he could literally rule the world. Swallowing sharply and drawing a quick breath, he said, "Who knows about this?"

"Everyone in this room," Pendleton said, not realizing he was the only one in the room who enjoyed the witticism.

"This is to be kept between you and me," Bjorkman ordered.

Stevie Pendleton nodded, his own grin running ear to ear.

"Use whatever means necessary to perfect this . . . this chemical."

"SPAAM."

Bjorkman began to mouth the word but couldn't bring himself to actually say it. It simply felt too childish. "I want test results in four weeks."

"I'm on it," Pendleton promised, already heading for the door.

SIX

The local radio station was situated inside a small brick building next to a horse pasture on the west side of town. To the visiting blond, it seemed like *every* business in- or outside of Logan's city limits was next to a horse pasture. This backward municipality was nothing like her hometown metropolis of Las Vegas.

The young woman called herself Jacqueline. She had always liked that name. It was the one she'd chosen for her part-time night job and ended up keeping for her new full-time job at Scandia Labs. The pseudonym seemed the perfect mix of glamour, power, and seduction. Her real name was known only to her. She preferred it that way.

As Jacqueline approached the mirrored entrance of the radio station, she paused briefly to admire her reflection. She carried a slim attaché case and wore a severely fitted, maroon camel-hair business suit, complete with a dangerously short pencil skirt, four-inch heels, and a light cream blouse that at first glance gave the illusion that she wasn't wearing anything under the blazer. It was a completely different look from the casual jeans and shirt she had sported a few weeks ago on the USU campus.

A smile lurked just behind her lips as she remembered her encounter with poor Peter Stokes. The smile turned seductive as she continued to ogle herself in the reflective glass. *Men don't stand a chance,* she thought. *But just to make sure . . .* She undid the top button on her blouse and entered the building.

A young female receptionist was talking on the phone. Behind her, a glass partition allowed visitors to watch the DJ work his or her magic over the airwaves. The receptionist held up a finger indicating she was almost finished with her call.

"Yes. Yes. Yeah, sure, I'll tell him," she said into the handset. "Okay, thanks for calling. Good-bye." She hung up. "Can I help you?" she asked her visitor.

"I have an appointment with your program manager."

"An appointment?" the young woman asked, leafing through her daybook.

"Yes, with Mr. Hampton. My name is Jacqueline Mills." A fake last name, too.

"Ah, yes, here it is," she said, pointing to the entry. "I'm sorry, but Mr. Hampton hasn't returned from his previous engagement. Would you like to wait?"

Jacqueline glanced at her watch. She had to call in by five o'clock that evening—about ninety minutes from then. The plan was simple: have the station give a specific set of music tracks a lot of airtime on specific days.

Knowing it was not company policy to play unsolicited or unauthorized recordings on the air, Jacqueline had a few preplanned answers to cover anticipated concerns. If that didn't work, she might have to use her employer's seemingly bottomless checkbook to make it happen. And if *that* didn't work, she always had her womanly wiles.

"If you're in a hurry, I can let you talk to his assistant, Mrs. Zollinger," the receptionist offered.

"*Mrs.* Zollinger?"

"Yeah, but we all call her 'Dear Gabby.'" Leaning forward, the young woman whispered, "Fair warning: if you don't want the entire valley to know about something overnight, don't even hint about it to her."

Jacqueline laughed good-naturedly. The young receptionist had an innocent yet calculating manner, as if she knew the score on everything that went down at the station. Her nametag read TAUSHA. "Thanks for the tip, Taush," Jacqueline whispered back.

"You bet. Should I ring her?"

Jacqueline chewed on her lower lip a bit and glanced at her watch again. "No, I'll wait a while first."

"No problem, Ms. Mills."

"Jacqueline."

Tausha smiled and tilted her head to one side. "Are you a model or something?"

Jacqueline laughed again. "Heavens no. I'm a business liaison. That's all."

"Too bad. You're way gorgeous," the receptionist expressed with gawky admiration.

"Thanks," Jacqueline said, moving to a seating area littered with archaic radio paraphernalia. Opening her briefcase, she removed the CDs she had been instructed to persuade the station manager to play.

If you can't accomplish it through business means, use whatever measures are necessary to complete the mission, her boss had instructed her.

Her training had been brief but thorough. She'd already possessed many of the skills necessary to "infiltrate the test area." That's the way Stevie had put it. The word *infiltrate* made her feel like a CIA operative. In reality, it simply came down to some basic acting ability and having the wherewithal to make things happen—regardless of what was asked of her. In exchange she had negotiated a substantial remuneration that made everything well worth it.

Dwight Hampton, a man in his mid-fifties, showed up ten minutes later. "Sorry I wasn't here to greet you, Ms. Mills. Traffic."

Jacqueline remained seated for a moment, knowing her skirt was hiked ever so slightly higher in that position. If Mr. Hampton noticed the extra skin, he certainly didn't linger on it. He smiled graciously and gestured with his hand toward the hallway. "This way, please."

"Whatever you say," Jacqueline said.

Hampton's office was plastered with radio memorabilia and photos of various celebrities, past and present. He offered Jacqueline a chair, closed his glass-front door, but kept the Venetian blinds open. "How may I help you today?" he asked, rounding his desk.

Jacqueline quickly surmised that Dwight Hampton was a serious man of business. No hanky-panky. Not easily distracted. If her planned assault was not successful, she'd have to change tactics on the fly. She hefted her attaché onto her lap. "First off, I'd like to thank you for your time this late in the afternoon. I know you're a busy man, so I'll come right to the point."

Hampton nodded, seemingly pleased.

"My employer has asked that you give these recordings significant airtime for the next thirty days," she said, handing him four plain-jacketed CDs. "Each disc has just one track on it; there's one disc for each week of airtime we'd like to purchase."

The CD jackets listed nothing more than the song title, the duration of play time, and the designation of week one, week two, week three, and week four, respectively.

"Now here's the catch, Mr. Hampton: each CD plays the same song but with a slightly different emphasis on specific instruments; one has more bass, another more high-end instruments, and so on. We're doing a test-market analysis and are interested in the responses a rural setting like Cache Valley will have to this genre of music, and more significantly, which version gets the best response."

Hampton donned his reading glasses and shuffled through the four compact discs. "And what genre is that, Ms. Mills?"

"I prefer Jacqueline," she said in a lilting, coquettish tone, hoping to soften him up a bit.

"Thanks, but I'd prefer to keep things on a professional level for the time being, if you please," he replied without censure, an unreadable and unyielding look on his face.

"Of course." She nodded. "Your reputation as a strict man of business is well earned," she added with a non-flirtatious smile. "The recordings you hold are categorized as world music. The name of the song is "Toad Stomp"; the artist is a rapidly rising group from Australia called Ayers Rock."

"The huge stone monolith in the middle of the continent. I believe the Aborigines claim it's a sacred site."

Jacqueline paused to note something on a PDA. "I'm impressed."

Hampton chuckled unexpectedly. "Don't be. We get the Discovery Channel here too, you know."

She nodded. "Yes, of course. I didn't mean to—"

"I know you didn't," he interrupted. "Listen, Ms. Mills. I see three things wrong from the outset. First, there is no ASCAP, BMI, or other unionized registry on these discs. We follow strict FCC rules here and can only play copyrighted music on a regular basis. One-time airplay of a local musician is allowed now and then, but you indicated a fairly lengthy and frequent broadcasting schedule from an established group. We have to chart the playtime of any and all music for royalty purposes, you understand. Secondly, it has to be a recording that's available in local stores, or one that can be requested by local vendors. Online-only sales do not qualify."

"And the third concern?"

Dwight Hampton's stony toughness softened before her eyes. A shy grin spread across his face as he leaned forward and clasped his hands together. "Well, you see, we're still pretty much a cow-town here where radio's concerned. We play lots of country and pop and classic rock. And on Sundays we offer a mix of religious tunes, but that's about as broad as we go. No jazz, no new age, no reggae, and certainly no world music. Now, that's not to say we won't someday. This valley's growing pretty fast—a bit too fast for some folks. But I can tell you exactly how aboriginal grunting and chanting will be received: Half the valley will call in asking, 'What in tarnation was that?'"

Jacqueline laughed at the program director's candor. "I'll bet," she agreed as she slid a professionally bound prospectus toward him. "As far as your first concern goes, here are all the proper royalty and FCC compliance documents you need. Sorry the ASCAP imprint is not on the discs, but as you can see, the burn numbers match the paperwork. As for the second concern, our initial sales will depend on how well the music is received. We've already arranged for copies of "Toad Stomp" to be available at a few local retailers. If it flies, we'll consider a full marketing blitz with national outlets. Lastly, the music is much more than unintelligible tribal grunting. You're welcome to listen to the any of the discs before making your decision, but I assure you there's nothing offensive about it. As you and I both know, KUSU plays Celtic and folk music on a regular schedule, so these four CDs shouldn't be too big of a shock to your audience."

"Four CDs with the same song on each?" Hampton asked as if making sure he'd heard correctly.

"Four discs, each with a *unique* recording of the same song. To keep our analysis simpler, we'd like only one version of the song played each week. As you can see, the discs are clearly labeled as to which is to be played each week. Ayers Rock gets plenty of airtime Down Under, but they're just breaking into the U.S. market and are practically unheard of in remote areas like Cache Valley, Utah. That's why we want marketability studies done here. If we offered too many selections at the same time, the population might be understandably overwhelmed. But if we play just one song, then each week ask, for example, 'Have you heard that new Australian tune?' they'll know exactly what tune we're talking about."

"Phone surveys?"

"To begin with, yes. We've already contracted with a local tele-marketing group to make the calls."

Hampton's serious demeanor returned as he flipped through the pages of flawless legal-speak. Jacqueline slowly crossed her toned, tanned legs and noticed the program director's eyes flicker momentarily toward her exposed calves and thighs. *Maybe he is human after all.*

"Well, all this certainly seems in order," Hampton said after his brief perusal. "One last concern is our sponsors. If they disapprove of any of our selections, we hear about it within the hour. I'd hate to lose a client over some Ubangi bongos and clattering rain sticks."

That's African music, you country imbecile, Jacqueline thought with a deceptive smile. "Trust me, Mr. Hampton. Ayers Rock mixes tradi-tional Australian instruments with modern accompaniment. It's incredibly distinctive and quite catchy. Kids love it, and most adults don't seem to mind it either. It's music that covers the whole demo-graphic, much the same way the French group Enigma did in the early nineties. Music that appeals to everyone. What more could you ask for?" she added with a confident smile.

"Well . . . I guess I can give it a spin once or twice, but any more than that . . ." he mused hesitantly.

Jacqueline reached into her attaché again and handed Mr. Hampton a contractual agreement. "Here's the schedule we'd like you to follow for requested airtime. To help negate any potential loss of revenue, my company has agreed to pay your radio station $11,000. That works out to $66.66 per play, four times daily, once per each six-hour block in a twenty-four-hour period—and one extra spin per the DJ's choice—for thirty days, including Sundays. That's all we ask."

"But that's only . . . what? $10,000," he said, calculating the sum in his head.

"The remaining $1,000 is to help with any unforeseen expenses you deem necessary. However, no accounting is required for these expenses. How the money is spent is totally at your discretion."

The implication was obvious. Whether Dwight Hampton would take the bribe was the lingering question. Jacqueline leaned back and folded her arms, signifying that her gauntlet had been thrown.

Hampton carefully looked over the contract and accompanying check. Finally, he removed his reading glasses and favored his guest with a fatherly frankness.

"While I appreciate your employer's generosity, I will more than likely use the extra funds for our upcoming Christmas Party. The station is actually a conglomerate of investors, and we keep tight tabs on all tips, gifts, and gratuities for tax purposes. We run a clean spread here, Ms. Mills; you can count on that. We make copies of all agreements and get authentic signatures on each."

Jacqueline nodded briskly. "Of course."

Hampton stood and tapped the CD labeled WEEK ONE with a finger. "I'll play this—"

"Toad Stomp."

"Yes, 'Toad Stomp,' at our seven o'clock board meeting tomorrow morning. If it's like you say, we'll give it the airtime you request, beginning this Sunday."

Jacqueline stood. "Thank you, Mr. Hampton. I'll stop by Monday around nine to pick up copies of the signed agreement. I am certain you won't be disappointed."

"I hope you're right," he said, extending his hand. "And call me Dwight."

WEEK ONE

SEVEN

Monday, October 5

Dr. Ethan Greene sat at his desk, staring blankly at a stack of papers in front of him. His eyes were glazed and unfocused from anger and betrayal. He felt crushed, belittled, stabbed in the back.

With the recent expansion of Scandia Labs' test facility in Henderson, Nevada, several new positions had opened, including the director of research in New Compounds. He was a shoe-in for the job. He had corporate seniority, years of experience with government research grants, and an ego-wall covered with awards, patents, and accolades attesting to his brilliance and expertise. Only now, their significance seemed to match that of the finger paintings he'd created in the third grade.

Earlier that morning, with butterflies thrumming in his belly, he had entered the boardroom for the monthly senior staff meeting, where all big announcements were made. He had worked on a short, gracious acceptance speech, knowing full well he would get the director's position. Still, not being one for the limelight, even amongst friends, he was nevertheless nervous about having to say anything as he accepted the position. He tried not to think about the increase in salary. He tried even harder not to dwell on the potential for six-figure bonuses and subsequent royalty earnings.

He was greeted with knowing smiles and extra-warm handshakes as he made his way to his chair at the large table. It was apparent that everyone present foresaw what was coming, and most seemed very happy for him. In spite of the company's mandate on secrecy and continuous, stringent enforcement of anti-rumor policies, the eight men and two women in the boardroom had rarely been surprised when such decisions were announced.

Dr. Steven Pendleton sat across from Ethan. They exchanged brief smiles. The light chatter in the room fell silent as Gunter Bjorkman entered with a thick manila enveloped clasped in one hand. His mouth was set in a hard line, and his eyes were unrevealing as always. He had an unfailing poker face, one he utilized not only at work, but also quite successfully at the gambling tables in neighboring Las Vegas. He pushed aside the large captain's chair at the head of the table and tossed the envelope in front of him.

"Gentlemen, Drs. Cole and Cutler, I apologize for being late," he began, even though he was easily three minutes early. "As you may know, Scandia Labs has had a less than stellar year. We are risking much with the addition of our new test facilities, but I have every confidence we can achieve great things with its state-of-the-art accoutrements. Already Drs. Greene and Pendleton have developed some very promising results, as have Drs. Durfey, Peterson, and Aucoin. I have also just learned that Dr. Cole has had some insights into a chemical that will break new ground in the treatment of obesity, which should fatten all our wallets." A few chuckles bounced across the wide table.

"As you are also aware," the CEO continued, "the expansion facility will require a new director of research to coordinate all investigative projects, both ongoing and proposed. The future of this company is very bright, my friends. It needs a leader with new ideas and fresh enthusiasm. And I have selected a man who I feel exemplifies these traits and thus the future of Scandia Labs. In fact, he already has a study in progress that should ensure our place as the leader in chemical research indefinitely."

As Bjorkman paused for dramatic effect, Ethan felt a number of eyes turn to him. The butterflies doubled in number and began rising into his chest. He forced himself to keep his emotions in check. The last thing he wanted was to adopt the dopey, grade-school grin Stevie was known for. But at the moment, he wasn't sure how successful he was being. He felt downright giddy.

Bjorkman unclasped the envelope and withdrew a stack of professionally bound reports. "I have here the prospectus on Scandia's future. It is a future we can all achieve if we work together. It is a future we *will* achieve under the brilliant direction of Dr. Steven Pendleton."

An audible gasp from all but two around the table seemed to suck the air from the room. Ethan knew all eyes had turned to him, waiting for his reaction. The butterflies morphed into a legion of spiny-skinned harpies threatening to claw through his throat. He swallowed what felt like a clump of razorblades and slowly stood. Forcing himself to breathe, he leaned across the table and extended his hand to Dr. Pendleton.

"Way to go, Stevie," he said as cordially as possible.

Stevie Pendleton took Ethan's hand reservedly, as if he suspected his colleague of setting a trap. "Thanks, Ethan," he said.

There was a lengthy pause as the others in the room shook off their astonishment and followed Ethan's example. The prospectuses were passed around the table, along with murmurings of speculation and surprise. Ethan heard his name exchanged in hushed tones, as if those around him didn't want to reveal that he was the focus of their conversations.

Gunter Bjorkman stood smugly at the head of the table with his arms folded across his chest and a knowing grin on his face. Ethan caught his eyes in an attempt to glean some answers. Bjorkman's hooded expression remained as cold as blue ice. But the condescending grin spoke volumes.

Ethan picked up his prospectus and left the room.

* * *

Later that afternoon, Pendleton poked his head into Ethan's office. "You got a minute, Ethan?"

Ethan was calculating the estimated stability of a new chemical in a neutral pH environment. "Not really."

Pendleton entered anyway. "Look, I know this is a shock to you. It sure was to me, I can tell you."

"You'll get over it."

Pendleton brayed his annoying, donkeylike laugh. "I guess I will. But listen, the real reason I stopped by was to let you know I've decided not to pursue the THIQ line."

"That's just ducky," Ethan replied in mocking hyperbole.

"Yeah. The follow-up of the initial tests results were not as remarkable as we had anticipated."

"Really?" Ethan wanted to believe the man, but he knew better. Stevie was known to exaggerate the truth, especially when it came to his personal exploits. The unethical—not to mention illegal—potential of their discovery had kept Ethan up for several nights. He certainly didn't want to get his hopes up, but if Pendleton and Bjorkman had worked something out and decided to scrap the THIQ project, then he was glad to let it be water under the bridge.

"Scout's honor." Pendleton grinned.

"So what was Mr. Bjorkman referring to in the board meeting?"

"Oh, that. I'm partnering with Dr. Cole to look into that new appetite suppressant—the one that enhances grehlin catabolism."

For once, he could actually be telling the truth, Ethan thought. "I remember reading her notes on it. Grehlin's the body's natural appetite booster, right?"

"Yep. That's the one."

"You think you two will be able to down-regulate that hormone?"

Pendleton shrugged. "I figured if THIQ has such a controlling effect, perhaps a grehlin reducer could be synthesized in the same way."

"Any guesses on why it doesn't break down in obese patients?"

"Not yet. But this project won't be just for treating lazy fat people."

Ethan cringed at Stevie's inaccurate, highly derogatory generalization. "That's rather harsh and insensitive, don't you think?"

Pendleton held up both palms as if suggesting surrender. "Hey, it's a potential boon for everyone: all eaters great and small," he said with another bleating honk.

"That's *much* more considerate," Ethan replied with unmasked cynicism.

"Just think: a chemical that keeps people from ever being hungry. *Ka-ching*," the young scientist sang, mimicking a cash register's ring.

"Well, I wish you and Dr. Cole all the success." Ethan had already decided he'd verify Stevie's story later with Deonn. Because she was already well into her study, it didn't make sense to take on a partner at this stage. Perhaps it'd been at Bjorkman's prompting.

"Thanks, Ethan. And good luck on whatever you're working on."

Ethan Greene waved off his ex-partner with a good-natured smile, but deep down he still wondered if he could ever fully trust the man.

EIGHT

Trevor Murdock watched as his supervisor marched toward him in a measured stride, his work-worn clipboard gripped tightly in hand. The man's perpetual scowl seemed darker than usual, accenting his beady-eyed, bulldoggish appearance. Normally Trevor tried to avoid Mr. Thompson at all costs, especially this early in the morning. But today it was as if the boss had been waiting in ambush at the Pepsi-Co distribution center.

The deliveryman drew a deep breath and steadied himself. The two had a mutual dislike for one another, and Thompson seemed to take sadistic glee in riding Trevor mercilessly.

"Murdock," Thompson snapped, "got another stop to add to your route."

Trevor nodded. He knew better than to complain about his already overflowing workload. "Okay."

"There's a few crates of Tribe in my office. They need to get to the commissary in the Taggart Student Center up at USU today before noon."

"Boss, my truck's already loaded with Tribe, all five flavors. I can use some of that load to—"

Thompson stepped into Trevor's comfort zone, and his scowl deepened even further. "No, you will *not*," he barked between clenched teeth. "You will empty a space in your truck and fill it with the crates in my office. I got a priority invoice from HQ says those crates are a special consignment for the Taggart at USU. A gal from corporate personally dropped them off herself last night. That tells me they're high priority. She said they're going to be tracking them, so make sure you don't get 'em mixed up, or it's my keister. And if it's my keister, it's your keister, too. Got it?"

Trevor took a step back. "Yeah, sure, boss. I can handle it."

"I doubt that, but I got no one else. Remember, I'm watchin' you, Murdock."

Trevor bit at his lower lip and walked quickly to his delivery truck. Why headquarters wanted a special delivery of an energy drink to a specific location before a specific time, he didn't know. Nor did he care. He had better things to worry about, including a brutal drafting test later that evening.

Although sometimes physically demanding, his job was not very mentally challenging, which was a good thing. That allowed him time to think about his future. He didn't plan to deliver soft drinks for the rest of his life. At night he took courses at Bridgerland Applied Technology College in computer-assisted drafting. He endured the delivery job because it offered a decent paycheck and benefits, but mostly so his wife could stay home with their new little daughter.

Trevor opened the retracting, corrugated metal door and looked over his inventory. He had six crates of Tribe Boomerang Blast, nine of Tribe Koala Kick, six of Tribe Barrier Reef Buzz, seven of Tribe Wombat Wallop, and five of Tribe Dingo's Dance. Each crate held forty-eight cans of product. He checked his case lots against the invoice sheet. Everything looked accurate.

Tribe was not a Pepsi product, but the soft drink giant was licensed to distribute it in the United States. Trevor was certain that in light of its astounding popularity, Pepsi-Co would buy out the Australian company in no time.

Heading toward Thompson's office, Trevor rechecked the product request printouts he got from the stores on his route and determined he could substitute a few crates of Koala Kick for whatever his boss had in his office.

Mr. Thompson's office door was slightly ajar, but Trevor knocked politely anyway. When no one answered, he slowly nudged open the door. The office was empty. In the corner sat four crates marked with simple lot numbers. He opened one of the plastic crates and slid out a tall, dark can. Dingo's Dance. *What the . . .* More of that stuff? He already had plenty of it in his truck.

Grumbling, he replaced the beverage and closed the lid. Using a dolly, Trevor wheeled all four crates to his truck and hefted them into the spot vacated by the Koala Kick.

Trevor muttered a contemptuous oath under his breath as he wrote the four crate numbers in his ledger, indicating their special delivery status. He then climbed into the cab, fired up the noisy diesel, and drove out of the loading area, still grumbling to himself. He hated having to negotiate his big panel truck through the narrow, pedestrian-choked byways on the USU campus. Still, the super had made it clear he needed to get this done before noon. And he took Thompson's threats literally.

By the time Trevor arrived on campus, it was 12:19. Praying that word of his tardiness would not filter back to Thompson, he drove quickly toward the student center, narrowly missing a couple of bicyclists and one jogger. Backing into the loading area of the Taggart Center, Trevor was greeted by a young woman wearing a stained, white biblike apron. He unloaded the first crate and placed it on the service dock.

"Whatcha got here?" the girl asked.

"Special delivery," he said, handing her the invoice.

The girl did not look happy as she looked over the rumpled paperwork. She opened the crate and removed a can of the energy drink. Turning it sideways, she inspected the lot number and compared it to the paperwork. She nodded curtly.

"That the right stuff then?" Trevor asked.

"So far," she affirmed, replacing the can and removing the next.

Trevor couldn't believe his eyes. Was she going to check every can? That would take forever. "You want some help with that?"

"No," she replied bluntly.

Trevor had the girl sign his clipboard and then tossed it back into his truck as she continued to check the lot number on each can. She looked vaguely familiar, but he wasn't positive. The name embroidered on her apron read *Salvador,* so that didn't help. It didn't matter. With the frequency the students rotated through the food service positions on campus, it was actually more of a surprise to see the same face twice.

He glanced at the scrawl on the "received by" line. Trudy? Judy? He couldn't make it out. No matter. He watched as the stocky brunette continued to work her way through each of the forty-eight cans.

What was the big deal with this particular delivery anyway? He bit his lip and choked down a well-earned expletive. Returning to the open panel on his truck, he unloaded the other three crates, wheeled them to the dock, and released a long, aggravated draught of air.

"Hard work, isn't it?" Trudy Whoever asked without looking up.

"Just running a bit late," Trevor grumbled.

"Well, it looks okay so far. I think I'll finish this inside. You have a nice day." Her farewell was delivered without much sincerity.

Shaking his head, Trevor climbed back into his truck. He'd made the extra stop. As it stood, he now had to blow through his other deliveries to finish on time. The exam in his CAD class that evening was rumored to be one of the worst, and he had hoped to get there a bit early to review.

Consulting his watch, and in the privacy of his truck cab, he finally used his pent-up expletive. There was no way he'd finish his route before nightfall.

NINE

Homer parked the Forester under the shade of a huge black willow and jogged into the single-story brick building. Bridgerland Developmental Academy was only in its fourth year of schooling the mentally challenged, and yet it had already garnered two coveted education accolades: one from the National Institute of Mental Health and the other from the Northern Utah Autism Program. But at the moment, none of that mattered to him.

"Hey, Cynthia," Homer said as he approached the front desk.

"Oh, hi, Homer. I'm sorry to call you from work."

"That's okay. How's my little genius?"

Cynthia's incessantly cheerful disposition had lost much of its luster. "Well, as I mentioned over the phone, we had a bit of an incident. I'm not sure whose fault it was, but it ended up pretty bad."

"How bad?"

"Zach's totally regressed. I am so sorry. We tried to help him understand, but it all happened so fast. We—"

Not waiting for the woman to finish her confession, Homer jogged down the hallway to his son's classroom. The other children, nine in all, were busy with crayons and large sheets of paper. Each child had lain on the paper while their counselor traced their outline in silhouette. The child was then given a choice of crayons to draw in their own face, clothing, hair, and such. For a bunch of grade-school–aged children, the room was surprisingly quiet. But that wasn't so usual in *this* school. Unless throwing a fit, most autistic children kept to themselves.

Standing in the doorway, it took a few moments for Homer to locate his son.

Zachary sat under a work table with his knees pulled to his chest. He was holding a glossy 5x7-inch card and staring at it with profound intensity while he rocked back and forth in a steady rhythm.

"I do apologize about this, Mr. Winegar," one of the counselors offered as she approached.

Ignoring the woman, Homer dropped to his hands and knees and made a slow, circuitous route to his son. Zachary's eyes never moved from the card, but Homer knew his son's peripheral vision worked just fine. Homer took his time sitting next to his son, matching the tempo of his rocking.

An angry gash over Zachary's left eye had crusted over but was still swollen and glowing. The glossy card in the boy's hand was a photograph of a fringed, horned lizard with bugged-out eyes, a long sticky tongue, and a prehensile tail.

"Chameleon," Homer said softly.

Zachary did not respond.

"Chameleon," Homer repeated, hoping to tune into his son's level of regression so he could help guide him out. He knew that at times like this, Zachary was dangerously sensitive to abrupt noises, glaring lights, and unsolicited, pressured interaction.

When still learning how to deal with his adopted son's autism, Homer had found himself losing patience and trying to force acknowledgment from Zachary. Without fail, the intrusion into Zach's emotional withdrawal would cause an instantaneous tantrum to erupt, which usually led to a full-on fit and a subsequent seizure. After that, Zachary was in total shutdown for up to seventy-two hours. He didn't eat or drink or move or speak or even sleep, really; instead, he became catatonic, tucked into a fetal position with his mouth clamped shut. When he eventually came to, it was as if nothing had ever happened, except for having a sore jaw and an empty stomach. The trouble was, according to medical experts, *coming to* was not always a guarantee.

Homer reached out slowly and pointed to the photograph. "Chameleon."

When Zachary still did not respond, Homer closed his eyes and said a quick, fervent prayer. "Chameleon," he said again.

Zachary moved his lips slightly, but no sound came out.

"Chameleon," Homer repeated softly.

Zachary's rocking slowed.

"Chameleon."

Zachary repeated the word in barely more than a whisper. "Chameleon."

"That's right, son." Homer moved his finger closer to the photo. "Chameleon."

"Chameleon," Zachary echoed softly.

"Chameleon. It's a lizard."

"Lizard."

Success.

When Homer stopped rocking, so did Zachary. "Kinda silly looking, isn't it?" Homer said.

Zachary angled the photograph so his dad could see it better. "Has funny eyes."

Homer chuckled gently. "It does have very funny eyes. They kind of look like Daddy's."

Zachary looked closer at the lizard then turned to his father. Homer had crossed his eyes and stuck his tongue out one side of his mouth. Zachary giggled.

The crisis was averted but not completely over. It took another ten minutes before Zachary came out from under the desk. A few minutes after that, he was enjoying a small bag of fruit chews while his father talked with the counselors.

"I'm not entirely confident how it started," counselor Geraldine Flander-Holmes was saying. "Zachary was listening to the radio as he usually does after exercises. It's an older model with knobs and dials. He loves to slowly scan through all the channels, listening to them tune in and out. Sometimes he'll just listen to the static between stations. It's not an unusual or unhealthy practice for a child with Asperger's. As you know, their interests are often piqued by the slightest thing, as long as it's not too abrupt."

Homer nodded. "He does that at home a lot, too. He loves music of any kind."

"Precisely. Only this time one of the other boys became interested in what Zachary was doing and tried to work the radio knobs too. You are aware that autistic children can be very self-centered. They simply don't understand the concept of sharing. Well, Isaac Willie tried to take the radio away from Zachary. I was very impressed with Zachary at first because he didn't immediately refuse. But after a few seconds, he insisted on taking the radio back, and Isaac lashed out. Being a larger boy, Isaac can be intimidating to the others, but not to your son. Zachary grabbed the radio, and that's when Isaac pushed him. Zachary stumbled into the bookstand and caught his eyebrow on the corner."

His patience already worn thin, Homer stood there trying to calmly receive the play-by-play synopsis of the event. He didn't like this counselor's syrupy, often patronizing manner. She was never wrong—the parents were not allowed to forget that. Every child under her tutelage was treated with equanimity far beyond the national standard for mental health programs. The fact that Zachary had a unique form of autism that made him more responsive than the other kids didn't matter. If one child could not progress beyond a certain point, none of the children should be allowed to either. It wasn't fair to the slower students. That kind of politically correct pandering always irritated Homer. To his way of thinking, it bordered on socialism. And it never failed to prick a particular nerve when it came to his son.

Homer acknowledged that his mindset was somewhat atypical. He had infinite patience with children, but not with adults. He figured "grown-ups" should intrinsically know better. They had the option to use logic. Children typically did not. The trouble was that many adults never progressed beyond childhood mentally . . . or behaviorally.

He felt Albert Einstein said it best: "The difference between genius and stupidity is that genius has limits."

"Thank you for your explanation," Homer told counselor Flander-Holmes. "I can see it was an accident. I trust you explained to Isaac what his misdeed was?"

Geraldine Flander-Holmes looked appalled. "I most certainly did not, Mr. Winegar. Honestly now. Autistic children do not understand the concept of right and wrong. To punish them would be a pure act of violence that could cause further mental—"

"I did not say *punish;* I said explain," Homer corrected the counselor. "Even autistic children can be taught the difference between good and bad behavior. They may not understand *why* it's good or bad, but they can understand that there *is* a difference. I thought that was one of the objectives of sending them to a school such as this."

Counselor Flander-Holmes tried to remain passive-faced, but underneath her granite exterior, Homer could tell she was incensed. "Mr. Winegar. Our programs here are top-notch, backed by the latest research in the field of developmental psychology. We are a fully accredited institute. We have won several awards in a short amount of time, proving our techniques are above par on a national level."

"Yes, I am aware of that, Gerri. That's why my wife and I chose to bring Zachary here."

"Then I would appreciate it if you, as the parent of an autistic child, would allow our professionals the right to perform their functions as they deem appropriate."

Homer stared hard at the woman.

"And it's Geraldine or Counselor Flander-Holmes, not Gerri," the woman huffed.

In his mind, Homer rehearsed at least a dozen comebacks and a score of alternate names with which to excoriate the self-righteous instructor. But he held his tongue. After all, she was the professional. He was merely a father.

"As you wish, counselor. I'm sorry if I came across too harsh. Let me put it to you this way: may I ask what you plan on doing to prevent such incidents in the future?"

The smug radiance of victory fairly oozed from the woman's expression. "We haven't addressed the options yet, but I assure you a rational course of action will be determined."

Homer wanted more specifics, but he knew that Counselor Flander-Holmes was hedging behind her authority and would not revisit the issue since she had just "won" the debate.

"I see," he said. "Then may I speak with Isaac for a moment, please?"

"Absolutely not," she asserted. "He does not respond well to strangers, and it's my professional opinion that you are in no mood to properly address a child, especially one as emotionally unstable as Isaac."

Homer mentally reviewed the way he had just brought his son out of a severe withdrawal and was surprised that the counselor hadn't even commented on his success.

He nodded curtly. "Fine." Then, grabbing Zachary's coat, he said, "I am taking my son home now. I'd like our family doctor to look at that gash above his eye."

"I do not feel that is wise, Mr. Winegar. It would be disruptive to the children's schedule. As you know, they are creatures of habit."

"Oh? Is it Isaac's habit to push the other children around?"

"Don't be absurd."

"Then this is a special circumstance. I am taking my son to his doctor."

Geraldine Flander-Holmes slowly folded her arms. "I want it noted that I recommend against that."

"So noted," Homer said, bundling up his son. He then knelt to face Zachary. "Son, look into my eyes, okay?"

Zachary did.

"You understand that Isaac didn't mean to hurt you, don't you?"

The boy nodded.

"I need a verbal answer, little man, just like we practice at home."

Zachary said, "Yes."

"When Isaac pushed you and you fell, did you try to hit him back or throw anything at him?"

Zachary shook his head.

"Zach?"

"No."

"Even though you know what Isaac did was wrong?"

"It's okay," Zachary said, touching his injured eyebrow then examining his finger. "No more blood. See?"

Homer tousled his son's hair. "That's my boy. You are a very good boy, Zach. Smart too. You did exactly the right thing."

"We go home now?"

"Yes, Zach. We're going home now," Homer said tenderly.

"Okay." Zachary then picked up the radio and took it over to where Isaac was coloring his self-portrait. He placed the radio in front of the other boy. "Your turn."

Isaac immediately dropped his crayon and greedily grabbed the radio.

"Maybe you can hear whispers too," Zachary said before returning to Homer. "All done," he told his dad.

Homer, beaming with pride, looked straight at Counselor Flander-Holmes, and said, "I've heard it said the best lessons are taught in the home." Placing his hand on Zachary's shoulder, he continued. "I believe that to be a fact. Have a nice day, Gerri."

And with that, father and son left the school hand in hand.

TEN

Friday, October 9

Thick cumulous thunderheads churned in the west, bruising the already purple sky with the shadowy contusions of an impending storm. The encroaching tempest spread an ever-darkening veil over the Wellsville mountainside, dulling the brilliant, orange fall foliage to somber shades of gray and black. It was a typical autumn afternoon in Cache Valley, Utah, one that usually brought Morgan Winegar a sense of tranquility in spite of the gloomy weather. But not today.

From her vantage point in the Old Main building on the Utah State University campus, Morgan was not examining the oncoming squall. Rather, from the opposite side of the building, she watched a disturbance brewing around the arching, modern art in the courtyard below.

It had started out as one student sitting cross-legged at the base of the *Synergy* sculpture, staring up at it as if in a trance. At first Morgan thought nothing of it, as many liberal art students often spent time soaking up the Kirlian aura they claimed emanated from the piece. But the lone student was soon joined by another, then another and another. Before long there were seven students encircling the polished, stainless-steel edifice, sitting stone-faced, frozen, silently staring at the near juncture of its apex.

This was more than just a sit-in or a group of art students studying form and function. It looked strangely like a séance; eyes open but unmoving, lips slightly parted, breathing slow and deep.

When passersby asked what was going on, none of the participants responded. The small group sat in catatonic stupor, oblivious to their surroundings.

Morgan had opened her window to try to catch bits of talk from those looking on. The whole scene felt wrong. There were nervous chuckles and jesting slurs, but the comments were all one-sided. Not one of the students sitting on the damp lawn made a sound.

Morgan shuddered as a brisk breeze nipped at her face. The chill in the air matched the icy feeling along her spine. She watched in fascination as a couple of frat boys jostled one of those in the gathering, calling him by name then adding an off-color remark. Knocked to one side, the young man quietly righted himself and continued to stare without uttering a word.

Within a matter of minutes a slightly larger crowd had formed around those staring at the arching, bipedal statuary. It was evident that this was more than a practical joke. Expressions of confusion, concern, and uneasiness rose to Morgan's ears. The longer those sitting remained unresponsive, the more fretful the outer crowd became. This was no prank—something was affecting these seven students in a psychologically negative way.

The campus police were summoned. Someone suggested calling 911. A few people took snapshots of the event on their camera phones. When Morgan recognized one of the university's superintendents questioning those surrounding the group, she rushed down to meet him.

"Hey, Harry, what's going on?" she asked.

"Oh, hello, Morgan. I was hoping you could tell me. You're the expert in this stuff."

"Beats me." She shrugged. "I was in my office correcting some papers when I looked out and saw this crowd gathering."

"I'll see what I can find out," he said, excusing himself to confer with the campus police.

Morgan worked her way to the front of the crowd to get a better look. The first few drops of chilled precipitation bit her skin as they fell from the sagging clouds. The sporadic drops quickly turned to a steady drizzle. As the wind also picked up, the skeletal branches of the

Norway maples in the courtyard clicked, scraped, whistled. The ambient temperature of the Old Main courtyard plummeted. Sodden leaves teased by the wind stuck to the ground or glued themselves to those sitting around the sculpture. The entranced students didn't seem to notice. But many in the outer crowd did and decided to leave before a real drenching began.

Morgan knelt beside a girl she thought she recognized. "Hey there, hon. Are you okay?"

No response. No indication that the girl had even heard her.

Morgan placed a hand on the girl's wrist. "Can you tell me what's going on?"

Still nothing.

"I'm very concerned about you, okay? You need to hear and understand what I'm saying. You have to get inside before this storm really hits."

A sudden, harsh gust of moist air plastered a dead, mottled leaf to the side of the girl's face. She didn't even blink. Morgan gently pulled the leaf away, bringing with it a strand or two of hair. Unmoving, the girl remained fixated on the polished steel statue.

Anxiety fluttered in Morgan's chest as she rose to her feet and studied the other students, searching for a more familiar face.

"Professor Winegar?" It was a young woman's voice.

"Yes?" Morgan said without turning to see who was talking. Strangely, just as the circle of students seemed to have a bizarre, inexplicable bond with the statuary, so Morgan could not unglue her eyes from the students. Her analytically trained eye cataloged that the students were from mixed ethnic backgrounds, both genders, and different social standings, but their unvarying, zombielike behavior made them appear as one homogenous clan. It reminded her of something she couldn't readily put her finger on. Something she had seen long ago . . .

"Professor Winegar?"

Finally drawn from her own surreal trance, Morgan looked at the girl standing next to her. "Yes?"

"Julie Perkins, Human Dynamics 220."

"Yes, Julie."

"Have you ever seen anything like this before?"

"I'm not sure . . . Certainly not in person, anyway. I've read cases of similar phenomena occurring, but it was usually in conjunction with hallucinogenic drug use or becoming spiritually frenzied or hypnotized by a second or third party."

Julie cast her eyes back on the small group and moved a bit closer to Morgan. After a pause, she whispered, "It's creeping me out." A nervous tremor, tinged with fear, weakened her voice.

"Yeah," Morgan agreed. "Me too."

"Will they be okay?"

Morgan shrugged and managed a wan smile for her frightened student. "I wouldn't be too worried. They look healthy enough, so it must—"

The tolling of the school's carillon interrupted Morgan's assurances with its eight-note, Westminster melody. The descending and ascending tune was followed by a monotone repetitive strike counting each hour passed. Presently it was five o'clock. At the sounding of the last clang, the gathering of art worshipers snapped from their catatonia and looked around with questioning glances. The drizzle had turned to a steady rain, and everyone was soaked. Some smiled; others frowned. Most looked manifestly scared.

Questions flew. What happened? What's going on? What am I doing here? Why am I sitting on the ground soaking wet?

When the awakening students were asked by outsiders what the sit-in was all about, no answers came. Fortunately, except for being cold and wet, those afflicted by the strange fugue seemed to have no residual ill effects. No one had a headache or any disorientation other than an acute, understandably eager confusion regarding their unanswerable whys and whats.

Because of the increasingly inhospitable weather, the excitement quickly faded from perplexing to miserable. Most of the onlookers shuffled away, some talking of drama department hoaxes or secret science experiments—or even candid camera high jinx. The remaining students simply left the scene speechless and confused.

Before returning to the Old Main building, Morgan quickly gathered the names of the affected students. She then went to the restroom down the hall from her office and used a small towel to dry her face. She did not know any of the sit-in students personally, but as a professor she had access to all undergraduate and graduate files.

Replaying the brief encounter in her mind, she found it impossible to believe that the sit-in had been a hoax or that it had been premeditated on the part of the students. Surely there had to be something else to explain the unexplainable event.

ELEVEN

Saturday, October 10

"It was the strangest thing I've ever seen," Morgan said over store-brand ravioli and generic garlic bread. "They were in a group trance, like a communal fugue. Nothing seemed to get through to them. Then all of a sudden, *snap,* they were lucid again. I just can't figure it out."

"Snap," Zachary echoed while attempting to make the sound with his thumb and middle finger.

"A fugue?" Homer asked.

"Yeah. It's a type of partial seizure where people can perform complex tasks without knowledge of what they're doing," Morgan explained.

"Were the students all from the same class?"

"No. In fact, only one or two knew each other. The rest were total strangers."

"What brought them out of the trance?"

Morgan chewed and swallowed a square of ravioli as she concentrated on some point behind her husband.

"I'm not sure," she mused. "It may have been the carillon chime. It may have been the cold weather and the rain. I haven't had a chance to talk with many of the students yet. But I did collect their names and phone numbers immediately after the event."

"Are you planning on interviewing all of them?" Homer asked as if dreading the task for her. "It seems like a lot of effort for what sounds like a staged sit-in."

Morgan's blank stare intensified as she relived the fugue in her mind. Her knuckles whitened around her fork, and her voice gained a palpable edge to it. "Homer, you weren't there. It wasn't staged. It was . . . *strange*." She shook her head, still not meeting his gaze. "No, it was more than strange. It was eerie, hypnotic—downright scary."

Zachary stopped eating and placed his hands in his lap. "Mommy's angry."

Sighing apologetically, Morgan said, "Oh, sweetheart, Mommy's not angry. I'm just a little frightened, okay?"

The boy nodded but refused to make eye contact. "Is Daddy in trouble?"

Morgan smiled. "No, Zachary. Not this time."

Homer guffawed. "What do you mean 'not *this* time'?"

"We'll talk later," she said with a nod toward their son.

Zachary returned to his pasta while the Winegar parents had a brief, private chuckle. As soon as he was full, Zachary cleared his plate and dropped it in the sink. He then spent the next few minutes washing and rewashing his hands, an OCD habit common in autistic children. Moving to his side, Homer handed Zachary a towel. "That's enough, son. Your hands are perfectly clean by now, so dry them off, okay?"

Zachary took the towel and wiped his hands. "We go Charlie's now?"

"Charlie's Ice Cream again?" Morgan asked in guarded surprise as she began to clear the plates from the table.

Homer shrugged. "I told him we might go after supper. You game?"

"Honey," she appealed plaintively. "I've been doing so good with my weight. These pants are finally feeling loose again. I don't want to fall off the wagon."

"Fine," Homer said. "You can just wait here while Zach and I go."

She huffed and smacked him on the shoulder. "Like that's going to happen. Zachary, *now* your daddy's in trouble."

"I can live with that." Homer smiled.

Homer knelt in front of his son, but Zachary looked off to one side, refusing to make eye contact.

"Zachary, look at me please."

The boy's eyes passed quickly from one side of his father's head to the other.

"Zachary?"

Slowly, Zachary's eyes drifted to meet his gaze. Homer waited until they appeared to register a look of cognitive correlation.

Homer beamed. His son had such clear, liquid, bottomless blue eyes framed by thick, dark lashes. Persuading Zachary to make eye contact was always a challenge, but it was always worth the effort. "Is your room clean?"

"Yes," the boy said slowly.

"Can I see?"

"Okay."

Zachary took Homer's hand and drew him to his room. Sure enough, the boy had made a passable effort to tidy his room. It wasn't perfect, but Zachary was clearly proud of the work he'd done.

Homer knelt beside his son. "Excellent job, little man," he said, embracing him in a generous hug. "Charlie's, here we come."

"Hurray!" Zachary cheered, returning his father's hug.

* * *

Homer and Morgan sat in their bed, both with books in hand, neither of them reading. Zachary was fast asleep in his room down the hall.

"You're sure the fugue wasn't a staged practical joke?" Homer asked again.

"It just doesn't make sense, Homer. I called one of the guys earlier this morning, Jared Lucas. He was a little embarrassed about the whole thing, but he swears he had no clue what was happening."

"And he didn't know anyone else in the circle?"

"He knew a few faces, but no one by name."

"Did this Jared kid look like someone who might use drugs?"

Morgan shook her head. "No. None of them did."

"But you really can't tell, can you?" Homer said as he rubbed his tired eyes. "You remember Gregg, the pharmacist down at the clinic?

We were discussing this once, and he says that even though you can't always know for sure, there are certain drug-seeking behaviors that always stand out. He says the abusers think they're being clever when they make the same old excuses for early refills and such, but most pharmacists can see right through them."

"But these kids didn't act high," she argued. "And they all looked pretty clean-cut to me." Setting her book aside and taking her husband's hand, she said, "Maybe I'm making too much of the whole thing. Should I just forget about it?"

"No . . . I think it's worth following up on. The bright side is that no one was hurt, right?"

"Yeah, as far as I can tell."

"Well, that's what's important."

He leaned over and gave her a soft kiss, cupping her face with one hand. It was tender and brief, but it still sent a warm shiver down her spine. It always did. Homer said good night, settled in, and almost immediately began breathing slow and steady.

It always amazed Morgan how he could fall asleep so easily. It was an enviable skill. Gently tracing her fingers through his hair, she thought about how they met. A loving smile warmed her face.

Morgan had just finished administering her first midterm exam to her USU students. She had picked up Zachary from a neighbor who ran an in-house daycare and was headed for home—a destination she almost dreaded. Two weeks' worth of laundry had overrun her bathroom, and Zach was completely out of clean underwear.

After a quick dinner, she pulled on a rumpled oxford button-down shirt and running sweats, dressed Zachary in his pajamas, and made her way to the Wash Hut six blocks over from her apartment. Bringing Zach with her always slowed things down, but she didn't have much choice. Just getting into the Laundromat took three trips from her car: two with basket-loads of laundry and detergent, and one with her laptop, a stack of exams to grade, and her son. Morgan always chose the nook in the far end of the Laundromat where the end of a row of dryers and the last machine in a row of washers formed a three-sided barrier with the building's back wall. It was easier to keep an eye on her son that way.

At nearly six years old, Zachary was a natural explorer, especially in a place filled with rumbling mechanized wonders. Morgan had given him a book of dot-to-dot puzzles—which usually engrossed him completely—and was busy trying to balance her laptop on her thighs while comparing an answer sheet with a stack of tests—while at the same time keeping an eye on the dryer and on her son.

Without Morgan seeing him coming, Homer appeared next to her and said it looked like she needed a third arm. Sad but true. He then asked if he could help.

Morgan gave him the once over. She had heard rumors about men who loitered in Laundromats looking for single women, but this guy seemed harmless enough, and there were several other people in the Laundromat in case he wasn't. "Have a seat, and thanks."

She handed him the tests and answer sheet and had him read off the responses to each question per student as she entered them in her computer. She liked to catalog the accuracy of each answer to better analyze how well her students understood each concept. An overall test score didn't tell her much, and since behavior studies and general psychology were so subjective, it simply made sense to put in the extra effort.

"You're a psychology professor?" Homer asked.

"Guilty," she said wearily.

"That's good to know. I'll try to watch my Freudian slips."

Morgan scoffed. "Freud was an incestuous creep."

"All the more reason." Homer sniggered.

It was only a matter of minutes before Zach came up to his mother whimpering that he had broken his pencil. Without missing a beat, Homer pulled a mechanical one from his pocket, showed Zachary how to click it to dispense the lead and how to hold the end to push the lead back in, should it end up too long. Young Zachary, normally leery of strangers, was instantly fascinated by the device, tried it a few times, and then carried it back to his corner without further complaint.

Morgan was floored. "You have a way with kids, I see."

"It helps to relate to them when you haven't grown up much yourself."

Morgan shivered. "Ugh, please don't say that. You'll remind me of his father."

"Sorry," Homer offered before returning to the tests.

When a completed dryer cycle demanded Morgan's attention, Homer offered to continue entering the data so she could attend to her clothes. Because he had caught on so quickly to the way her software worked, she agreed.

A full five minutes passed in rapt concentration before she realized she was folding and stacking her bras, panties, and slips right next to this stranger. Mortified and red-faced, she quickly piled her things into one of her laundry baskets and placed it out of sight. She was certain the helpful man had noticed her faux pas, but he had said nothing. He didn't even act embarrassed. The natural ease he exuded was a curious comfort to her. And the fact that he had made friends with Zachary so quickly lessened her intrinsic trepidation toward him.

As Morgan took over the last of the data input, Homer crawled over to where Zachary was scribbling away. Being a psychologist, Morgan was intrigued by the man's approach to her son. Normally, a grown person would walk over to a child before engaging him. By crawling on hands and knees, he had put himself at Zachary's level even before approaching him, thus diminishing the potential for intimidation.

When Homer asked to have his mechanical pencil back, Zachary refused. When he said please, the boy immediately got that look on his face Morgan knew was a preamble to a tantrum. Homer must have seen it too, because he quickly said never mind, and began drawing imaginary pictures with his fingertip on a blank piece of paper. The impending tantrum faded quickly as a fascinated Zachary watched the make-believe penmanship of the stranger's index finger. When Zachary went back to scribbling with the mechanical pencil, Homer backed away and sat by Morgan.

"Sorry about that," she said with regret. "He's autistic and doesn't always understand. I'll buy you a new pencil."

"Nonsense," Homer said cheerfully. "Your son has already mastered it, so naturally he should keep it. You and your husband must be very proud."

"My *ex*-husband could care less about Zachary. He probably doesn't even remember his name, let alone mine."

"What a loss," Homer said in a disgusted tone. "Your son is obviously a very bright boy. Your ex is going to miss out on some happy times with the two of you."

Not only did Morgan's inward defenses instantly vanish, but she actual felt a bond form with this man. He had called her son "bright." *Bright!* Most people referred to him as "special," a term she had grown to loathe. Additionally, this guy didn't appear to be scared off by a young, single mother with a unique-needs child.

Morgan casually checked out his left hand. No ring. But that didn't always mean available. There was one way to find out, but she was hesitant to try. This gentle stranger could be some creepy predator stalking an attractive, albeit stressed, young woman—or worse, stalking her son. Yet somehow Morgan knew that wasn't the case. His natural calm, his plain looks, and his nonaggressive manner instilled in her an uncharacteristic ease. Intuitively, Morgan knew he was safe.

Gathering her courage, she asked him over to dinner. "Not only as payment for Zachary's new pencil, but for helping me with my paperwork."

He smiled and readily agreed.

"By the way, my name is Morgan. Morgan Young."

"Homer Winegar."

She smiled back. "Homer?"

He shrugged. "Yeah. My dad loved that old movie *The Best Years of Our Lives*. It won best picture back in nineteen-forty-something. His favorite character in it was a disabled sailor named Homer Parrish—'a young man who took all that life could throw at him and still kept smiling,'" Homer said as if quoting his father. "I was doomed even before I was born."

She laughed out loud. "Well, maybe after dinner we can watch the DVD together so I can find out what you're really supposed to be like."

He agreed.

The rest was history.

WEEK TWO

TWELVE

Kayson Maughan rendezvoused with his classmate at the outdoor café connected to the Merrill-Cazier Library on the USU campus. Flopping his backpack on the small table, he groaned loudly. Brennan Hatch calmly slid a can of Tribe energy drink toward him. "Hair of the dog?"

Kayson popped open the can of Dingo's Dance and drank deeply. After a loud belch, he exclaimed, "That exam was brutal, Bren."

"Severely nasty, Kace," Brennan concurred.

"Unrighteous dominion."

"Machiavellian anarchy."

"Dante has nothing on that inferno," Kayson moaned, nodding toward the Widtsoe Science Building.

"I totally bombed the nucleophilic substitution equation."

"Not alone there, man."

"So, what do you think?"

"I'd rather not."

"I'm guessing a C plus."

"I'll be lucky with a D minus."

"Dude, your parents'll go ballistic."

"Total nuclear meltdown."

Brennan unzipped his backpack. "So, you wanna review it?"

"Maybe in another life."

"As in reincarnation or just taking the class over?" He chuckled.

"As in this one's all but over."

Brennan's empathetic grin faded quickly as the categorical extent of his friend's depression impacted him. The look on Kayson's face was one of abject despondency. Forcing levity in an attempt to hide how concerned he was, Brennan said, "Hey man, don't say stuff like that. It ain't the end of the world."

"Says you."

"Come on, Kace. Even o-chem ain't worth dying over."

After a long pause, Kayson mumbled, "Then again . . ."

Brennan and Kayson had been friends since middle school. They took many of the same classes together and often helped each other fight the melancholy that followed particularly grueling exams by commiserating through humor and sarcasm.

But Kayson did not feel like being funny right now. His head pounded relentlessly, and his spirits were at an all-time low. With his nerves still short-circuiting on the copious amount of energy drink he had consumed to help him cram into the wee hours of morning, he hoped Brennan's can of Tribe would indeed be the tonic needed to even out his emotions. Instead, the stuff he just drank was giving him a strange sense of . . . *potential*. His nerves slowly settled, but his emotions were amped to a compelling overload. It was as if he were on the edge of a precipice awaiting an impulse, a command of some kind. The liberating rush was moments away from fruition but for some reason would not come. The floodgates were bulging, straining, ready to burst any second. All he needed was the go-ahead for release, and then all would be well.

He heard Brennan calling his name, but his friend seemed so far away. "Kayson!"

"Yeah?"

"Relax, dude. You're sweating like a pig."

"I need . . ."

"Need what, bro?"

Kayson didn't answer because it wasn't the right thing to do. His entire body was craving the rush, demanding to be sated in ways he couldn't readily discern. But he knew he must find out how. And soon.

"Geez, relax, Kace. Come on, man, you're scaring the crap out of me."

Suddenly, the desperate need swelled to an extreme intensity. His mind was inundated with a compulsion that subjugated all other thoughts, emotions, and controls. The *need* dominated his entire being, promising a scintillating fulfillment beyond comprehension; one of rapture, euphoria, transcendental ecstasy. All he had to do was obey. It didn't matter what the task was.

"I *need* it."

"Need what, dude?" Brennan's voice was thin, worried.

His heart pounding with the ravenous burn of expectancy, Kayson's religious upbringing took a definitive second place to the potential he knew was suddenly within his grasp. Consequences did not exist. Morals evaporated. All that mattered was reaching that plateau where his spirit promised to separate from his body in a rush that could only be described as a *cleansing*.

Kayson stood slowly, deliberately. His eyes were glassy, his expression vacant.

"Come on, man. This isn't funny," Brennan pleaded.

Kayson's tone was eerily fervent. "I *need* it."

"Need *what*, Kayson?"

"I need it. I need. I need. *I NEED!*"

Brennan was near panic. "Please, Kayson. Just calm down and tell me what you need."

Kayson looked around slowly before answering. "To be free."

Leaving his backpack on the table, Kayson strode directly across the sidewalk to a large building project adjacent to the library. Many portions of the five-story structure were still skeletal and wrapped in plastic tarps to keep the wind and weather off the construction workers within. On the south end of the project sat a huge tower crane with an extension boom elevated some one hundred feet in the air.

The protective, yellow caution tape encircling the construction site did little to prevent Kayson from shuffling under it and scurrying to the crane. Climbing a ladder to the cab, he no longer heard the cries of concern from his classmate following him. A group of students materialized in seconds shouting protests and pleas as Kayson rounded the cab and began to clamber up the frame of the tower. Within minutes he was at the juncture where the vertical tower met the horizontal boom.

"I need to be free."

An erratic breeze buffeted Kayson as he tightrope walked to the end of the boom.

A siren wailed somewhere in the distance.

Desperate pleas rose from below.

I need, I need, I NEED!

Looking upward, he closed his eyes and leaned forward. Gravity pulled mercilessly. Floating, Kayson felt a blissful release.

"I'm freeeeeeeee!"

THIRTEEN

Wednesday, October 14

"We may have a problem," Dr. Steven Pendleton told CEO Bjorkman.

"What problem?"

"With our SPAAM trials in Logan."

"Logan?"

Stevie grimaced and frowned. "Dang. Forget I said that. I meant with the field tests up north."

The CEO leaned back in his chair. "What problem?"

Stevie hesitated as if building up courage. "Our contact says there might be an issue with the SPAAM causing . . . adverse reactions."

Bjorkman stared icily at the scientist for a time. With a level voice, he asked, "Serious adverse reactions?"

"Well, we're not really sure it had anything to do with our tests."

"Dr. Pendleton, I am a very busy man; therefore, I appreciate direct, concise answers."

Stevie slipped his hands into his smock pockets. "Some kid committed suicide."

"That's not so unusual. Might there be a connection?"

"Maybe. See, we're putting the SPAAM in a very popular energy drink at a specific location. Keeping it isolated helps to better monitor the outcome. We think a problem may arise when someone ingests the chemical but *doesn't* hear the subliminal commands."

Bjorkman leaned forward and began tapping his fingers together. "And by your tone I assume that could be dangerous."

Stevie's forehead began to bead with nervous sweat. "Maybe. The parent compound is one of those chemicals everyone responds to differently. One of the first tests we ran was on an old drunk who, we think, started hallucinating, and then stepped out in front of a delivery truck. A few other tests showed the same results, so I got the idea of incorporating an auditory trigger to control the subject's direction of thought. To make it less obvious, we've come up with a way of enacting subliminal triggers and commands."

"But if someone ingests your chemical and then does not receive the auditory prompt . . . ?"

The young scientist fidgeted. "We're not exactly sure. Most likely nothing."

Bjorkman brought his fingers to his pursed lips and let his gaze burn an imaginary hole between Stevie's eyes. "You mentioned you did some animal trials earlier?"

"Yeah. They all went great. It was awesome. There were no sympathomimetic abnormalities or changes in congenital catecholamine release—"

Bjorkman's brow knotted into a perturbed scowl. "Dr. Pendleton. If you please," he said in way of a request and a reprimand.

"Oh, sorry," Pendleton backpedaled. "As per the norm, we tested the chemical in lab rats; Norway rats to be specific, or *Rattus norvegicus* in Latin. They respond much better than black rats, a.k.a. *Rattus rattus*, the carriers of the bubonic plague back in—"

The CEO closed his eyes and drew in a slow, exasperated breath.

Luckily, Stevie caught the implied message. He paused to clear his throat. "You see, a rat's chemical system is surprisingly like a human's. But there's a huge difference when it comes to brain function. There's practically no way to measure a rat's emotional likes or dislikes, or its ability—if any—to rationalize. More importantly, we can't measure its dreams, phobias, or aspirations—especially those in the subconscious.

"The same holds true in the human subconscious. Since SPAAM has an unparalleled ability to influence all those parameters, we're just not sure how it will affect anyone who doesn't have the concomitant auditory stimulus."

"You're saying to achieve the results we want, *both* parameters must be met?"

"We think so. The subliminal audio prompt is a regulatory mechanism more than anything. It directs all impulses to fulfill a specific set of tasks with the promise of a huge dopamine surge as a reward."

"So what do you *assume* happens without the audio prompt?"

Stevie shrugged. "It may still work just fine; or worst case scenario, it may make cravings and mental issues worse—even uncontrollable."

Bjorkman caught on quickly. He was not happy. "You mean if some sociopath drinks your stuff, and he's not controlled by your auditory trigger, it will *amplify* his manic tendencies?"

Stevie slid his hands farther into his smock pockets. "Maybe. But it could also cause a regression of his impulses. Who knows? It might even help cure him."

Bjorkman flattened his palms on his expensive desk and rose to his feet. "But it *could* make them worse. What you're saying is that it could turn him into another Hannibal Lecter?"

"Except that Hannibal is a fictitious character, sir."

"Hannibal Lecter, Charles Manson, Jack the Ripper—take your pick. You know what I'm getting at," the CEO snapped.

Suddenly, Stevie's voice held none of its characteristic boyish enthusiasm. "We—that is, the research team—really don't know."

"You mean *you* don't know. Last I heard, *you* were in charge of new compounds research."

"Mr. Bjorkman, this is all speculative," Stevie said plaintively. "I said we *may* have a problem, not that we have a definite one. Honestly, there's nothing conclusive that links that kid's suicide to our drug. One of the first rules of science is that correlation does not equal causation. It's highly unlikely minor quirks and habits are affected by SPAAM, and perhaps only a few of those who are predisposed to severe emotional psychoses will be influenced by it. From the rat studies, we've learned that the drug's triggering effect only seems to last about four or five days. After that it gets metabolized into an inactive compound. So even if someone ingests the SPAAM but never hears the audio prompt, the chemical will be eliminated in a relatively short amount of time anyway."

"That doesn't really blow any air up my skirt, Dr. Pendleton."

"Sorry. Look, please don't worry. I just wanted to keep you abreast of everything that's going on."

The Scandia CEO's subzero glare dropped a few degrees lower.

"But just to be certain," Stevie quickly added, "I'll make sure our field agent documents everyone and everything that may be linked to our tests."

"Agent—singular? You only have one person monitoring this potentially volatile experiment?" Bjorkman's tone now matched his glare.

Pendleton shivered. "Yes sir. But she's really very good at her job. She won't miss a thing, I promise."

"She?"

"Yeah. Her name's—"

"Dr. Pendleton, the less I know about how you proceed with your experiments the better. What I am interested in are results. Positive results, if possible. Run the tests you have scheduled, but also have your agent keep an eye open for *any* unexpected behavior—both in and outside of your test population."

"Yes sir."

"More importantly, I don't want a speck of evidence left anywhere when she's done. Is that understood?"

"Yes, sir."

"Does your agent have the ability to do whatever is necessary to . . . to cover things up if things get out of hand?"

"Oh, yeah. She has no qualms about using *any* means," Stevie said with lascivious glee.

"Good. Tell her that her bonus will be substantial if all goes well."

"Yes, sir. I'll get right on it," Stevie said before literally running from the office.

Bjorkman stood in silence for some time before moving to a wall-sized rosewood filing cabinet across the room. He opened the glossy cover panel to expose a set of drawers surrounding an inset safe.

Dialing the combination, he removed a thick portfolio and returned to his desk. From it, he removed a stack of financial documents whose numbers were listed mostly in red. The CEO reflexively clenched his teeth and pushed those documents to the side. Underneath was a prospectus that always made him feel much happier.

His rise to power was clearly outlined in this dossier. It was ambitious, heady, perhaps even foolhardy, but now, suddenly, quite obtainable. His plan had been to run for governor of Nevada next year. But the governorship currently seemed sophomoric, trivial. With the aid of Pendleton's new drug, there was no limit to where he could go. And that thought alone made all the red numbers in the previous stack seem quite rosy.

FOURTEEN

Thursday, October 15

That morning, Homer followed Zachary into the Bridgerland Developmental Academy. His son entered the building without any hesitancy. This was part of the boy's routine. The incident from the previous week was long forgotten. And although Zach loved being at home, he also loved the consistency found at school. The academy had a schedule of lessons and activities in which each student partici- pated, in addition to scheduled amounts of free time. But even "free time" was well structured and orderly. It was a tried and true method for teaching autistic children.

"Good morning, Zachary. Morning, Homer."

"Good morning, Cynthia," Homer said to the receptionist. "Is Gerri Flander-Holmes in? I think I owe her an apology."

"You don't. But you also don't have to worry about her anymore. Even though she's only been here six months, we all knew she was waiting for an administrative position in Salt Lake, and she finally got it. Her office was empty by the end of the day. She didn't say good- bye to anyone, and you know what? I don't think anyone cared."

Homer laughed. "So your day must be pretty good so far."

The receptionist forced a smile that didn't quite work. "I think I'd rather go back to Monday."

"Uh-oh. What's the matter?"

"Just the usual: two of the staff called in sick, one of the children has already thrown up, I have a migraine, my son's in jail, my husband's LDL is too high, and we've got a big Health and Human Services audit coming up next week."

Homer blinked. "What was that just before your husband's cholesterol?"

Tears glistened in the woman's eyes. "Dang it, Homer, you're going to make my mascara run again."

"Sorry."

Homer knelt in front of Zachary to help him undo his coat and to allow the receptionist time to regain her composure. The boy wriggled from the winter jacket the moment the buckles were unclasped. Five seconds later he was halfway to his classroom.

Homer stood and folded Zachary's coat over his arm. Turning back to the receptionist, he asked gently, "Anything I can help with?"

Dabbing her eyes with the end of a tissue, she said, "You're so sweet, Homer, but no, I don't think so. Robbie went with a bunch of friends to a party last night and got into a bit of trouble."

"A 'bit' doesn't usually land a boy in jail," Homer said lightly.

He knew this was a hard topic for Cynthia. They had been friends for three years and had learned to trust each other's company and confidentiality. She had done so much for Zachary even as just a receptionist that Homer always had a listening ear when she was feeling blue.

Cynthia was a stocky woman in her late fifties. She was the mother of four boys, three of whom had already moved away from home. The remaining son was a perpetual source of consternation. He was into everything counter-culture. If the current trend was long hair, he'd shave his head. If it became cool to not smoke, he'd puff away like a locomotive. If a certain rock band was hip, he'd listen to the next harshest thing. He fit in by standing out. That was his style, and all his friends seemed to gravitate to him because of it. If there was one regularity in his life, it was chronic depression. A psychiatrist had told Cynthia as much.

"Robbie fights the system because it makes him feel alive. His doctor says he finds purpose in accomplishing something for which he is being recognized, even if it causes everyone else grief," Cynthia explained. "He acts out to bring himself back from the darkness. But he refuses to take medication, so all we can do is encourage him to choose the right paths and associate with friends that'll help him through the tough times."

"Does he have many friends?"

"Oh, he has a lot of friends, but none I would call mentor-worthy," Cynthia said. "His doctor recommended befriending someone in the Church or having a Church member befriend him— someone to take the lead in a steady relationship."

"Steady relationship? Was he suggesting a girlfriend?"

"Oh, no. He expressly discouraged a regular girlfriend at this point in time," Cynthia explained, checking her makeup in a small hand mirror. "He said the emotional rollercoaster kids go through in teenage romance would cause more damage than good."

Homer chuckled good-naturedly. "It doesn't seem that long ago that I was on that same rollercoaster."

The receptionist sighed heavily. "Me too. Only I fit in the little cars better back then."

Cynthia went on to divulge that, in spite of the doctor's counsel, the very next day Robbie had hooked up with a young fifteen-year-old whose real name was Katie Jo but who went by Vixen. She was a dishwater blond who dyed her hair jet black and who had enough chrome studs and loops protruding from her face to receive XM radio. She had a colorful tattoo of a snake that slithered from her right shoulder, over her collar bone, down her sternum, and disappeared into the front of her tank top. Cynthia initially wondered how far down it went, then quickly decided knowing that particular detail would keep her up at night.

Homer tilted his head to one side. "You sure you're going to be okay?"

The woman blew her nose and forced another smile. "Yes. I'm sorry, Homer. Robbie is such a good boy inside. I just hate to see him acting this way."

"So why did he end up in jail?"

"Oh, it's just misdemeanor stuff, but it all adds up. There was some underage drinking and some drug paraphernalia. He wasn't caught with any, but he has a bit of a record already. I should have seen it coming a long time ago." She forcefully shook her head and swiped at her eyes again. "Stop it, Cynthia, you're just being a boob," she openly scolded herself.

"Don't beat yourself up, kiddo. It's not your fault," Homer said. "Everyone has their agency to make good and bad decisions."

"I know you're right, of course, but it doesn't make it any easier on a mother."

"Or a father. I lost my mother to heart disease when I was fourteen, and my father wasn't much of a role model for a kid fumbling his way into manhood. When I started hanging out with the kids on the wrong side of the tracks, he didn't even notice. By the time he did, we were well beyond the constructive criticism stage."

"Really?" Cynthia asked.

"Oh, yeah. At first the best he would do was offer an occasional black eye and some bruised ribs, but he soon saw that the harder he pushed, the harder I resisted. One night he followed me to a dive we used to sneak into. It was a good thing he did. One of my buddies got into it with a steelworker from a local iron foundry, and before I knew it, we were all throwing punches. Suddenly there was a knife in some gorilla's hand, and just as suddenly I was bleeding like a stuck pig."

Homer rolled up a sleeve to show Cynthia a thick keloid scar that ran the length of his left forearm. "The dang thing took forever to heal, lots of infection and tearing and such. Anyway, before I knew it, I was on my back and this big ape was kneeling on my chest, about ready to make a jack-o-lantern out of my face, and then I heard a gun shot. The guy fell to one side, and my dad was arrested for possession of a concealed weapon without a permit, aggravated assault, use of deadly force, and manslaughter. It didn't matter that he saved my life—when the police asked what had happened, I first told them I didn't even know the guy."

Homer frowned and bit his lip. He picked up a paperclip from the receptionist's desk and randomly twirled it in his fingertips. "I guess it was my way of payback. I later told the truth, but it was only to keep Dad from going to prison for the rest of his life. It wasn't until I was in the army and learned what it meant to cover someone's back that I realized that my dad was trying to tell me with action what he couldn't with words."

Cynthia started dabbing at her eyes all over again. "I don't think your story is helping my makeup any," she teased.

Homer chuckled. "Sorry. I guess what I'm trying to say is that even if your *words* aren't getting through, your *actions* will. Just give Robbie time. Don't pander to him; keep right right and wrong wrong. But always show him your love and concern. Eventually he'll get the message."

Cynthia rose from her chair, rounded the desk faster than Homer thought was possible, and caught him in a formidable bear hug. "Thanks, Homer. That's exactly what I needed: encouragement instead of pity."

Homer gave her a couple of tender pats on the back and stepped away. "You're a good mother. Don't ever forget that."

"I won't," she said, pulling another tissue from a pocket. "Thanks."

* * *

Exiting the school, Homer ran to his car because it had begun to rain. He didn't know why he had shared that bit of history with the receptionist. She was a good friend, and Zachary liked her too. Fighting conflicting emotions, Homer sat in his car for a few minutes just thinking. He shouldn't have told her that much about his past. That was one of the warnings he'd received years ago from the FBI. But he hadn't mentioned any cities or locations, or even names. No, what he'd done for Cynthia was a good thing. And he'd grown to like doing good things for a change.

FIFTEEN

"Did you hear the official conclusions on that Maughan kid?" Professor F. Scott Key asked in his stuffy, Bostonian accent.

"*Kayson* Maughan," Morgan clarified, not looking up. Having just finished reading a note from the dean asking that she personally get to the bottom of the fugue, she was trying to formulate a logical investigative strategy.

"Kayson? Yes, yes. That's the boy."

"Of course. It's all over campus."

Helping himself to the chair next to Morgan and thoughtlessly setting his Starbuck's cup on a corner of her paperwork, F. Scott interlaced his fingers behind his head and casually took in the teacher's lounge through smug eyes. "A horrific tragedy. I never would have expected him to be suicidal."

Removing the coffee cup from her papers, Morgan said, "You knew him that well, did you? A moment ago you didn't know his first name."

Dr. Key exhibited a condescending smile of beautifully veneered teeth. "My dear Professor Winegar, you know as well as I do that my utmost concern extends to each and every student under my tutelage."

"Really?" Morgan scoffed. "Is that why you traditionally fail half of your classes, Francis?"

Placing a manicured hand to her shoulder, he said, "I don't fail them, my dear; they fail themselves. And please don't call me by that hideously effete, bourgeois nickname. I prefer F. Scott—or for you, pretty lady," he paused for anticipatory emphasis, "Scott will suffice. Besides, Scott is much more masculine, don't you concur?"

Shrugging from his slimy touch, she said, "Whatever."

F. Scott nodded slowly, as if making a magnanimous sacrifice in accepting her answer. He sipped his latte with a pinky extended in an air of superiority.

"A bit nippy this morning, wouldn't you say?" he asked in an effort to continue their conversation.

Morgan hated conversing with Francis Scott Key, Ph.D. She hated being in the same room with him, and subsequent to meeting him, she now hated anyone with a Boston accent.

Raised in Worcester, Massachusetts, and schooled at Boston College, F. Scott Key had an insufferable ego and an arrogant, snobbish personality to match. His pomposity was off the charts. He wasn't there to nobly bestow his vast knowledge of musicology on his pupils; they were there to glean what they could from his superior mind and astounding talents. If the students couldn't rise to the challenge, that was their fault, not his.

F. Scott Key believed he was more than a few rungs higher on the intellectual ladder than most everyone else at Utah State—especially since it operated out of a lowly hamlet like Logan—and he wasn't afraid to say so. More importantly, at least to him, was his ability to trace his prodigious genealogy back to Francis Scott Key, heralded author of the "Star Spangled Banner" and the patriot after whom he was named. Thanks to superior genetics, his brilliance was manifestly inbred.

To Morgan, his pompous mannerisms were as repugnant as rancid cooking grease and left an equally foul taste in her mouth. There were so many negatives about the man that she couldn't put her finger on which characteristic repulsed her the most. Perhaps that's why she always felt a need to shower after conversing with him.

"Morgan? A bit chilly, yes?"

"No colder than your heart," she said just under her breath, not wanting to encourage chitchat.

"What's that, my dear?"

"I suppose," she said, again busying herself in her papers.

Ignoring the brush-off, F. Scott continued: "And what of the sit-in the other day? I hear the students are calling it the 'Aggie Trance.' My word, this reminds me of the student protests of the seventies and eighties. Rather stimulating in a way. That's probably why they chose to congregate around that enigmatic *Synergy* sculpture. Oh, the foolhardy rebelliance of youth." He chuckled warmly.

"'Foolhardy rebelliance,' huh? Those kids got soaked in a freezing rain."

"My point exactly! Of course, I was never as pugnacious as that; but I did sit on the administration steps at Boston College for four hours once, protesting apartheid in South Africa. Does that shock you?"

"A whole four hours, huh?" Morgan said without looking up.

"Well, perhaps it was only two or three. I took an extended lunch break to cool off. It *was* an insufferably hot summer, after all. But there was a modern art sculpture next to the admin building, so I guess that counts."

At the risk of reliving the glories of his fleeting human rights experience, Morgan said, "I'm pretty sure that particular statue had nothing to do with it."

Dr. Key leaned forward and placed his hand on Morgan's wrist, clearly stimulated by the repartee she offered. "Never mind that. What I'm interested in is what you make of the sit-in, as a professional, that is."

"Nothing yet," she said, removing his hand.

"But surely as a psychologist you must have professional opinions on the matter," F. Scott persisted. "I would love to discuss them over dinner tonight."

"I have a few thoughts, but I'd prefer to keep them to myself, if you please," Morgan said, becoming unendurably annoyed by his persistence. "And I still have a ring on my left hand that actually means something to me, even if the one on yours doesn't. I really wish you'd stop asking—"

Just then a voice bellowed across the lounge, "It's happening again!"

Both Morgan and F. Scott looked up.

"Another sit-in," the young man exclaimed. "Over at the french fry stack by Ag Science."

Morgan quickly gathered her papers, crammed them into her voluminous shoulder bag, and headed toward the exit. F. Scott was at her side doing his best not to spill his precious latte.

"Slow down," he whined. "If it's anything like the last one, they'll be there for an hour."

Jogging toward the north end of campus, Morgan saw that a crowd had already grown thick. The students talked in exaggerated whispers as they stared at the twenty or so kids seated around the modern art display. A glazing of sleet had fallen the night before, and the outdoor temperature hovered near twenty degrees. Yet, to everyone's surprise, none of the students wore winter coats.

Morgan recognized most of the students from the first episode, but there were some new faces too, including a girl from her Sociology 101 course. Kneeling beside the girl, Morgan asked, "Holly? What's going on? Are you okay?"

The girl did not respond. She stared slack-jawed at the assemblage of yellow metal beams that resembled a loose pile of ten-foot-long french fries. The chill of the afternoon air condensed her breath in a vaporous cloud with each exhalation. Like the others, the girl wore no coat, but she did not appear to be cold.

"Holly? Can you hear me?" Morgan persisted.

No answer.

Morgan gently nudged the girl. She did not stir. She then gripped the girl's shoulder and shook it. Still no response. She snapped her fingers directly in front of the young girl's face and repeated her name. The girl didn't even blink.

Placing two fingers on Holly's wrist to feel her pulse, Morgan timed the young girl's heart rate—at least 140 beats per minute.

"Holly, stand up for me, okay?"

Nothing.

"Is she drugged?" Dr. Key asked, coming up behind Morgan.

"No, not her."

"Are you sure? Kids will be kids, after all."

"Look, Francis, I know this girl. Like many on this campus, she's staunch LDS and wouldn't be caught dead near illicit drugs."

"Oh, I don't know," F. Scott said before taking a thoughtful sip from his steaming cup. "Sometimes it's the sweet, innocent ones that are the real hell-raisers."

"Not Holly. I'd bet my life on it."

Just as Dr. Key predicted, the trance lasted about an hour. During that time, Morgan asked that none of the students be moved. She was concerned about the potential for shock if they were forced from the fugue prematurely.

There were twenty-three this time. Again, they varied in age, gender, and socioeconomic backgrounds. Ten were white males, seven white females, three Asian males, two black males, and one Middle Eastern male. Because none of them wore coats, Morgan asked if those observing could share any extra clothing they could spare until emergency services could be summoned.

At precisely five o'clock, the carillon began its Westminster chime, then meted out five hollow gongs. Just as before, the students snapped from their communal fugue and asked if they had just experienced the Aggie Trance. For a few of them, it was at once frightening and exciting. But the majority had negative feelings. Some of the boys were visibly shaken; some of the girls started to cry.

Holly was sobbing.

"Hey, I've got you, hon," Morgan said, putting an arm around the girl. She was trembling uncontrollably. "Let's get you inside where it's warm. Where's your coat?"

"I—t-took—it off—in—the—the b-building," she stammered.

"Why?" Morgan asked as she escorted the girl through the scattering crowd.

"I d-d-don't know."

Dr. Key strode ahead and opened the glass door for the two women. He glanced inside, then turned back. "You're not going to believe this," he said with wide-eyed amusement.

Inside the vestibule of the Ag Science building lay an orderly row of winter coats and jackets; twenty-three in all, matching the number of students that had just experienced the trance. Morgan had a student run back to the french fry stack to inform the others as to the whereabouts of their outerwear. As the students came to grips with what had just happened, they began exchanging information. Not one of them remembered why they had taken off their coats in the first place.

Morgan quickly gathered everyone's name and phone number. She also asked each student to write down the last thing they remembered doing just before they came out of the trance at the modern art sculpture.

"Please include everything, no matter how trivial it may seem— what you were reading, what you were eating, the class you had just come from, what you had for breakfast and lunch, who you were with, and drugs you are using, both prescription and illegal, everything. Also list any health issues such as recent headaches, fatigue, relationship issues and the like, and even any extra stress you may have felt from midterms—especially if you're in one of Dr. Key's general ed. music appreciation classes," she added to lighten the mood. The students all laughed knowingly. F. Scott Key smiled at the inference.

"I assure you, all information with be kept strictly confidential," Morgan continued. "I give you my word none of it will go beyond my office, and it will not be used against you in any way. I don't care who you are. I don't care what you were doing—other than how it may relate to these trances. I don't even care why you were doing it, and I will pass no judgment on anyone. But I can do nothing without your help. So please, help me help you, okay?"

Morgan didn't realize the fervency of her pleading until she had finished. Her entire body trembled from intensity. Her breathing was shallow, staccato. The students all gawked a moment before uniformly saying yes.

She then turned to Holly. "Do you have a minute to come with me right now?"

The girl wiped her eyes, nodded, and took Morgan's hand as if she were a little child who had just woken up from a nightmare. Morgan wasn't sure who was comforting who at that moment.

SIXTEEN

Morgan first took Holly to the campus infirmary to get her checked out. The attending PA could find nothing wrong other than the after-effects of a mild panic attack. The girl's heart rate was still elevated—around 105 bpm—but that was probably due to the anxiety of the moment.

"Would you like a prescription for some Xanax?" the PA asked. "It'll help calm your nerves so you can sleep tonight."

Holly looked to her professor for guidance. The trepidation in the young girl's eyes belied her uncertainty and incapacitating fear.

"No, thanks," Morgan answered for the girl. "We'll figure something else out."

The PA noted their decision in his chart, recommended that Holly go home and get some rest, and then excused himself.

Morgan then escorted Holly to her office. She made some hot cocoa for warmth and comfort. She figured it would do almost as much good as the addictive prescription would have.

"I think we should call your parents," Morgan suggested after Holly had settled a bit.

Holly paled. "Oh, no, please don't."

"Are you sure? I really think they should know about this."

The girl fidgeted a moment before answering. "It's a long story. Kinda embarrassing, too. You see, we're from Lehi—you know, down in Utah County? Anyway, my parents wanted me to go to BYU, but I didn't want to."

"Why not? It's not a bad school."

"Oh, I know. Both my parents went there. That's where they met."

"Ah. And you wanted an education rather than an MRS degree?" Morgan asked with a grin.

"Yes and no. It's just that Utah State had such a bad reputation as a party school when my folks were in college. They claimed that more than half the kids they knew who came here ended up excommunicated from the Church."

"I don't know that it's ever been *that* bad," Morgan said. "Besides, I used to hear equally ugly rumors about BYU. For instance, any girl caught kissing on a first date was put on scholastic probation for violation of the honor code."

Holly laughed. It was a welcome sound.

"But you got to come here anyway," Morgan persisted.

"Yeah. I've always loved Cache Valley. My grandma lived here her whole life. I used to visit her each summer before she passed away. It's silly, but I've always felt I should come to school up here. But to do so, I had to promise my parents I would keep my grades up on penalty of transfer to another school."

"Well, you're certainly doing well in my class."

"In all my classes," Holly divulged. "I carry a 3.8 GPA. I got an A minus in Dr. Key's class."

Morgan expelled a burst of air and shook her head. "I'm confident that was not your fault."

Holly shrugged, then stared blankly into her cocoa mug. "Anyway, if my parents think I'm into some kind of partying or drug culture, I'm out of here for sure."

Morgan moved to her desk and grabbed a pen and a notepad. "I am determined to get to the bottom of this thing, Holly—that's a promise. As far as school goes, I'll make sure you're staying here. And until I figure out what's going on, it'll be our secret. Okay?"

Holly responded with a halfhearted smiled.

Morgan started writing. "Now, I'm going to list each day of the week, beginning two weeks ago. We're going to record everything you have done since then, day by day." She paused and waited for her student to make eye contact. "You're going to have to trust me here, Holly. Not only will everything you tell me remain in the strictest confidence, but I will pass no judgment on your lifestyle and choices, nor will it affect your grade in my class. However embarrassing it may be, I need to know what's going on with these trances, and right now you're my best source."

Holly took a deep breath and held it, focusing on her decision.

"More than anything," Morgan continued, "I want to make sure that no one is harmed from these episodes, physically or emotionally."

Holly released her breath and agreed. Not wanting to get into a lengthy explanation over the phone, Morgan left a message for Homer on their answering machine saying she'd be home a bit later than usual because of an issue at school.

The two women spent the next four hours going over everything Holly could remember from the last two weeks. As she moved along in her narrative, one incident would spark a memory from earlier in the week, or would substantiate a reason for an action later on. Morgan scribbled constantly, noting not only the actual facts, but also her initial thoughts on each.

By the time they were finished, it was past nine o'clock and very dark. Morgan offered to drive Holly to her apartment. The girl readily accepted.

* * *

By the time Morgan got home, she had a headache, bloodshot eyes, and a queasy stomach.

"You look terrible," Homer said with compassion as his wife changed into her sweats.

"Thanks a lot," she groaned. "Honey, I'm really getting worried about these episodes on campus—these mass hallucinations or fugues, or whatever they are."

"Fugues . . . plural? There was another one?"

"This afternoon. A couple of the kids may have gotten frostbite from it."

"Wow. What does the dean think about it?"

Massaging her temples, Morgan said, "He's asked me to head the committee to figure it out."

"What committee?"

"Me, myself, and I."

"Great. Where're you going to start?"

"I did an in-depth interview with one of the girls who was affected, but nothing stood out."

"Have you compared her responses to the other students you've talked to?"

"Only briefly. I haven't had time."

Homer stood behind his wife and started rubbing her neck and shoulders. "Well, I'm sure something will come up."

"I know. I just hope I can figure it out before they get any worse."

"Me too, sweetheart. You want some dinner?"

She shook her head. "I'm not very hungry. Maybe just a bagel."

"You got it," he said, folding her hair aside and brushing his lips on the nape of her neck. Then, heading toward the kitchen, he added, "If you like, I can help you analyze the information."

"That would be great. Midterms are next week, and I'll be swamped. My TA, Lanh, is going to organize the data, and then I'll bring home a copy. But I'd still like to take a stab at it myself."

Homer dropped two halves of an Asiago cheese bagel into the toaster. "How about I get a head start on it while you're into your tests? I don't have your psychology expertise, but I do know a thing or two about data analysis."

Morgan walked up behind her husband and slid her arms around his waist. "You're the best, you know that?"

"Only because of you and Zach."

She hugged him tightly. "You know, if they made more guys like you, there'd be a lot more happy women in the world."

"Now *you're* the one hallucinating," he chuckled.

"No. I'm afraid I know all too well what's real and what isn't. And to be honest, these mass fugues scare me to death."

WEEK THREE

SEVENTEEN

Monday, October 19

Morgan perused the *Statesman*, the university's tri-weekly newspaper, during one of her free periods. Emblazoned across the front page was an article on USU's rout of Boise State in the latest WAC football game. Below that was a clip from an AP affiliate castigating the lack of U.S. representation in the current Helsinki summit on global warming.

At the bottom of page two she found a small follow-up article on the suicide of Kayson Maughan. *Suicide* seemed the only viable explanation. Kayson's friend Brennan Hatch had commented on Maughan's despondent behavior just before the tragedy, but he'd also said that his friend had been subject to mood swings and lacked self-esteem as long as he'd known him—they had become friends at Logan Middle School.

"It really sucks that professors put so much pressure on students by giving insanely hard tests," Hatch was quoted as saying. "Kayson loaded up on Tribe just to make it through that exam . . . Dudes like Kayson take it so hard when they get a bad grade . . . the system's totally whack."

The article, written by a senior staff editor, had a clear bias toward the plight of the poor student, making all instructors—from student teachers to tenured professors—out to be the bad guys.

Morgan had seen this angle before and could never understand it. If the entire class did poorly, then something might be amiss with the instruction. After all, there *were* professors like F. Scott Key. But if only one or two students failed to make the grade, then that was a personal issue.

What Morgan was looking for was tucked back on the fourth page, nestled in between a schedule of upcoming soccer games and a listing of movie times in local theaters. It was a small piece on the Aggie Trance.

The reporter listed a few "educated" guesses as to the cause of the events and in the end speculated that it was simply a hoax. No one had yet come forward to claim responsibility for the trance, but the writer estimated that with the coming of winter, such happenings would soon be nothing more than a laughable memory. No one wanted to sit outside in the snow just for a lark.

Morgan was appalled. It baffled her why the university was not giving these mass fugues more attention—or concern. It was almost as if the matter garnered the same importance as the spreading of a seasonal flu bug. Be extra vigilant in washing your hands and covering your mouth when you cough. Drink lots of fluids and take a daily multivitamin. *Come on!*

She had discussed aspects of the fugues with other professors in her department, but no one had any more of an explanation than she did. It all came down to raw data. And she had precious little to work with.

What she needed was to amass all the information she could from every student who had gone through an episode. There was no way that each participant in the two gatherings could stick to a concocted story. Someone would blow it. Morgan knew she could find a slip, a chink in the narrative that would expose any subterfuge.

The newspaper article had presented the episodes much like a humor piece. But Morgan knew firsthand that many of the students involved felt otherwise.

Dwelling on it caused a dark feeling to stir inside her. It wasn't merely the frustration of not knowing; it was a shadowy whispering that hinted of evil portents. Disturbing questions without answers plagued Morgan's thoughts. What if the trances weren't isolated events? What if someone was organizing them, studying them?

As she folded the paper, Morgan paused, struck by another unsettling thought. A sour feeling curdled in her stomach as her eyes rested on the Kayson Maughan article once more. What if the fugues were only part of larger, more sinister plan? The thought sickened her. To find out what, she needed specific, isolated data.

Morgan called the *Statesman* and asked for the person in charge.

"Editorial, this is Sam," a female voice announced.

"Hi, Sam. This is Morgan Winegar—" She stopped midsentence, unsure of how to approach this. *Just dive on in,* she decided. "Listen, I need to make a comment on the article covering the Aggie Trances and perhaps ask a couple of questions."

"Sure. What year are you, Morgan?"

"I'm not a student. I'm a teacher."

"What department?"

"Sociology and Psych."

"Oh, *Professor* Winegar," the young woman said. "This is Samantha Cuthbert. I had your class last term, you remember?"

"Sure I do. You were lots of fun," was Morgan's sardonic reply.

Samantha made sure that every lecture Morgan gave ended up in the paper's opinion column, but never with the same emphasis or conclusion in which it was given. It was a forgone guarantee that Sam would present the topic in a negative light. She claimed it simply made for better copy. The articles always spawned a legion of reader comments and criticism—which was the reporter's specific intent.

Fortunately, Morgan was never quoted directly. But those in her class recognized the topics. It always made for a lively discussion the next time they met.

"I'm surprised you remember it as *fun,*" Sam said with a chuckle. "Now, is this on or off the record?"

"On, I suppose, but we've got to be careful how it's presented."

"Fair and impartial are my middle names."

Morgan choked back the acrid comment burning her tongue. "Sam, I need to gather all the information I can on every person that has experienced the Aggie Trance."

"That's odd," Sam said in a detached tone. "I have witnesses that say you were at both occurrences. And I heard you got a lot of copy at each."

"Some, but not all. Plus, I'm betting the trance—or something close to it—has happened elsewhere, both on an off campus."

"Is that a bet or a fact?"

Morgan blinked. "What's that supposed to mean?"

"Well . . . some people in my department have speculated you were behind the trances in the first place. You know—some kind of human behavior experiment, *Professor* Winegar . . ."

"That is totally absurd," Morgan barked. "There have been serious repercussions to these events. Some of the students have needed counseling and medication because of them. How dare you infer I was behind this madness."

"Whoa, rein it on in, professor. I was just throwing out ideas, you know?"

"Well, you can throw *those* ideas right out the window. I want to prevent more damage from occurring, not simply study it out of curiosity."

"Okay, okay. Sorry," the young woman said with little sincerity. "How can I help?"

"What I need is an article—" Morgan paused for emphasis and to control her emotions. "A well-written, non-sensationalized article on the seriousness of the trances. I'm going to provide medical aid and crisis counseling with certified disaster therapists for anyone who has experienced a trance or who knows someone who has. They need to contact my office as soon as possible to answer a few questions. All calls will remain anonymous. Everything will be handled with utmost confidentiality."

"This sounds serious," Sam said with significantly less sarcasm.

"Serious enough to cause suicide," Morgan hinted, which was picked up immediately by the perceptive journalist.

"The Maughan kid? You think there's a connection?"

"Off the record, maybe. But that's between you and me, Sam. Okay?"

There was a long moment of silence on the other end. "An article like this could go the other way, you know."

"What—make it worse?" Morgan asked.

"I've seen it happen," Sam confirmed.

"Then let's make it as panic-proof as possible, but with enough urgency to prompt the students into action."

"So . . . a 'Your Life May Be at Risk' header is not what you had in mind?"

"Hardly. But I do want it to have the same impact. Have you got a writer who can do that?"

"You bet, professor. His name's Dickson. I'll get him right on it."

"Thanks, Sam."

The girl chortled. "Hey, it's the least I can do after what I put you through last term."

"No argument there, Samantha."

EIGHTEEN

Wednesday, October 21

"I think it has something to do with an energy drink," Homer told his wife. "But there's got to be more to it."

"What—like Red Bull?"

"Yeah, but the newer one: Tribe. And not just any flavor. It seems to only be the Dingo's Dance that affects the students."

Morgan left her desk and moved over to the small couch in their study. Homer had highlighted various sections on all the interviews with colored markers, and laid them in three rows at his feet. Discounting normal activities like bathing and eating, Homer had focused on anything that deviated from everyday life. He was surprised at the number of students taking prescription stimulants like Adderall and Concerta; most legally, others not. But not all the students had taken them, thus removing that factor as a potential cause of the trance.

What he *did* find was equally surprising. Fluorescent yellow markings showed that every student Morgan interviewed had mentioned drinking a Tribe Dingo's Dance sometime before the trance. The next closest connecting link was that each student had recently seen the latest blockbuster installment of the *Jurassic Park* movies. A third link revealed that all of the students had been listening to music, either on MP3 players or the radio. A fourth grouping indicated that all had experienced difficulty sleeping because of extra-vivid dreams that week.

Starting with the first corollary, Morgan asked, "Do you think there's something wrong with the drink?"

"I did a quick Web search but couldn't find any product recalls."

"Could it be some contagion no one has discovered yet? I mean, like some unknown bacteria or contaminate in the drink?"

Homer rubbed the back of his neck. "This data is a good start, but it's not enough to base any conclusions on."

"Should we report this to the manufacturer?" Morgan asked.

"I think we'd better," Homer agreed. "And to be extra safe, maybe we should ban the sale of it on campus for a while."

"Just on campus?"

"For now. A number of these interviews mention buying a Dingo's Dance at the Taggart Center," he said while still massaging his neck.

"What's to stop the kids from buying it at Macey's or Lee's?"

"Nothing. But I have a feeling something is going on at the campus level—you know, like a single batch that went bad. I could be way off, but that's the pattern I'm seeing."

Morgan scooted closer to take over her husband's attempt to relieve the kink in his neck. As her fingers grappled and her thumbs gouged, Homer let out a deep groan of satisfaction. "I'm going to insist you let me take you out to Blackstone's for this."

Morgan leaned close and kissed his ear. "As much as I'd love a nine-ounce filet mignon, you know we can't afford that. But thanks for the offer."

As Morgan massaged away Homer's tensions, he kept looking over the patterns and anomalies he'd found in the interviews. He was close to something, but there had to be more. Just as a microscope reveals an unseen world, Homer knew some vital piece of information loomed just beyond the limits of his vision.

A minute later, Zachary walked into the room with a credit card–sized sports radio and a single earphone. "I want the whispers song," he said, holding up the unit.

"What song is that, little man?" Homer asked.

"The whispers song."

"Do you know the artist, honey?" Morgan asked.

Zachary shook his head.

"Was it just playing?"

Another shake.

"Can you sing us some of the words?"

"No words."

"Can you hum the melody?"

"Uh-uh."

Homer closed his eyes and leaned into Morgan's massage. "Then I'm afraid we can't help you, son. We'd like to, but we need more inform—"

"I want the whispers song!" Zachary interrupted, causing both parents to flinch.

Morgan reached a hand toward her son. "I'd like to hear it, too, sweetie—"

"I want the whispers song!" Zachary belted out, slapping her hand away.

"Zachary," Homer said sharply.

"Whisperrrrrs!" the boy screamed.

"Zachary, sweetheart, you know we don't yell for things," Morgan said.

"I want the whispers song, please," he said in a slightly lower volume, holding out his radio.

"Okay, son. We'll try to find it tomorrow," Homer offered.

"No! I want it now!" he cried, throwing the radio to the ground.

"Zachary," his mother scolded.

Homer slid from his chair to his knees. "Zach. What's this all about?" he asked softly.

"Whispers, whispers, whispers!"

Homer reached for the radio only to have Zachary try to grind it underfoot. The boy's cries became harried, frantic.

"It won't play it anymore. It won't, it won't."

"Zachary, I'm going to need you to focus for me, okay?" Homer said.

Morgan joined them on the floor in the middle of the room. "Zachary, let's focus like we practiced."

Zachary was near tantrum stage. His fists were clenched white on either side of his head; his face was turning purple from inner rage. His voice had quickly gone raw from screaming. Now all that issued from his lips was a scratchy revelation: "Whispers hide. Whispers hide. Whispers, whispers, hide right there."

"They hide right where, sweetheart?"

"Whispers hide. Under the music. Whisper, whisper, whisper, whisper!" he whimpered.

As Morgan reached out to stroke Zachary's arm, the boy fainted. Homer's reaction was incredibly fast; he caught his son just before he hit the floor.

Homer checked Zachary's breathing and heart rate.

"Is he okay?" Morgan was near tears. "I've never seen his tantrums that intense before."

"Me either."

"So is he okay?" she repeated, wiping at her eyes.

Homer nodded. "He's just resting now. His back is relaxed and his jaw is loose. He's terribly hot, but I don't think he's going to seize this time."

Homer stood with Zachary in his arms and took him to his bedroom. Morgan followed close behind. As their son lay on the bed, Morgan removed his shoes and socks while Homer got a cool cloth to help bring down his temperature.

"Should I call Dr. Owens tomorrow to see what he makes of this?" Morgan asked softly.

Homer gently dabbed Zachary's forehead and wiped down his arms. The boy was breathing easier now, and his temperature was dropping. In a slightly strained voice, Homer said, "That's okay, hon. If he's not feeling well in the morning, I'll take him to the clinic."

Morgan nodded.

After a few minutes of silence, Homer asked, "What do *you* make of it?"

She shrugged. "Something he heard on the radio, I guess. And probably not just once."

"The *whispers* song . . . Does that sound familiar to you?"

"No. You?"

Homer thought for a moment. "I'll ask a couple of the techs I know at work. They're always listening to music on their headsets. Maybe they'll know."

Changing the subject, Morgan asked, "And what about the energy drink?"

"Well, if it's possible, I'd like to get a hold of every can of Dingo's Dance that USU food services has."

"What're you going to do with them?"

"I'll have one of the scientists at SatchBo help me fractionate them. I have a hunch we'll find something that's not supposed to be in there."

Morgan agreed. "I had the school paper run a piece about the trance, indicating that it was a serious issue. They mentioned my name and told anyone with concerns or information to contact me."

"Any bites yet?"

"No. Most kids still seem to think it's a hoax."

"Not me. Not anymore."

"Me either."

Both parents looked on their son sleeping peacefully. It was hard for either to believe he'd thrown such a fit only minutes before.

"I guess we're smack-dab in the middle of this now." Homer's voice had a worried, almost hopeless edge to it.

Morgan took the washcloth and dabbed the sides of her husband's face and neck. "I bet this whole thing blows over soon. You'll see."

Homer wished he could agree with his wife, but deep inside he suspected something far worse.

NINETEEN

Morgan sat in the back of the Kent Concert Hall on the USU campus. The speaker was F. Scott Key. Trying to personify his role as a quintessential old-school professor, the New Englander had donned a tweed sports coat, an oxford-cloth shirt, a clashing silk bowtie, and blue jeans. His lecture was on the brain's subliminal response to mathematically dominant music—somewhat of an offshoot of the Mozart Effect.

Morgan attended the lecture with reservation. As much as she detested the man, she hoped his information would help her understand what was plaguing Zachary. Her son had become obsessed with the "whispers song." Every day was spent scanning radio channels, searching for the song. After twenty minutes of failure, Zachary would regress into classic autistic behavior, becoming noncommunicative, short-tempered, and often violent.

At school it was even worse. Zachary refused to work with the teachers and wanted nothing to do with the other children. It was suggested that Zachary spend less time at school and more at home. Either that or put him on an ADHD medication, even though such therapy was controversial in the treatment of autism. The idea of drugging her son simply to keep him quiet was repugnant to Morgan. Her husband agreed. Yet, until the semester ended at Christmas break, Morgan could not stay at home with Zach. She and Homer had arranged with the principal of Zach's school to work extra hard with their son at home, and agreed to consider medication should his tantrums increase to the point that they endangered the other children.

Morgan had called the local radio station asking about any new song that mentioned "whispers." They had no idea what specific song it could be. There were several older recordings that mentioned *whispers* in the lyrics, a few that had *whispers* in the title, and even a band called *The Whispers*. The station receptionist suggested Morgan try searching an online music seller, then play through sample selections to find the particular tune.

Bringing Zach home from school, Morgan did just that. Sitting her son in front of the computer, she played through one snippet after another. Zach made it through almost fifty recordings before becoming frustrated to the point of lashing out.

Morgan flinched as a shrill whine blared through the Kent Concert Hall. "Sorry about that," Dr. Key mumbled. "Let's try this again, shall we?"

After a short, grating buzz, a familiar selection of music began to play. F. Scott tinkered with a mixer at his lectern until his voice could be heard over the music he was discussing. Morgan recognized the selection as Mozart's *Eine kleine Nachtmusik*.

As Francis Key droned on, Morgan surveyed the concert hall. It was about three-fourths full, which surprised her. Although USU had a renowned music department, she didn't think so many students would have an interest in this topic, especially with Key's poor reputation. Perhaps it was an assigned lecture in numerous classes, one on which they would be tested later.

Without warning, the music changed to a selection of freeform piano jazz. F. Scott said the artist was Suzi Child. The tune was fluid and moving but had a rebellious edge to it. It was captivating stuff. Morgan let the music wash over her and tried to tune out the professor. She preferred to let the artist's music speak for itself.

After that selection, the genre switched to a Baroque piece featuring a violin, a cello, and an oboe. The professor identified various mathematical aspects of the arrangement and commented on how they affected human brain chemistry.

The next selection was a Motown artist whose name Morgan thought she recognized. Again, Key emphasized primary rhythms, contrapuntal rhythms, and syncopated secondary melodies. He equated the tune's complexity to fugues by seventeenth-century composers. He noted that the underlying beat and melody captivated the listener, but it was the background percussion and instrumental underscoring that stimulated the subconscious.

"The penultimate examples of this complex form of composition are found in the basest of primitive cultures; for example, the Djenne Tribe from West Africa, and the Pitjantjatjara Tribe in Central Australia. Here are some excerpts from early recordings of their music."

The drums, congas, reeds, and a score of unidentifiable percussion instruments created myriad tonal vibrations in Morgan's head. She closed her eyes and tried to absorb the subtle undertones the professor talked about. It was fascinating to consider how she probably would have totally missed the polyrhythms and other musical nuances had she not be told what to look for. As much as she hated to admit it, F. Scott knew what he was talking about.

"Modern composers will sometimes, albeit unwittingly, mimic the tapestry of melody, rhythm, and even harmonics of these early musicians. Here, for example, is a brand new recording I just acquired from a group called Ayers Rock, named after the huge monolith in the center of Australia, not far from the Pitjantjatjara. The tune is called 'Toad Stomp.'"

The music began with a seductive cadence of low bass notes and percussion. A few cymbals and rattles joined in, offering counter rhythms and an intriguing depth to the sensuous underscore. After a few measures, an Australian didgeridoo began a warbling buzz, which added a dimension that was mesmerizing and haunting, bizarre yet unavoidably hypnotic. The song went on for about three minutes with a reed pipe playing a low, ululating melody.

Just as the tune was winding down, approximately fifty or more students suddenly stood up, gathered their belongings, and headed toward the main entrance. They did not converse with each other or with those they stepped over as they made their way into the aisles. It was almost as if their mass exodus had been prearranged, choreographed for a specific moment in time. F. Scott Key stopped midsentence, staring dumbfounded at the students.

Morgan's breath caught in her throat. Her mouth went totally dry.

Because she sat just off the center aisle in the back, she had a good view of the exiting students as they passed by her. None of them made eye contact with her. They all had the blank look on their faces she had seen before. And many of them were students who had gone though this before.

It was happening again—only this time on a much larger scale.

TWENTY

Morgan followed the group of students, as did a large mob of curious onlookers. The walk was a long one. There was no snow on the ground, but you could smell it in the air. If the flat, opaque sky did not bestow a downy white blanket that evening, it certainly would sometime the following day. The chilled atmosphere bit the skin and stung the eyes. Winter was coming early this year. Morgan loved this kind of weather, but not today, not now. Presently, the dull light and low clouds gave her a claustrophobic feeling that bode of danger and mishap.

As the ever-growing crowd passed the Widtsoe building, Morgan saw that a smaller crowd had already assembled in front of *Phra Apaimanee,* the statue of a Hindi goddess holding a magical, jewel-encrusted flute to her lips. The entranced students formed a tight circle around the statue. After a moment's pause, the students all removed their winter coats and set them by their feet. They then commenced to remove their shoes and socks, and knelt facing the goddess. Morgan counted more than eighty students and some faculty affected by the trance, including all those whom she had interviewed twice before. After about ten minutes, they moved as a body into a cross-legged lotus position and clasped hands with the person next to them.

A stiff breeze blustered between the buildings where the statue resided. Plumes of condensed vapor billowed from those entranced in perfect, uniform synchronization as they sat yoga-like around the Hindi goddess. Yet none of them appeared to be cold. They were so focused on the statue that they blocked out all external stimuli, including the temperature.

Morgan couldn't believe what she was seeing. Not only had these people experienced a simultaneous "call-to-arms," as it were, but their physical processes seemed to harmonize with each other. They inhaled at the same rate and exhaled as a single body. She wondered if they would all have similar heart rates, too.

Morgan tried to recall any historical documentation of mass hypnosis but could not recall any verified events. It was known that certain charismatic speakers throughout history had the ability to hype listeners into extreme states of euphoria. Jim Jones was able to convince 918 followers in Guyana to drink cyanide in an act of "revolutionary suicide." Adolph Hitler had effectively convinced a nation of their superiority and their moral responsibility to rid the world of inferior people through genocide. Ancient cultures often used natural hallucinogens to facilitate clan members performing outrageous acts of courage and bravery. Some scholars believed the word *assassin* came from the term *hashish*, the Middle Eastern name for marijuana, used to embolden mercenaries to commit murder.

Currently, religious fanaticism dominated the news with reports of suicide bombings, random acts of terrorism, and wanton violence. Such episodes were often preceded by a chemical delusionary or an indoctrination that triggered such destructive behavior.

But Morgan had witnessed no such trigger in the concert hall. Or had she missed it while worrying about Zachary?

Just then, a hopeful thought sprang to mind. The department always recorded such lectures for those who could not attend.

"Professor Winegar!" a young man called out. It was Lanh Tran, her Vietnamese teaching assistant. "This so cool, isn't it!" he exclaimed.

"No, it is not cool," Morgan snapped. "Something is definitely premeditated here; something that goes deeper than we assume. Frankly, it scares me to death."

"Yeah, but no one ever get hurt," the TA argued.

"None that we know of at least. I'm guessing Kayson Maughan may have been part of this mess."

"Really? A lot of people saying he just cracked. Too much stress from study, I think."

"Your sympathy is underwhelming."

"Hey, I feel for the guy. But it happen sometime, right? You remember last year after homecoming?"

Morgan didn't have time to discuss every suicide attempt that had happened on campus. "Listen, Lanh. I need a huge favor. I'm going back to the Kent to check on something. I need you to monitor this fugue. When they come to—"

"If," Tran interrupted.

"Okay. *If* they come to, I want you to ask as many of them as possible two questions."

"But professor, there got to be a hundred kids here."

"Enlist the help of a few others if you need to. Tell them I asked."

He shrugged. "What question?"

"What did they have to drink lately—and especially if they've had any Tribe."

"Tribe? You mean the energy drink?" he asked as if questioning the validity of her request.

"Yes. Ask them when and what kind of every drink," she commanded over her shoulder, already heading back to the concert hall. "I'll be right back."

"You got it, professor."

TWENTY-ONE

Inside the Kent Concert Hall, Morgan was surprised to see F. Scott Key still addressing the remaining audience as if nothing had happened. Another piece of classical music played in the background as the man droned on about the mathematics employed in period music. It was interesting material, but Morgan was no longer concerned with picking up details. She knew that the trigger she was looking for had come and gone.

Exiting the hall and locating the door to the audio-visual control room, Morgan entered without knocking. A couple of young men were stationed at some electronic apparatus—hopefully one that captured audio.

"Have you gentlemen been recording the entire lecture?"

"Yes, ma'am," the senior of the two responded.

"Any way I can review what just happened?"

"You mean the mass exodus?"

"Yes. I need to see it right now," Morgan stated in no uncertain terms.

"Um . . . but the lecture isn't over," the younger man said.

Morgan's eyes narrowed. She didn't have time for this. "The important part is."

"Ma'am, we're graded on how well we record this lecture," the older student explained. "It's for the students who couldn't be here as well as for those who want to reference it later. So in a matter of speaking, it's not only our grades on the line, but everyone who is supposed to be in this concert hall."

Morgan considered his words before nodding curtly. "Okay. You've got a point. When's it supposed to end?"

"In just a couple of minutes."

The two men stared at each other briefly before the younger one asked, "You're Professor Winegar, right?"

Morgan nodded.

"My sis had one of your classes last semester. She said you were freakin' awesome."

"Tell her thanks. And thanks for your help with my request. I know it's a bit out of the ordinary."

"Not really. And it's no problem, really."

Morgan thanked them again and moved to the back of the small room. Opening her cell phone, she speed-dialed her husband.

"B lab," a young female answered.

"Hey, Melissa, is Homer available?"

"Oh, hi, Mrs. Winegar. You bet. Hold on, please."

Morgan could hear the hum of flow hoods and the whir of centrifuges in the background. She could almost detect the odor of chemical reagents though her cell phone. Having visited Homer's workplace several times before, she was familiar with the malodorous trappings of his job.

"Hi, hon. What's up?"

"I'm going to be stuck at school for a while again, perhaps very late. Can you get off early to pick up Zach?"

"Yeah, I guess. Is something wrong?"

"You could say that. It happening again: the mass fugue. Only this time, it's affected nearly a hundred kids."

"You're kidding! A hundred?"

"I didn't have time to make an exact count, but I've got a few students helping me gather information, including a body count."

"Interesting way of putting that."

"That's how it feels."

As if sensing the fear in her heart, Homer gently said, "Hang in there, babe. What information are you getting?"

"What we talked about earlier."

"That energy drink?" Homer said.

"Yes, but there's more. Do you remember what you said about there being a second part to it—that it wasn't just the drink?"

"I do. Some kind of trigger."

Morgan could not keep her voice from trembling. "I think I may have a recording of it."

"No kidding," Homer said in a low voice. "You serious?"

"I'm not certain, but I think so."

The younger AV tech turned in his chair. "He's just wrapped it up, professor."

Morgan heard muffled applause from the concert hall on the other side of the glass partition of the AV booth. She gave the tech a thumbs-up.

"Hon, I've got to go. I'll call you the minute I find something, okay?"

"I'll grab Zachary. Is it okay if we stop for a pizza? It'll help distract him from you not being there."

Morgan smiled and shook her head. "Boy, you're good at that."

"At what?" Homer asked innocently.

"At getting what *you* want by claiming it's for Zachary."

There was a long silence on the other end of the line. Then, "Rats. You see? You can get to the bottom of any mystery."

"The connection between your mind and your stomach is no great mystery, dear."

Homer laughed. "I can't hide anything from you, can I?"

Morgan smiled in spite of her anxiety. "Don't even try."

TWENTY-TWO

Jacqueline stood inside the Widtsoe Building looking out a second-story window at the group surrounding the *Phra Apaimanee*. She smiled, pleased with such a large turnout. She had begun to think that the self-centered professor wasn't going to play her CD. Evidently, however, her rendezvous in his office that afternoon had not been a total waste.

She had given Dr. Key a copy of the third week issue of "Toad Stomp." It didn't really matter. If everything went according to plan, this extra airtime wasn't really necessary. But Stevie thought it would be a justifiable safeguard in case some students never listened to the radio. It was the same reason he'd had her contract with the Taggart to play the song throughout the hallways of the student center. Additionally, she had melded into small gatherings at lunch time with a discreet boom box to play it to the crowd.

She still was not completely sure she understood the mechanics of the project, but that didn't matter. She had done all that was asked. She reported in via an encrypted Internet link and sometimes on a cell phone with a dedicated bandwidth. More importantly, she had watched the digital readout of her bank account increase with each report. By the time this project was over, she'd have two and a half million in her private account in Belize. Not bad for a two-month field job.

The girl's lips curved into a slight smile. *Phra Apaimanee*, the mystic soother—or some other such nonsense. To Jacqueline, the bronze Thai artifact was more like the Pied Piper of Hamelin, drawing kids after her like puppets on a string, directing them along unmarked pathways while instilling dread and horror in those who stood by powerless to stop her.

Jacqueline reveled in her position as puppeteer. Sure, her contact in Vegas was the creator of the instrument with which to control anyone he wanted—or anyone who drank the poison. She'd figured that much out already. But here in the field, she had the last say. It gave her the feeling of a siren.

She didn't know exactly what was said in the music that caused the mass transformation, but she guessed it was a powerful subliminal command. She'd listened to the music herself but had not sampled the energy drink. Stevie had told her there was a correlation. The tune was some sort of primitive Australian music played on modern instruments and given a techno-pop edge. It reminded her of the stuff played during her aerobics classes. There were no vocalizations, no singing or grunting or even native aboriginal wailing in the background. Stevie had explained that each week's subliminal embedding commanded the listener to seek out the following week's broadcast. Including that specificity ensured that as soon as a person was hooked, they'd stay that way.

Jacqueline smirked as her gaze swept over the swelling crowd. The onlookers muttered words of concern and wore worried expressions. A few even appeared to be crying. As in the other fugues, those affected were oblivious to anything but the object of their attention. The vacant stare in their eyes bespoke an altered state of consciousness. What a bunch of little kids. What a bunch of lemmings. Perfect. Stevie had said a university was an ideal choice to isolate the results because most test subjects would not stray from the "field" for a set period of time. A university in an isolated small town would make it even easier to observe and control the outcomes. Located in conservative, rural, *boring* Cache Valley, Utah State University *was* perfect. With raised eyebrows, Jacqueline nodded sharply in admiration of the little geek's decision.

Jacqueline's smirk twisted into a slight frown as she reflected on the woman she had seen in the crowd a few moments earlier. The woman, whom she knew to be Professor Winegar, had caught

Jacqueline's eye as she walked among the students. Jacqueline had seen the young, attractive woman at the other gatherings, and she had watched her interview a number of post-entranced students. She seemed very intent on helping each student, perhaps even trying to figure out what was causing the trances.

Jacqueline's smile returned, and she laughed out loud. Good luck with that. If *she* didn't know the exact process, how was this Winegar woman going to figure it out?

The professor had conferred with an Asian student before running back toward the concert hall. Perhaps she was on to the music connection. Jacqueline would have to look into exactly what this professor suspected. If the woman was getting close to the truth, she would call Stevie for direction. Until then, Jacqueline would find out what she could on her own.

Jacqueline watched as the young Asian man began recruiting a few others around him. He pointed to various sections of those squatting in front of *Phra Apaimanee*. She knew a plan was being formulated—one that she probably should be aware of.

Leaving her watchtower, Jacqueline ran down the stairs and out into the plaza between the Widtsoe and Animal Science buildings. She quickly wormed her way over to the young man. He was kind of nerdy-looking and appeared to be having trouble convincing others to help him. Perfect.

"Lance, you and Jenny ask the first twenty student on north side. Kristy and Josh, you ask as many as can just south of them. SueAnn, LaVal, ask next twenty continuing south. The rest pair up and try to get others to help: about two for every ten or twenty in group. Be quick. Professor Winegar thinks the fugue could break any moment. It's going on almost sixty minute now."

"Can I be of any help?" Jacqueline asked the young man, flashing him a coy smile.

He gawked as if he'd forgotten how to speak. She knew why.

"Please?" Jacqueline asked.

"Uh, yeah, sure," he stammered.

Moving closer, she spoke very softly. "To be honest, this really frightens me. Would you mind if I partnered with you?"

The young man's face turned crimson, and his narrow eyes widened. "Really? Uh, yeah, sure. And don't be scared. This is nothing," he said gesturing toward the entranced gathering.

If you only knew. Jacqueline touched his arm tenderly. "I'm sorry to be a bother. I know you're very busy."

"No sweat. My name is Lanh Tran."

"Thanks, Lanh. I'm Jacqueline."

"Pretty name for pretty girl."

She smiled. "Easy there, chief."

Together, they headed around a small group of onlookers and worked their way to the front of the crowd.

"What exactly are we supposed to do?" Jacqueline asked.

"As soon as they wake up, ask them what drinks they had in last couple day, and ask what kind. If they say Tribe, ask which flavor."

She snorted scornfully. "Tribe? What for?" she asked to ascertain how close these people were to uncovering Scandia's experiment.

"Professor Winegar think there is correlation."

"Who's he?" she asked.

"She's a woman. She teach advanced psychology and sociology. She's totally brilliant, but way cool, too. If anyone figure this out, she can. Here," he said, handing her a mechanical pencil and a notebook. "Write just what they drank and when."

"What does she plan to do with the information?"

Lanh shrugged. "Analyze it, I guess."

"What if it *is* something in the Tribe?"

"Her husband work at Wasatch BioChemical."

"Is he a scientist?"

"No, he just work with numbers."

Jacqueline cocked her arm to read her watch. "When are they going to come out of this?"

"I think when carillon gong."

"The carillon?"

"Yeah. Any second now . . ."

The eight note Westminster tune chimed across the campus. As soon as the first note struck, the entranced students calmly got to their feet, turned to the person next to them, and slugged them hard in the face.

Gasps and screams went out from those watching. A few of the affected students fell unconscious. A number of them had blood running from crushed noses or split lips. But no one in the gathering cried out. It was as if they were impervious to the pain.

As soon as the carillon struck the last of its five hour-chimes, the trance lifted. A number of the girls began to cry, both from pain and from fright. Most of those watching rushed to give aid. The atmosphere crackled with the electricity of pure terror.

Lanh immediately knelt beside a young woman. "You okay?"

The girl nodded and touched a huge lump forming under her eye.

"I'm with Professor Winegar. I need to ask you questions. What have you had to drink the past few day?"

"I—I'm not sure," the girl stammered.

"Think hard. Did you drink any Tribe?"

She thought for a minute. "Yeah. I think I had a . . . a Dingo's Dance."

Lanh looked up at Jacqueline. "And that how it's done."

Jacqueline nodded and moved a few people down to ask the same questions. Then she looked back to make sure she was out of earshot from the professor's TA. When she turned back to the students, she saw a familiar-looking young man.

"I'm with Professor Winegar. I need to ask if you drank any Tribe in the past few days."

The young man nursed a swelling lip and pondered her question. "Yeah. A couple of 'em."

"Do you remember which kind?"

"Um . . . a Barrier Reef Buzz and a Dingo's Dance."

"Can I get your name, please?"

"Peter. Peter Stokes."

Ah-ha! That's why he looks so familiar. Jacqueline wondered how thoroughly her first contact with the young music and French major had been removed from his memory. "Do you remember me or know who I am?" she asked.

Peter looked at her with a mix of confusion and hopefulness. "No, but I'd sure like to."

She smiled and stroked his arm platonically. "Maybe later. I'll get back with you as soon as I'm finished here, okay?"

"Yeah, sure," he answered, dabbing his lip with the back of his hand.

Jacqueline finished up about the same time as Lanh Tran and his impromptu cohorts. Nearly everyone in the Aggie Trance had been questioned. Most had recovered from the initial shock of their abuse, but nearly all would need some form of first-aid. One girl was still unconscious. She had been standing next to a lineman from the football team. The large Samoan knelt beside her, nearly in tears himself.

Jacqueline handed her papers to a random team member and left. She knew she had to report this immediately.

TWENTY-THREE

Morgan took her copy of the audio recording to her office. Lanh was waiting outside her door with a stack of rumpled papers.

"How many did you get?" Morgan asked.

"Almost all of them."

"Then why the worried look?"

He shook his head. "It just doesn't make sense. Why did they hit?"

Morgan had heard the news of the violence and couldn't believe it herself. "I don't know, Lanh. That's something else we have to look into. What about the Tribe drink?"

"All the interviews match except this section," he said tapping a few pages.

Morgan unlocked her door and entered. "Let's take a look."

Lanh followed obediently.

Morgan booted up a grid page on her computer and typed a few headers. "All right. Just go through the list, naming each flavor. I'll make a new column for each drink and mark it each time it's repeated."

"Right. Tribe: Dingo's Dance."

"Check."

"Tribe: Dingo's Dance."

"Check."

"Tribe: Barrier Reef Buzz."

"Check."

"Tribe: Dingo's Dance."

"Check."

"Sobe: Lizard Lightning."

A pause as she entered the new column. "Check."

"Diet Mountain Dew."

"Check."

The list went on with the majority of checks falling under the Dingo's Dance column. About every third claim went to water, but Morgan did not feel that needed to be recorded. A large number of Coke and Pepsi products were cited, as well as many other drinks in the Sobe line. There were only three alcoholic beverages mentioned until Lanh reached the bottom of his stack.

"Then there these pages," the TA said, tapping the papers with a skinny finger. "Only one student said he had Dingo's Dance. The rest is Pepsi, Coke, Gatorade, Sprite, and a fruit drink. Then there about twenty student who said beer, wine, wine cooler, vodka, or other alcohol. It make no sense."

"You're right. Who took that survey?" Morgan asked.

"Don't know. It look like a girl's write—" He stopped short as his mind focused on the image of a very pretty face. "I think her name Jenny or Jacqui."

"Jacqui who?"

"I . . . I don't know," he admitted.

"Would you recognize her if you saw her again?"

"Definitely. She kind of girl my mom not approve."

Morgan chuckled. "Blond and blue-eyed, right?"

"Woman of my dreams."

Morgan took the papers and reviewed them briefly. "Any reason to suspect that she might have intentionally altered the answers?"

The young TA cocked his head to one side. "Why she do that?"

"I don't know," Morgan admitted. "Just wondering."

* * *

Driving home, Morgan listened to the CD of the lecture the tech had burned for her. Although the fugue happened toward the end of the lecture, she listened to the entire recording to be sure she didn't miss anything.

She blocked out the fact that it was F. Scott Key speaking and concentrated on what was being taught. Morgan was surprised at how much of what he'd said had slipped by her—information that explained a lot of Zachary's behavior toward music. It suddenly occurred to her that Dr. Key might actually be involved in the fugues at Utah State. After all, he had specifically asked her opinion on them, and he had been the one to discover the discarded winter clothing in the science building, and the lecture itself . . .

The clamor of spring-loaded chairs identified the exact point of the exodus from the concert hall. Morgan backed up the CD to replay that point again. F. Scott was discussing the various instruments used to create the Australian tune. Morgan could detect nothing in his syntax or a tonal change that might indicate a trigger. He may have used a key word, but which? Several words jumped out as potential prompts: the tribal names, the Australian instruments, etc. Morgan felt like she was circling an elusive insight that, once seized and opened, would unfold into a dreadful revelation. And yet she knew revealing that insight would help many lives, perhaps even save them.

She decided to have Homer listen to the recording. His honed analytical skills might grab the "something" she was missing. Then she'd confront Dr. Key with their evidence.

By the time she pulled into her driveway, it was just after ten o'clock. Entering their 1990s rambler, she heard a horrific noise coming from Zach's bedroom. It was a desperate, painful mewl accompanied by fierce growls and snarls. But mixed in the cacophony of animal noises was the laughter of a little boy.

Morgan dropped her satchel on the table and ran down the hallway that led to her son's bedroom. Throwing the door open, she saw Homer jostling on his hands and knees with Zachary riding on his back. Homer pawed at the carpet and made hideous noises from deep in his chest and sinuses. Zach was doing his best to hang on while laughing, both his arms and legs wrapped around her husband's torso.

"If you fall off, I'm going to eat you up," Homer growled.

"No, Daddy, don't eat me!" Zachary giggled.

Morgan couldn't bring herself to be angry at her husband for keeping Zachary up so late. After the day she'd had, the sound of a child's laughter was just the tonic she needed.

"You know," Morgan said, entering, "I haven't tasted little boy in a long time either. Dear, what do you say I get some fresh bread and we'll have a Zachary sandwich?"

"That sounds delicious, hon," Homer said pulling one of Zach's arms toward his mouth.

"No, Mommy. No Zachary sandwich."

"Oh, that's too bad. I'm very hungry," she said dejectedly.

"We're playing," Zachary said.

"I should have had the leftovers warmed up for you. I guess we got carried away," Homer admitted. "We actually ate hours ago."

"And I know a little boy who should have been in bed hours ago, too," Morgan said trying to rein in the excitement.

"No, Mommy. We're not done."

"I think we are, little man," Homer said, sliding Zachary from his back and lifting him onto his bed.

"Okay, Daddy. Prayers again?"

"Sure, son. It's always a good idea to pray."

Morgan joined her boys at the bedside and knelt for family prayer. After kisses, she turned out Zachary's bedroom light but left his door slightly ajar, then met Homer at the dining room table.

"I bet you worked up a second appetite with your horseplay. Would you like a snack before bed?"

"Whatever you're having sounds good to me, hon. You want some help?"

"Yes," she said kicking off her shoes. "But not with dinner. I need you to look over some stats I brought home and listen to a recording from the lecture I told you about."

"Did it turn out?"

"Yes, and get this: the fugue happened during a lecture on how music influences brain function. Rather interesting timing, wouldn't you say?"

"Yeah, I'd say that."

Forgetting about dinner, Morgan unloaded her satchel and quickly organized the papers. "You were right about the energy drink."

Morgan handed Homer the results of the survey Lanh and his friends had taken. "As you can see, we tried to categorize the different beverages consumed over the past three weeks. It's pretty obvious which was the dominant drink." Moving to their entertainment center, she loaded the CD. "And then there's this."

She started the recording just before the beginning of the aboriginal sampling. "Listen close. In a moment you'll hear when all the students stand up to leave."

The music throbbed and pulsed as it filled the room. It was bizarre but strangely captivating. Homer moved to the couch, sat, closed his eyes, and leaned into the music.

"You found it!" a little voice cried from the hallway.

Homer and Morgan stared at each other, completely awestruck.

Zachary hobbled into the living room with only one leg in his pajama bottoms. His eyes were as wide as any child's at Christmastime.

"The whispers song. It's the whispers song!"

TWENTY-FOUR

Morgan and Homer continued to gawk at each other, unbelieving. Her eyes betrayed shock, fear. His eyes were filled with confusion and amazement.

"The subliminal message is the *song,*" Morgan articulated in little more than a breath.

"Probably a sub-track recorded with the music," Homer guessed. He too spoke softly, as if their sudden breakthrough was so crystalline it would shatter if mentioned out loud.

"The whispers song, the whispers song," Zachary sang, as he fell to the floor trying to insert his other leg back into his pajama bottoms.

"I thought it was in something Professor Key said," Morgan admitted. "You know, a word pattern or phrase matrix. I've listened to the song a half dozen times already, but each time I was concentrating on what he was saying in the background instead of the music itself."

"Incredible."

"Wait—but there's no lyrics," she remembered. "It's all instrumental. Where's the trigger?"

"Zach says this is the song. Right, Zach? You hear whispers under the song?"

"Inside."

"Inside?" Homer and Morgan said at the same time, again staring at each other.

Homer increased the volume a bit as they concentrated harder on the pulsating music. Zachary crawled onto the couch to sit by his father. Standing off to one side, Morgan had her eyes closed, concentrating on every nuance in the tune. Leaning forward again, Homer's elbows rested on his knees, his hands clasped tightly together.

The family held these positions for a full minute before Homer realized Zachary was swaying rhythmically, waving his arms, directing the song. He watched closely as his son brandished and flourished and gesticulated in perfect cadence with the beat.

Then Homer noticed something else. Zachary's lips were moving very quickly, as if he were reciting a memorized passage to himself.

"Zachary?" Homer asked softly. "Can you hear what's being said?"

"Whispers."

"They must be very soft whispers. I can't hear them at all," Homer admitted.

"Very soft whispers," Zachary confirmed. "Very fast. Inside."

"But you *can* hear them?"

"Yes. Very soft."

"What are they saying?"

"Too fast," Zachary said shaking his head.

Morgan had moved closer and knelt in front of her son. "Honey, are there words under the music? Is that what you hear?"

Zachary shook his head. "Inside the music. Very fast."

"Inside. What does that mean, son?"

"Inside. Between the notes."

"Oh, I see. Are they strange words—words you don't understand?"

"Lots of words. Same words, over and over, very fast." Zachary's tone had gone from joyous to anxious.

"What words?" Homer asked a second time.

"Don't know. Too fast, too fast," the boy cried, his agitation growing by the second.

"Homer, let's not push it," Morgan said.

Homer held up his index finger, indicating he needed just a moment. "Can you tell me one or two of the words, son?"

"No. Too fast. The words are too fast!" Zachary's fists were now clenched. He was no longer moving to the music but seemed to cower from it.

Morgan's eyes fidgeted with concern. "Homer, no."

"Just one more second, hon."

The boy was trembling now. His head shook to and fro, not in cadence with the song but as if he was trying to expel the sound from his ears.

"Zachary, it's okay," Homer said firmly. "There's nothing to be afraid of. Mommy and Daddy are both here with you. We want to hear the whispers too."

"Too many. Over and over and over."

"Just one word, Zach. Come on, little man."

"It hurts, Daddy, it hurts my ears."

"Homer," Morgan whimpered.

"One word, son, then it'll go away. I promise."

The boy's trembling bordered on convulsions. His face was a furious shade of crimson. Morgan got to her feet and reached for the stereo.

"Morgan, wait," Homer snapped.

"Homer, it's hurting—"

"Zachary, please," Homer persisted, overriding his wife. "Just one word."

Zachary's fists flew against his frail chest, pounding his sternum. His breathing came in desperate gasps and explosive exhalations. In between these, he mumbled something through clenched teeth.

The music abruptly stopped. Morgan glared at her husband.

Homer draped an arm around his son's narrow shoulders and gently pulled him close. "Okay, Zachary. It's over now. No more whispers. It's okay."

The boy mumbled something again, his teeth still held tightly together, his breathing still staccato.

"Shh, little man. It's okay. It's okay. No more whispers."

Morgan returned to her spot kneeling in front of Zachary and held his balled fists in her hands. "Zachary?"

"Ward." A sharp breath followed.

"Ward?" Homer asked, still holding his son tightly.

Zachary shook his head. A couple more breaths. Then, "Weward."

"Weward? Oh, you mean 'reward'?" Homer asked, clarifying what his son had just said.

"Reward." Pulling a fist from his mother's grip, he knuckled a tear from his eye. "Ulimate."

"Reward. Ultimate? An ultimate reward?"

The boy jerked once and then relaxed, as if he'd just vomited a poison. He nodded.

"Okay, buckaroo," Homer said, kissing the top of his son's head. "You did very well. I am so proud of you."

"So am I," Morgan added as she slowly helped the boy's fists to open and massaged his tiny hands. "I am so happy you're my son. I love you very much."

"I love Mommy."

"And Daddy loves you too," Homer said. "More than ice cream."

Zachary looked up and smiled. "You're silly."

The crisis was over.

Homer looked at his wife with a measure of shame in his eyes. "I'm sorry for pushing him."

Zachary glanced at his parents. "Does Mommy love Daddy?"

Morgan leaned over and gave her husband a kiss. "Mommy loves Daddy more than ice cream, too," she said, inches from his face.

TWENTY-FIVE

Saturday, October 24

Lanh Tran left the Merrill-Cazier Library, still feeling like he had accomplished something important. Professor Winegar had been very pleased with the thoroughness of yesterday's Aggie Trance data. This was his fifth year at USU, his second as a teaching assistant to the professor. And with each passing semester, he'd become an increasingly important part of the system. In his mind, he was just one step closer to becoming a true American, his goal since the day he had entered this country for an education.

As the TA crossed the central courtyard and then rounded the Old Main building, a strange feeling haunted him, a sensation that he wasn't alone. The sun had dropped behind the Wellsville Mountains, but enough natural light remained that the lampposts and decorative lights along the walkway were not really needed.

He paused at the top of the long flight of cement stairs that extended down Old Main hill, a distance roughly the length of a football field. During the winter months, the snow-covered grade was a favorite spot of sledding extremists and reckless, fanatical tobogganers. Unfortunately, the steep hill led right to a busy street, which necessitated the stacking of hay bales to halt the thrill-seekers' meteoric descent. It was also a place frequented by the Logan City EMTs—for obvious reasons.

At the head of the steps the disconcerting feeling became stronger. Again, he felt like he was being followed. Looking around, Lanh could see no one nearby. A few students walked briskly along the street at the bottom of the hill, but that was all. The lack of people didn't really surprise him. Not only was it a weekend, but it was almost dark, and the air had turned uncomfortably cold. He'd have to watch for black ice as he made his way down the concrete steps.

When he was about a third of the way down, he heard a chirping scream behind him. Turning quickly, he watched as a girl tumbled from the sidewalk and rolled toward him on the frost-glazed grass. Lanh moved quickly from the steps and braced himself to stop her descent. Luckily, the girl slowed somewhat just before colliding with him.

The poor girl was breathing sharply from fright. Lanh knelt beside her, placing a gentle hand on her shoulder. "Hey, are you okay?"

The girl looked up wildly, terribly scared and confused. Realizing what had happened, a soft bleat of air burst from her lungs as she crumpled into his arms and laid her head against his chest. "Oh, thank you," she said in an explosive whisper.

"Sure. No problem. You okay now? You feel broken bone or anything?"

She squirmed back and forth, checking her condition, but continued to hold Lanh close. He was embarrassed by the intimacy of the act but didn't pull away. He wasn't stupid. Something like this only happened once in a lifetime to a guy like him.

After a moment she said, "No. I think everything's okay. The only thing hurt is my pride."

Lanh laughed. "Don't worry. My pride has scar tissue."

The girl laughed merrily as if suddenly all was right with the world.

Lanh rose to his feet and helped the girl to hers. She had the most remarkable purple-blue eyes. Perhaps it was just the subdued light of dusk.

"Do I know you? You look familiar," he said.

She rolled her eyes. "Like I haven't heard *that* one before."

"Hey, that wasn't a line. I mean—you really look familiar. Like—" He stopped midsentence. "Wait. You're the girl who helped collect data during Aggie Trance yesterday. Uh . . . Jacqueline, right?"

"Wow. Good memory."

"Thank you."

"No—thank *you* for saving me. I must have tripped or something. I can be so clumsy at times. It's embarrassing. Would you . . ." She paused as if shyness inhibited her next request. "Would you mind if I held your arm the rest of the way down?"

Lanh stared at her as if she had just asked if he wanted a million dollars. "Uh, sure. You—you go ahead," he stammered.

"So are you an exchange student?" Jacqueline asked, slipping her arm into his and gazing at him wistfully.

He shook his head, both to clear a fog of disbelief and to make sure he wasn't dreaming. "No, I am visa student working on my master's and later my doctorate. I was born in Haiphong, close to Hanoi. It's Vietnam third largest city. My family is still there, but I been in States almost six year."

"I figured as much," she said, giving his arm a playful squeeze. "Your English is very good. Only a hint of an accent."

"Thanks. So where you from?"

"Santa Barbara," she said after a slight pause.

"A beach girl?"

"You know it. I look great in a bikini."

Lanh swallowed hard. He had no clue where this was heading, but he was going to milk it for all it was worth. He'd never had a jaw-dropping gorgeous girl like this show any interest in him before.

They reached the bottom of the steps without further incident, but Jacqueline kept a tight hold on his arm. Maybe she was afraid because it was getting dark and she might fall again.

"So, which way you headed?" Lanh asked.

"Which way are you going?" she countered.

"Uh, straight ahead. My apartment is couple blocks down 600 North. You live close by?"

"No. I'm pretty much across town."

"What you doing at university on Saturday night?" Lanh wondered. He figured a girl with her looks should have every weekend booked with dates from now until New Year's.

"Actually, I was hoping to talk to you," she said with eyes lowered, as if embarrassed again. "It's about the Aggie Trance yesterday."

The TA smiled with all-knowing concern. "You still pretty scared, right?"

The blond nodded.

Gaining confidence from the fact that she still clung to his arm, Lanh said, "It's okay. Uh, my place is next block. You want to talk there? I can explain trance better, and it's much warmer than outside."

Jacqueline pushed away but still maintained physical contact. "Can I trust you, Lanh Tran from Vietnam?"

"You bet," Lanh said.

Jacqueline paused and scanned his face in the darkening twilight. She then cocked her head toward the street and took his arm tightly again. "Then lead on."

TWENTY-SIX

Lanh opened the door to his apartment and let Jacqueline enter first. It was a gentlemanly gesture, but one Jacqueline would have regretted had she owned the flat. The place looked like hurricanes Katrina, Rita, and Andrew had stopped by for a visit.

"My, this place looks well used," she teased.

Lanh appeared unfazed. "It's my roommate turn to clean living room, and they all gone for weekend."

"How unfortunate," Jacqueline said, her nose wrinkling at an odor she'd rather not try to identify.

A large overstuffed couch separated the living room from the kitchen. The dated piece of furniture was garnished with soiled clothing and sweat-stained sports apparel. A beanbag chair sat under a window without much of a view, and two milk crates supported a length of particleboard to form a makeshift coffee table. Assorted textbooks; a chaotic pile of papers; and two crusty, used cereal bowls competed for the narrow space with a laptop and a half-dozen empty soda cans. Facing the couch, a massive, high-end plasma widescreen sat atop a component system that probably cost more than its owner's tuition.

"Who owns the toys?" Jacqueline asked, nodding toward the electronics.

"Brig. He watch sports all the time."

With a roll of the eyes, she scoffed, "Up close and personal apparently."

Moving beyond the couch, Jacqueline saw that the small kitchen was equally cluttered. A hazardous stack of dishes and utensils teetered in the sink, and an equally precarious stack of empty pizza boxes balanced next to a bulging trash can on the verge of a Vesuvian eruption.

"Is Brig in charge of cleaning the kitchen too?"

"No, that wait for his roommate, Nephi."

"Nephi?" Jacqueline said, turning to face him. "What kind of a name is that?"

"It's from Book of Mormon. I never read it. Have you?"

"Oh . . . I've looked through it before. So," she said quickly changing the subject, "Nephi and Brig. Does anyone else live here?"

"No. I used to have roommate, but he got married. It's okay. I like room to myself."

"A room of your own? Can I see?" she asked innocently.

"Uh . . . sure."

Lanh kept his bedroom locked. Opening the door, he led Jacqueline into a space that was fastidiously clean. No clothing—dirty or otherwise—cluttered the area, and no trash littered the floor. His shelves were meticulously organized, and both twin beds were made to military standards. A single painting of Asian calligraphy adorning each wall gave the place a feng shui feel. She immediately went to his bed and sat down. Lanh paused a moment before sitting across from her on the unused twin.

"I need to ask you a few questions about Dr. Winegar," she began in a suddenly businesslike tone.

The TA's eyes narrowed, equally businesslike. "She's not a Ph.D. She got master's from UCSD, so we just call her 'professor,' not 'doctor.'"

"Fine. What is her full name?"

The young man looked confused, if not suspicious. Jacqueline knew that being so direct was risky, but she wanted to get this over with as soon as possible so she could report in. Her boss had said it was of the utmost importance to learn how much the professor suspected about their project. And, as always, her monetary bonus was in direct proportion to the outcome of the task.

"The university directory list 'M. Winegar,'" relayed Lanh. "But . . . why you not just ask her?"

"Well, being her TA, I thought you'd know of any nicknames or pseudonyms she might go by."

"No. It's just Morgan Winegar, as far as I know. She married before, but she don't talk about it much. I don't know her early name."

"Is she married now?"

"Yes. Her husband name is Homer."

"How long have they been married?"

Lanh frowned. "Wait—what's this all about? Why you ask these questions?"

"Just curious. Homer, huh?"

"Yeah. I meet him many time. He pretty okay guy. Very smart, but he hide it good."

Jacqueline's eyebrows rose a bit, questioning. "Interesting. So, did you find anything conclusive about the mass hypnosis events?"

Lanh did not answer. The look on his face was hard to read but indicated a level of mistrust. Jacqueline knew she was progressing dangerously fast, but she felt she had to. The evening was wearing on, and Lanh seemed to be hedging. Jacqueline figured she'd have to take this to the next level to get the answers she needed quickly.

"I'm sorry for asking all these silly questions," she said while slinking out of her winter parka. "I guess I'm still kinda scared over the whole thing." She patted the empty space next to her. "I'm not usually this forward, but . . . well, would you mind sitting next to me? I just need to talk through this to convince myself I'm not a total wimp."

Still wearing a leery look, Lanh said, "We can talk."

Jacqueline knew she presented an irresistible lure to most guys, but for some reason the TA was resisting. Lanh Tran was not unattractive, but he certainly wasn't every American girl's dream. He probably had trouble finding dates. Maybe he wasn't interested in dating. His look reminded her of an anime character—without blue hair and oversized eyes—and his manner was confident yet quirky; intelligent. Quite frankly, she wasn't sure how to read him.

Playing the innocent, vulnerable college coed was a gamble. Most guys fell for it, but some didn't. His daily proximity to Morgan

Winegar would provide the most reliable data, however, and judging from the hesitant, deer-in-the-headlights expression he was now showing, she figured the gamble would be worth it.

"Please, Lanh," she asked with plaintive, misty eyes, again patting the empty space beside her.

The TA stood slowly and shoved his hands in his pockets. He took a step then halted. Then another step and another pause. It was a slow process, almost painful to watch. But it was only a minute before he was sitting beside her.

Jacqueline leaned against Lanh Tran in total submission. "Thanks. This really means a lot to me."

"Sure," he said. "I don't mean to be cold. You just been asking a lot of detailed questions."

"I know. And you're a sweetheart for answering them. It's just my way of dealing with it, I guess. You know—finding out all I can so I can get my mind around it?"

Lanh nodded. "It's okay. I'm same way sometimes."

Jacqueline brought her knees to her chest, which caused her to loose her balance. Lanh instinctively put an arm around her to steady her—just like she knew he would. *Sucker.* "As I remember, you were trying to find out if anyone drank anything before they met at the statue of *Phra Apaimanee.* What did you find out?"

"Dingo's Dance," he confirmed. "Almost every student drink one before trance."

"Anything else?"

"Did they drink anything else?"

"No, silly," she said snuggling into his embrace. "Did they mention anything else that may have initiated the trance?"

"Not that we found. The professor think there is another key. Something they see or hear."

"So what's Winegar going to do next?"

"Keep looking. She got permission to get all Dingo's Dance off campus. Her husband work at Wasatch BioChemical in Logan. She probably have him analyze it."

"Serious?"

"Yeah. Like I say, he pretty smart."

Jacqueline took a deep, exaggerated breath. "What do *you* think he'll find?"

Lanh removed his arm from her shoulders and twisted around to face her. "I don't know. Professor Winegar has studied this phenomenon many time. She say this kind of trance never happen without an outside influence. There lots of record of mass hallucination. I read an account of Puritans in Massachusetts who were forced to join a night of intimate sin because a witch cast spell on them."

"Puritans?" Jacqueline chortled. "I can only imagine what *that* party was like. Somebody probably spiked the punch."

"Maybe just like Dingo's Dance. The professor's husband is going to check samples from campus and grocery stores too, but she think someone picked USU for experiment."

"Really? So what can they do even if they find out there *is* a drug in the drink?" Jacqueline asked, placing a hand on Lanh's knee.

"I think Wasatch BioChemical has government connection. They find who's behind the trance real soon," Lanh revealed, placing his hand on top of hers.

"That'll be good," she said, tracing a pattern around his knuckles with her free hand. "I may want to talk to the professor myself. You know—woman to woman. Do you have her address and phone number?"

"Yes. But why not go to her office on campus?" the TA asked, as if her last question was the most suspicious of all.

Jacqueline caught his tone and began to caress a finger along Lanh's arm. She felt him tense in response. He was such a little boy. "Oh, just to get another opinion."

Lanh Tran did not move. He did not speak. Jacqueline could almost feel his inner turmoil as he struggled to maintain his harried nerves. "Please, Lanh," she breathed into his ear. "I'll do anything to talk to her."

The young man was quivering. His glassy stare was fixed on the calligraphy across from them. "O-okay," he squeaked.

This was all too easy.

WEEK FOUR

TWENTY-SEVEN

Sunday, October 25

Stevie Pendleton answered the dedicated cell phone, "Don Juan's pad."

Jacqueline closed her eyes and shook her head. Every time she talked to the man, his geekiness increased and her opinion of him decreased. She fought the urge to tell him exactly what she thought of his little spy game routines.

No. Better to see it through, she encouraged herself.

"Is the man of my dreams at home?" She placed her forehead into her right hand, fought a gag reflex, and told herself that this stupidity would soon be over. At that point her bank account in Belize would be bulging, and her life would be a dream.

"He is if you know the code."

She took a steadying breath. "One, seven, one, one, four."

"Master number?"

"Five."

Jacqueline could not figure out why a scientist as brilliant as Pendleton would have such a strong belief in numerology. He preached about it all the time—to those who would listen.

Jacqueline had met Stevie at No Regrets, the Vegas club at which she danced. Because he was a very generous tipper, she had always gravitated toward him. At first he didn't talk much. Taking her cue from that, neither did she. But it wasn't long before he asked the manager for her personal attention every Saturday night. He'd come in other nights too, but he only asked for personal attention on Saturdays.

Jacqueline figured he liked Saturdays because that was when the club was the most crowded. That way, every guy in there would watch in amazed, bewildered jealousy as he captivated the attention of the hottest dancer there. It didn't matter if the crowd was a gang of greasy bikers, a bunch of rowdy college guys, or a gathering of conference-attending businessmen; even if the entire floor was populated with GQ models, he made sure that her full attention was always on him.

One night, he got up the nerve to ask her out. As a rule, Jacqueline never dated guys she met at the club. But Stevie was different; not too bold, not too forward, always a gentleman, even though he was in a men's club where that behavior was never expected. Eventually, she agreed to meet for dinner. She would not let him pick her up at her apartment. She didn't want *any* potential psychopath knowing where she lived.

Stevie booked reservations at the Picasso atop the Bellagio Hotel, a restaurant famed for its collection of original paintings and ceramics by the renowned Spanish artist. Jacqueline had never sampled the five-star French-Mediterranean cuisine and was actually very excited to go just to see the artwork.

The young man had talked incessantly. He was a chief scientist at Scandia Labs in Henderson. He had two doctorates: one in biochemistry and the other medicinal chemistry. He prided himself in being inventive, enterprising, driven. He claimed it came from the numerological breakdown of his name. When Jacqueline questioned what that meant, she got a mini-lecture on one of the oldest occult philosophies in the world.

"If you line up nine columns, then place the alphabet under them, one letter in each column, wrapping around into three rows as necessary, you get the cosmic algorithm of numbers-to-letters metaphysics," he had explained. "It turns out all of the attributes in our lives boil down to one number, a single integer—your master number. Unless of course you end up with one of the omnipotent master numbers—11 or 22 or 33; but that's something altogether different."

Grabbing a napkin he scribbled out a rough chart.

1	2	3	4	5	6	7	8	9
A	B	C	D	E	F	G	H	I
J	K	L	M	N	O	P	Q	R
S	T	U	V	W	X	Y	Z	.

"Your master number is derived from adding the value of each letter in your name—the one actually printed on your birth certificate. Mine is Steven Pendleton. That's 1+2+5+4+5+5+7+5+5+4 +3+5+2+6+5, which equals 64. Add the six and the four together and you get ten. Add those digits together, 1+0, and you get 1. *One!* That's my master number. Not only that, but my first name alone equals 22, an omnipotent master number. Do you know what a *one* personality is like?"

Boring? Psychotic? Jacqueline wanted to say. "Someone like you?" she asked instead, playing up to him.

"Exactly! And if that person also has omnipotent number 22?" The young man's excitement had him almost yelling.

"A demigod?" she answered cynically.

"A visionary, a pioneer, a master builder, and a creator," Stevie corrected her. "Someone who likes to push the edge of the envelope just to see what's on the other side. A guy who dreams up crazy things and then actually makes them happen. And, I might add, gets filthy rich in the process."

If the young man's eyebrows had arched any higher they'd have lifted clean off his forehead. Numerology didn't mean a thing to Jacqueline, but she was curious about his research—especially the "filthy rich" part.

"Create what, for instance?"

Thus began a relationship of give and take, with Jacqueline doing most of the taking. Within a month, the dancer left her career at No

Regrets for a much better one as Pendleton's personal assistant. She regarded their affiliation as an investment, an opportunity to accrue enough money to retire in style. Plus it was an easy job.

Jacqueline had been a Running Rebel. She attended UNLV during the day, majoring in both writing and finance. She was good at mixing facts and figures with unrestrained creativity. Her grades were impressive; she had brains as well as a body. She danced because it was a steady night job and the money was good. As Stevie's assistant, however, she would have the opportunity for travel, intrigue, accounting, some "undercover tasks," and, of course, the potential for more money than she could earn in a decade at the club. School took an easy back seat.

"What have you unearthed, Gypsy?" Pendleton asked over the encrypted phone, shaking her from her memories.

She hated that code name. *Just play along, girl.* "It's not good. There's a professor up here who specializes in abnormal behavior in random populations. Plus, her husband works at some research lab in the valley."

"Research lab? Which one?"

"Wasatch BioChemical."

There was a pause on the other end of the line. "I know that name. But I thought they were strictly a production lab."

"I can look into that," Jacqueline said. "Is it a concern if they also do research?"

"Possibly."

"They're already on to the energy drink. They know there's a link, but they're not sure what. They're thinking it may be chemical, but they haven't thrown out the idea of an external signal. What's tripping them up is the randomness of the gathering points. Besides that, I'd say the stuff is working fine. According to the phone surveys I arranged, the song's very popular among the younger generation, but not so much with the adults. You gotta remember this is a very rural setting. If the final gathering is successful, we'll be able to wrap things up and go into mass production."

"That's good news."

"*Great* news. This could be really big, Stevie."

"Don. Remember to use our code names over the phone."

Jacqueline rolled her eyes again. The man, as brilliant as he was, had just given away the fact that Don was a pseudonym to whoever might be listening in. "Sorry."

"Just in case, get whatever you can on this professor and her husband. We may need ammunition later on. If you can, create a distraction in their lives."

"Copy that." She also hated the spy jargon Stevie liked to use.

"Anyone suspect *you*?"

"Nope. I'm as pure as the driven snow."

She heard him snort, suppressing a laugh. *Jerk.*

"Keep up the good work, Gypsy. Let me know what happens at the final gathering. It should be interesting. Kind of like to be there myself," he added as an afterthought.

"Copy that. Out."

"Over and out."

She closed the phone and stared at it for a time. She wished she knew exactly what to expect at the gatherings, but in a way she was glad she didn't. Stevie had explained that knowing in advance would bias her observations. That made sense. He had told her not to get too close, as each consecutive test would involve a greater amount of violence.

To what extent Pendleton was willing to carry out this experiment on innocent civilians was the real question.

TWENTY-EIGHT

From the information she got out of Lanh Tran, Jacqueline was able to initiate Web searches for additional, very private information on the professor and her husband.

Morgan Winegar was born and raised in Brigham City, Utah. Her performance in high school was impressive, garnering a tuition scholarship at UCSD.

She had married two years into her undergrad work but divorced soon after. Public records indicated a breech of prenuptial agreements. She had not sued for child support or grievances of any kind. Curious. Apparently, the Marquis family was rolling in financial resources. Jacqueline would have jumped all over that money train in a heartbeat.

Morgan had earned her BS, added a master's to it, then hired on at Utah State in the psychology department. She'd married Homer Winegar about two years after that.

Through a high-tech, black-market spy browser, Jacqueline learned that Morgan belonged to the LDS church and practiced her religion faithfully. She had a VISA card and a MasterCard, both with average balances, but she carried no major debts other than a mortgage, a home-improvement loan, and a car payment, all of which she shared with her husband. She had one mentally disabled son from the previous marriage and had lost a daughter with her current spouse. The daughter, Emily, had lived for five months before succumbing to SIDS. That was sixteen months ago.

Morgan had no vices, no addictions that were evident online. All her personal Internet traffic was medical, school-oriented, or religious in nature, with only a few random searches for travel deals and what looked like Christmas shopping. Her tenure at USU was exemplary. Jacqueline could find no reprimands, no allegations, not even any student complaints. The woman had a rugged past but had come through squeaky clean.

When Jacqueline used her disreputable resources to search Homer's background, she was surprised to come up with next to nothing. Homer Winegar had a birth date, a birth place, a social security number, and some grade school transcripts. He currently worked at Wasatch BioChemical as a data analyst. He'd been there four years. He made about $55,000 a year. He had good job reviews and, besides a parking ticket, had no criminal record. He attended church with his wife, having converted to Mormonism shortly after their marriage. Jacqueline hit a wall—or rather, a deep void—when she searched for information between his childhood and his current employment—a space of about thirty-five years.

Taking a different approach, Jacqueline pulled up recent DMV records to obtain photos of both Winegars. Except for a few changes in hairstyle, Morgan's picture looked pretty much like Jacqueline remembered her on campus. The ex-dancer recognized the professor's natural beauty: her almond-shaped eyes, full lips and wide mouth, and high cheekbones. The psychologist was a very pretty woman—photogenic too. Jacqueline knew Morgan would be a hit at the clubs she had worked in Vegas. But because of the woman's stodgy religious convictions, the idea was manifestly laughable. When she down-loaded images of Morgan from her childhood, it was clear she'd been very attractive since birth. Lucky. Almost half of Jacqueline's beauty had come at the expense of surgical upgrades.

Jacqueline then downloaded the DMV image of Homer. He was plain-looking. Not ugly by any means, but simple, average, boring. It took some searching, but she was finally able to locate some child-hood photos of young Homer Winegar using his birth date and county records. When she did, her eyes widened. Whoever Homer Winegar used to be—unless he'd undergone some *serious* cosmetic surgery—the man married to the USU professor was not the same one on her computer screen. She double-checked his birth date, social security number, place of birth, county records, etc. Identical. Even the hospital in which he was born and the physician who delivered him were spot on. Yet the Homer Winegar who matched the numbers she'd unearthed was a little black kid.

TWENTY-NINE

Monday, October 26

Because the dean had been at a conference in Salt Lake, it had taken a full week for Morgan to acquire the letter of concurrence to collect every remaining can of Dingo's Dance from the Taggart Center and other food service venues on campus. The recall resulted in a total of only eleven cans. To avoid undue panic or potential lawsuits, the confiscation was performed with minimal explanation.

"We're running an experiment," she told the staff. "Don't reorder any Dingo's Dance for now. Make a log of the number of specific requests for it, but it's not necessary to get names or anything. I want to keep it low key. If people catch on, it'll skew the results."

"No problem, professor," was the typical response.

Morgan delivered the cans to her husband that evening. "Now what happens?" she asked.

"I'll take them to the lab. I'll get Mike to run some gas chromatography fractionations on them to see what the chemical breakdown is. I'll also grab a dozen or so cans from Albertsons and Walmart as a control."

"What do you think you'll find?"

"I'm afraid to guess," he admitted.

* * *

The following morning Homer knocked on the open door of his friend's office at Wasatch BioChemical. "Hey, Mike. Can I bother you a second?"

Hidden behind reams of papers, stacks of binders, piles of reference books, and a multi-screen computer, Dr. Michael Duce's attention was glued to one of his flat-panel displays. A rapid clicking accompanied the staccato movement of his eyes across the screen. Every now and then the clicking stopped, but his eyes never did. Focused to the point of oblivion, Mike didn't hear his friend's request. Homer could only imagine what kind of complex chemical conundrum the man was trying to solve. Although Homer had had some schooling in chemistry, he knew his brain power was a fraction of that possessed by his friend.

"Mike?" Homer said a bit louder, still standing in the doorway.

The scientist flinched. "Geez, Homer. Why do you always have to creep up on me in that slimy way?"

"Sorry 'bout that," Homer chuckled. "I got a question for you, but it looks like you're super busy, so I can come back later."

"No, no," Mike said, waving his friend in. "I'm just taking a moment to exercise the ol' grey matter, trying to keep my mind sharp."

Carrying a manila folder, Homer rounded the scientist's desk for a look at his monitor. He couldn't help but guffaw. "Spider solitaire?"

"I tell you, this game is addicting. But I've found that if you time yourself—you know, try to solve it in under two minutes—it actually sharpens the mind."

Homer gave Mike a skeptical raise of an eyebrow.

"Well, it's a theory anyway," Mike snickered. "Pull up a chair. What's on *your* mind?"

Homer looked around. All of the chairs in the man's office were covered with papers and books. Homer grabbed the one least encumbered and moved the books to the floor. Sliding the chair close to the desk, he noticed a placard that read, "A clean, uncluttered desk is the sign of a sick mind." *No worries here,* he mused.

While one monitor had a four-deck game of spider solitaire in progress, the other two displayed multi-grid boxes of data from various workstations throughout the complex. One terminal even had a CCTV camera display linked to each of the four labs at Wasatch BioChemical—or SatchBo, as the community liked to call it.

"Do you get over to the labs much?" Homer asked congenially.

"Heck no. I used to eat and sleep there, but not anymore. Ever since I started directing the tests instead of running them hands-on, I made a rather enlightening discovery."

"What?"

"It stinks in there. Literally. Some of those chemical fumes turn my stomach. They never used to. I've always hated deskwork, you know that. How you can sit and analyze data for hours baffles me. But now, having breathed clean air for a while, I hate the thought of going back in there. It makes me wonder why I used to love it in the first place."

Homer laughed. "Because that's who you are, Mike. You love the challenge of the unknown, same as me."

Mike rubbed his eyes and stretched against the back of his chair. "You're absolutely right, of course. But I still pity you and your number-crunching coworkers. I truly do."

"I love my job. It allows me to be me."

"A good thing, too," he said, clicking off the card game. "You're one of the best. Now, what can I do for you?"

Homer leaned forward, resting his elbows on his knees and holding his folder between his palms. "I need some help—well, a favor, really. There's some strange stuff going on up at USU. Morgan thinks it's responsible for one suicide already, and some random, violent acts. She's afraid there may be more very soon."

Mike reached under a stack of binders and retrieved a yellow legal pad and a pen. How he knew they were there, Homer couldn't guess. How the man could find *anything* on his desk was a mystery.

"You're referring to those mass hallucinations people are talking about?"

"The very ones."

"Great. Give me some details," the scientist said.

"Okay, but this may take a minute or two, and I guarantee it'll sound like pure conspiracy theory paranoia when I'm through."

"Let me be the judge of that, my friend. And as for spending time on it; hey, I'm salaried. As long as I'm at my desk, it counts."

Homer liked this guy immensely. And he trusted him just as much. He was the only one who knew Homer's true past—well, the part that mattered anyway. Mike had been Morgan's bishop when Homer was investigating the Church. The man knew more about Homer's past than anyone else on the planet—and that included the U.S. government. But Homer knew Mike was true to his Church calling. What passed between them stayed between them. Luckily, the FBI had granted a breach of the protection program this one time. Mike became part of their overall agreement. And the man had remained true to everything he had promised the government and Homer.

"Thanks, Mike." Homer took a deep breath. "We think someone is drugging the students at Utah State."

Making a few scribbles on his pad, Mike prompted Homer to continue.

Homer detailed the series of events Morgan had relayed, as well as the results of her interviews. He then opened his folder and pulled out a typed transcript of the dialogue. Handing it to Mike, he also passed along his breakdown of the results. "I know this is your field of expertise, but as you can see, I gave it a stab."

Mike waved him off as if to say, *yeah, right.*

"Here's what I came up with," Homer continued. "I need a second opinion. One I can trust. At the risk of seeding any bias, I'm hoping you'll tell me I'm wrong in my conclusions."

Dr. Michael Duce scanned the synopsis with steady eyes and an expressionless face. "Dingo's Dance?"

"It's one of the newer flavors according to Tribe's Web site."

The scientist read both reports twice without further comment. He flipped a page on his legal pad and began scribbling like mad. It was five minutes before he looked up. "I think you may be onto something, Homer. You wrote here that you've removed the remainder of the drink from the university?"

"It's in my car."

The scientist was clearly surprised. "Not very good lab technique, Homer. Temperature fluctuations inside a car can cause chemical degradation in all sorts of ways."

"Sorry. But it's pretty cool outside. I figured a few minutes wouldn't be too big a risk. Do you think it's worth testing?"

"Yes. As soon as possible, in fact."

"I'll go get it," Homer said.

"Take it to D lab. It's less smelly." The doctor of chemistry winked. "I'll meet you there in fifteen minutes."

"I owe you one, Mike."

"Actually, you owe me two or three hundred. But who's counting?"

THIRTY

A brisk, ice-spangled wind knifed its way under Homer's lab coat as he ran out to his car. Glancing around the parking lot, he fought the nervousness that thumped inside his chest. He'd considered the possibility that this whole USU mess was simply someone trying to find him again. But it sure seemed like a roundabout way of searching. Besides, it'd been years since he had started his new life. Although the whole thing had been meticulously planned and executed, he doubted many people believed the fake death—corpse included—and destruction of his old identity. Still, Homer prayed every night that the henchmen in his old life had lost interest in trying to find him.

Entering D lab, Homer saw that his friend was already at work setting up an HPLC—high pressure liquid chromatograph—used in analyzing the individual components of almost any substance. It was considered the gold standard in biochemical research.

"I've been thinking about your chemical," Mike said with his back to Homer. "It seems a drug by itself is not enough to elicit the kind of control you're suggesting. To date, I know of no way to obtain that kind of specificity with an oral substance. If someone *has* unraveled that mystery, then heaven help us all."

Even though he and Morgan had come to a similar conclusion, Homer decided to let Mike explain as much as he knew before adding any additional information. "How so?" he asked.

"As you know, certain chemicals can cause instantaneous addiction, even drug-seeking behavior, after just one dose."

"You're talking about crystal meth and crack cocaine."

"Among others, yes. But it's not just opiates and narcotics." He wheeled a tank of pressurized helium closer to his workbench and continued constructing his chromatograph. "Compulsive gamblers, pornography junkies, even some overeaters have similar surges in dopamine levels that prompt their addictions. In fact, some researchers say the dopamine surge associated with pornography is off the charts. So are oxytocin, serotonin, and other human neurochemicals; but dopamine is the major addictive agent."

"You're saying we can be addicted to our own hormones?"

"Sure. Old men crave testosterone partly because their body remembers what it was like to have it dominating their systems at eighteen," Mike sighed, as if he had experienced the same thing.

Homer began organizing the eleven cans of USU Tribe on a tabletop, along with a few "control" cans from other vendors in the valley. Unbelievably, the table surface was nearly clutter-free.

"See, we're all built with certain thresholds that regulate our hormonal and chemical impulses. That way we don't go around over- or understimulated all the time. Heavenly Father knew just what He was doing when He created these amazing bodies. We all have ups and downs, but hormonal and neurochemical fluctuations are generally held within a specific range. It's when we go out of those bounds that we need chemical intervention."

"Chemicals to counteract chemicals. Sounds like an endless cycle."

"Can be," Mike said, returning to his colossal chemistry set. "You just need to know your chemicals. Now all we have to do is isolate *your* mystery chemical and, more importantly, what other stimulant is involved."

"You sure there's another one?"

"Oh, yeah. Look at it this way: a wino is addicted to alcohol in general, not specifically Jack Daniel's or Dom Pérignon or Napa Valley Ripple. A smoker is addicted to nicotine, not specifically Skoal or Marlborough or Cuban cigars. So when you said the students that drank this Dingo stuff congregated at a specific location and all snapped out of it at a specific time, I have to assume there is something else instructing them once their systems are primed for input—something that would promise an ultimate reward of some sort."

Homer flinched. "Could this instruction come from a subliminal source?"

Mike's eyes never left Homer's face, but his mind was clearly elsewhere for a long moment. "Yeah, sure. Why?"

"My son may have discovered the input."

Mike grabbed his yellow legal pad and clicked some lead from his mechanical pencil. "Keep talking."

Homer took a deep breath while organizing his thoughts. "Okay. This may be a red herring, but Zach kept asking Morgan and me about a 'whispers song.' We could never figure out what he was talking about until Morgan inadvertently recorded it at a lecture. In fact, it was right after the song played that another fugue occurred."

"What's the song?" Mike asked excitedly.

"Some new age, instrumental world music. I think they called it 'Toad Stomp.'"

"Totally instrumental? You sure about that?"

"Yeah, I've heard it. But Zachary says there're words being whispered *inside* the music."

"What words?"

"He couldn't repeat them all. Or he didn't understand them all. He's only nine and, if you remember, autistic. But he did say something about an 'ultimate reward.' He said the words are repeated several times, very, very fast."

Dr. Michael Duce thought hard for a moment. "I've got a friend down in Houston who deals with this kind of stuff. Name's Kirk Lamont. He's a Ph.D. working for EnSat Communications; specializes in cutting-edge satellite signal encryption and deciphering. Says you'd be surprised at the junk that bounces between earth and outer space. If I can send him a good copy of the song, he's got the equipment to break it apart."

Hesitantly, Homer asked, "Can he be trusted?"

"Trusted? Sure. Why?"

Homer rubbed his eyes forcefully. "I have a sinking feeling this mess goes a lot deeper than any of us imagines."

"Then I'll give you his number so you can talk to him firsthand. Mention my name and our affiliation. If you think he's okay, then send him the file. Personally, he's top-notch in my book."

Homer took the number. "Thanks, Mike. I hope I'm wrong about this stuff."

"Yeah. Me too."

THIRTY-ONE

Tuesday, October 27

Homer took a half-day from work to run some errands around town. He first stopped by a florist to send Cynthia a cheer-me-up bouquet. He swung by the Pita Pit for a quick bite then drove to the radio station. Passing by the antique radio memorabilia in the vestibule, Homer approached the bullpen feeling apprehensive, worried. A disconcerting thought had just occurred to him. What if someone at the radio station was an intentional accomplice to the whole thing?

"Can I help you?" the young receptionist asked from behind a laptop on her desk.

Glancing at her nametag, Homer said, "Hi, Tausha. I need to find out about a specific song you guys have been playing."

"Sure. Do you know the title or artist?"

"I think it's an Australian group."

Tausha sniggered. "You'd be surprised how many people have asked about that song. It's called 'Toad Stomp.' Do you like it?"

"Well, to tell you the truth, I've only heard it once," he said. "It's something my wife wants."

"Seriously? That's a shock—unless she's in her twenties. Most people over thirty don't care for it."

"Well, she still looks twenty-three to me, but she's actually closer to thirty-five," Homer said with a wink.

"Good answer." Tausha beamed.

Tapping at some keys on her office PC, the receptionist quickly scanned a few pages. "Let's see . . . here it is. 'Toad Stomp.' It's by a group called 'Ayers Rock' from Brisbane, Australia. You can buy a copy of the song from the Book Table downtown and at Sandhill Crane CD in Providence."

"Seriously? They're selling it to the public?" Homer was shocked.

"Uh, sure. Why not?"

"Never mind," Homer said, scribbling down the information. "Thanks."

"You bet," she said, tapping the ESCAPE key. "Of course there's only one version available to the public."

Homer stopped short. "Excuse me?"

Tausha smiled as if having insider information pleased her immensely. "The label representative who purchased the airtime gave us four discs, each with the same song on it. She says there are minor differences in each, but I can't hear any. They're using Cache Valley as a test market to decide which version gets the best response."

"But they're all the same song?"

"Yeah. We play one each week. They're doing phone surveys or mailers or something to determine which is the keeper."

With a concentration-frown furrowing his brow, Homer asked, "How many weeks have you been playing it?"

Again referencing her PC, Tausha said, "This is the fourth week."

"And you started playing the last disc . . . ?"

"Sunday morning, before our religious programming."

Homer's heart skipped a beat at the implication. If each week had an increasingly harsher test asked of those entranced, then the last week might include a test that would be extreme, maybe even deadly.

He pulled out his wallet and removed his Wasatch BioChemical identification. "Listen, I work for a government-sponsored department at SatchBo. What do I have to do to get a copy of those discs?"

"Is there something wrong?" Tausha asked, clearly fearing she'd already said too much.

"That's what we need to find out. I promise I'll leave your name out of this. In fact, I promise no one will hear the recording outside my office."

Tausha fidgeted as she chewed on a fingernail, debating.

"This is very important, Tausha. It could mean life or death to the people of this valley."

Sucking in a gasp of air, she exclaimed, "Then we've got to tell our program director."

Homer's temper rose quickly. "Look, Tausha, this can't wait. If I have to, I'll call the mayor's office and get a court order," he bluffed. "Then there'll be no way to keep you out of it. I really need those recordings, right now!"

"I—I just can't *give* them to you, Mr. Winegar. We're still playing the fourth week's recording."

Glancing at her desk, Homer asked, "Does your laptop have a CD burner?"

Her eyes widened as if just now realizing that it did. "It sure does."

"Then it'll only take a few seconds. Please do this for me, hon. It really is that important."

The young girl walked into a back room while examining Homer's business card. She returned a few minutes later with four paper-jacketed discs and a plastic-encased blank CD. "If I get fired for this, I'm expecting you to get me a job at SatchBo."

Homer smiled. "We have great dental."

The four burns only took two minutes. Tausha was able to put all four recordings on a single disc. Homer thanked her, let her keep his card and, despite her assistance, left the radio station much more worried than when he entered.

* * *

The Book Table had a small display of the Ayers Rock recording on the checkout countertop. If it weren't for the display, Homer wouldn't have guessed the CD jacket contained the music he wanted. The cover art was downright creepy.

A murky black background was printed on some kind of prismatic paper so that when you tilted or turned the jacket, the artwork appeared to writhe and squirm with sinuous undulations. A barely distinguishable image lived within the molten background; a black specter, infinitesimally lighter than the background, a humanoid form with membranous leather wings and venomous, burnt-yellow eyes. Dark crimson letters that seemed to bleed into the background decreed the CD's only composition: "Toad Stomp." Ayers Rock.

For a song with such a comical title, the cover art did anything but convey a sense of humor.

"Have you heard it yet?" the cashier asked.

"A bit. It's for my wife."

"Really? Well, it's interesting stuff, but I can't listen to it very long. They played it in here all the time when it first came in, and I tell you what, by the end of the day, I always felt a need to don a loincloth and go out and kill something with a boomerang," the woman jested.

Homer smiled. Then he laughed. The woman looked to be in her sixties, if not older, and the idea of her running around like a scantly-clad aborigine was strangely very humorous . . . and somewhat disturbing.

After picking up Zachary, Homer drove home and immediately put the disc in their CD player. Morgan had yet to make it home from the university. Zachary sat at the kitchen table working another word search puzzle.

Homer pressed PLAY then hit PAUSE.

"Zachary? Can you come here a moment, please?"

The boy brought his puzzle book with him.

"Sit here on the couch. I'm going to play the whispers song again. Is that okay?"

He didn't answer. Homer wanted to make sure Zach knew what was about to happen. He didn't want to cause his son any sudden trauma. "Zachary?"

"Hi, Daddy."

"Hi, son. I'm going to play the song again. Are you ready?"

"Okay."

Zach was so intent on finding a word in his book that Homer wasn't certain he'd understood him. He made sure the volume wasn't too loud, then hit PLAY.

The music started as it had in the Kent Concert Hall recording. The bass underscore, the rhythmic percussion instruments, the buzzing warble of a didgeridoo, the breathy tone of the pan pipes were all just as Homer remembered. He turned to watch his son's reaction. But the boy never paused to listen; never batted an eye or cocked an ear.

"Hey, Zach. What do you think? Do you like the whispers song?"

Zachary kept circling words as he slowly shook his head.

"You don't like it?" Homer asked. "Do you want me to turn it off?"

"Not whispers song," the boy said without emotion.

Homer scooted closer to his son. "What do you mean, little man? The whispers haven't started yet?"

"No. It's not whispers song. No whispers inside."

"But . . . it's the same song. I made sure of that," Homer explained.

"Not the whispers song. Not the song in my radio."

Homer ejected the CD and put in the disc copied on Tausha's laptop.

"Okay, son, how about this one?" he asked as he pushed PLAY.

Zachary listened intently as the tune got going, then bounded to his feet. "Whispers! It has whispers. That's the one, Daddy. More and more and more whispers."

Homer ejected the CD before it got too far into the song. He was concerned that Zachary would react as he had earlier. Sliding the disc into the case, Homer found it hard to breathe. It was all too clear. The radio station played the recordings that had subliminal words imbedded in the tune, but the local stores sold unaltered versions. That way, no one who purchased a copy would be able to decipher the subliminal messages. And that meant that whatever message was being broadcast was indeed something worrisome, incriminating, or worse—deadly.

THIRTY-TWO

Homer called Mike Duce's friend in Texas from a payphone inside a Wi-Fi–accessible cafe. He figured a random, innocuous location would be safest—a paranoid emotion, but one cultured from years of experience.

"EnSat Communications. How may I direct your call?" a monotone receptionist asked.

"Dr. Kirk Lamont, please."

"One moment, please." Homer heard a click and some contemporary country music with crickets chirping in the background.

"This here's Dr. Lamont," the Southern-twanged voice answered.

"Hello, Dr. Lamont. My name is Homer Winegar. I'm calling because a mutual friend recommended you."

"A mutual friend? Who'd that be?"

"Dr. Michael Duce."

"No kiddin'? How is that myopic, neat-freak mad scientist these days?"

"Um . . . well, the mad scientist part is alive and well; he still wears glasses most of the time; but the neat freak isn't anyone I've ever met."

Dr. Lamont laughed heartily. Even across the phone line, Homer could detect a smile behind his boisterousness. He pictured the man as a barrel-chested, broad-shouldered, twinkly-eyed Santa Claus stand-in. If he had a thick white beard, it would not have surprised Homer.

"Just sniffin' you out, Mr. Winegar. And you come out fresh as a daisy."

"That's good to know, I think. And please, call me Homer."

"Fair enough, Homer. And you call me Kirk. You know, I used to share lab space with Mike long about a dozen years before he got his own spread. Now I've met packrats in my day, but Mike? Bless my soul, if you lined up the mess on his desk end to end, it'd stretch from God's mansion on high to Satan's cabin on Brimstone Lake. And get this—when he was awarded his own lab back in '03, and he got to cleanin' off his desk to move to his new spread, he uncovered a Valentine card to his wife, dated February of '01."

Homer chuckled. "Did he still give it to her?"

"He sure enough did."

"I'm surprised the man's still married."

"Hoo-wee, me too."

"He probably gave her a romantic subscription to *Science Digest* along with it."

The jovial man in Texas roared a second belly-laugh that without doubt was heard across the border in Mexico. Homer waited patiently for a chance to speak again, but Kirk beat him to it.

"I like you already, Homer. And if you're a friend of Mike's, you're a friend of mine. If you haven't guessed yet, I am an irrepressible optimist. Everyone starts out a friend until they prove otherwise. See, I believe a stranger is just a friend you haven't met yet."

A Santa Claus wannabe blended with a hometown helping of Will Rogers. Homer couldn't help but feel a bit worried about Kirk's qualifications. He sounded more country bumpkin than audio specialist. "Thanks. Listen, I need to ask you some questions of a very confidential, very technical nature."

"Y'all aren't gonna ask me to eavesdrop on your wife's cell phone calls, are you?"

"Not at all. Here's the deal . . ." Homer gave a quick synopsis of the fugues at USU and his and Morgan's suspicions about the cause.

"And you believe one kid has died because of it?"

"That's a definite maybe. But there may others we don't know about. That's what worries me."

"Well, it sounds like you're sniffin' down the right set of tracks."

"Yeah, but even if you're on the right track, you'll get run over if you don't get moving," Homer said, quoting Will Rogers.

Another round of *basso profundo* laughter caused the earpiece to buzz with distortion in Homer's ear. "I knew there was a reason to like you, Homer—besides bein' a friend of Mike's. Subliminal messages, huh? Creepy stuff, that. I used to dabble with it a smidge in grad school. Of course, that was back in the sixties when we first were discoverin' there actually *was* a subconscious. Speakin' of grad school, there was this one gal in my alternative communications class. Sweet little thing. Kind of a cross between Sally Field and Goldie Hawn. Cute as a bug's ear. Smart too. Tried hookin' up with her a time or two, but she—"

"Say, Kirk, I don't mean seem rude, but I really need to move on this thing. The pattern has shown that the trances are programmed for every Friday around four o'clock. Each gathering has been accompanied by a task more dangerous than the one before. I may be over-guessing this whole mess, but if I'm not, we've got to find a way to stop it before this weekend."

"Fair enough, Homer. Whatcha got in mind?"

Homer succinctly laid out his request to pull the subliminals from the "Toad Stomp" recordings he had. "I'm not a man prone to panic, but this could easily snowball into a very deadly avalanche. Can you help?"

"I reckon I can, Homer. How soon can you get it to me?"

"In two minutes if you give me your e-mail address. I'll send you an MP3 file of each song. If you want, I can also send a file without the whispers."

"Whispers? Oh, I gotcha—the subliminals. Why would you call 'em whispers?"

"It's a long story."

"Got a few of them myself. Okay, pard. Send 'em both. I'll run 'em through our siftin' processors. I just wrote a new algorithm that can pick up a lone flea sneeze from a whole pack of bloodhounds with the itch. If there're 'whispers' in your song, I'll find 'em, by gum."

"Thanks, Kirk. I mean it."

"Aw, now, don't go gettin' all sweet on me, Homer. You just try and keep Mike clutter-free. And don't let him stay in the lab too long.

I worry about that boy breathin' all them chemicals twenty-four-seven, 'cause he never goes home."

"It's a deal."

Homer jotted down Kirk's e-mail and hung up. He then opened his laptop, opened a mail file, and sent a copy of the radio-versions of "Toad Stomp" along with the store-bought version. Accompanying the files, Homer sent a silent prayer that the happy-go-lucky Texan would be able to help prevent a disaster.

THIRTY-THREE

"Is the man of my dreams at home?" *In my dreams if I was high on Peyote buttons and LSD maybe.*

"He is if you know the code."

"One, seven, one, one, four."

"Master number?"

"Five."

"Excellent. What's up, Gypsy?" Pendleton asked.

"You remember the husband of the teacher that's snooping around our project?" Jacqueline asked.

"Yeah. Some lab analyst, you said."

"I think he's a bit more than that. The guy's not much to look at: typical middle-aged, middle-class male Caucasian. You wouldn't think he could do more than punch a clock to stay ahead of his bills. Comes across as Joe Average, if you know what I mean. Used to see lots of his kind at No Regrets; only tipped in one-dollar bills."

"Sounds like a non-issue. So what's the problem?"

"I think the guy's a ghost."

"A what?" the scientist said.

Jacqueline paused to rub her eyes. Why was it she always felt a headache coming on when she tried to converse with this egghead? "Don't you ever read Clancy or Ludlum or watch spy movies?"

"Lame," Stevie sang in a falsetto, stretching the word into two syllables.

"A ghost. A spook. Someone who only *looks* harmless on the outside."

"You mean a spy?"

"There's a chance."

"Why in the world would you suspect that?" Stevie scoffed.

"His social security number, his birth date, all his records are fake. He borrowed them from a black kid who died from diabetes complications twenty-six years ago. I can't find a thing on this guy, except that he is married to Morgan Young Marquis and that he works at Wasatch BioChemical. It's like he appeared out of nowhere. A ghost."

"Wow. How did you find all that out?" Pendleton was truly amazed.

Jacqueline was getting extremely irritated. "I don't just sit around here waiting for your phone calls and picking the lint from my navel. You asked me to find out what I could, and I came up with a mystery."

"Roger that. Ah . . . good work, Gypsy. So then, what do you think? Is this guy going to be a problem?"

"Anytime I can't find out someone's shoe size, it worries me."

"Copy that. You think you can shut them down?" Stevie "Don Juan" Pendleton asked.

"Maybe. I have a few ideas, but I might need more time. Any chance of postponing the last gathering?"

Stevie hee-hawed a short laugh that hurt her ears. "You really don't grasp what's going on here, do you? Once the chemical is in a person's system and they hear the subliminal triggers, it's like programming a robot to perform a specific task. Since the last subliminal is already in play, the only way to alter the programming is to use a backdoor command to override the primary one before the event finishes."

"Like the one I used at first?" Jacqueline wondered.

"Precisely. The very one, in fact. But there's just no way of knowing who to give the command to until after the event begins," he explained. "And depending on the person's response, by then it may be too late."

Jacqueline thought about that for a moment. "So, should I know what the final task is before it happens?"

Pendleton didn't answer right away. "Well, it's one I wouldn't want to miss," he said as if in deep contemplation. "Without getting specific, I can tell you the final task is the most dangerous of all. It'll create a nationwide news flash that'll surpass Waco, Columbine, and Virginia Tech."

Jacqueline did not respond. Although she didn't particularly like the idea of hurting innocent young people, she realized the importance of testing them to the limits. If they would respond to something as morally distasteful as random violence, then there was no end to what could be asked. Besides, if these experiments panned out, there just might be some good money to be made in addition to the small fortune already promised her . . . and that always piqued her interest.

"Okay, Don Juan. I'll get right on . . . *disrupting* the Winegars."

THIRTY-FOUR

Over the past two weeks, Dr. Ethan Greene's ex-partner had become even more erratic than usual. Ever since he had hired on with Scandia Labs, Steven Pendleton had never been a favorite among research techs—or anyone else in the facility. His temperament was bipolar in nature. His methods were unconventional in the extreme. Hazardous chemical spills were a given in his lab. Accidents were to be expected. According to Pendleton, it was part of the thrill of the job, of discovery.

But lately, Pendleton had seemed overly agitated, nervous beyond the norm. The young scientist had taken to pacing the hallways, mumbling to himself. He threw things around the lab and used language caustic enough to ignite asbestos. Within the last two weeks, Stevie had gone through three secretaries and a half-dozen lab assistants. Nothing was ever done right. Nothing was ever good enough.

Ethan figured the proper thing to do was offer assistance; one scientist to another. After all, they worked for the same company, didn't they? Yet when Ethan extended his proposition, Pendleton exploded into a rampage. "Still upset that Bjorkman picked me over you, huh? Can't wait to get your hands on my chemical so you can steal the credit, right? *Right?* Always triple-checking everything, afraid to take risks. You're more of a lab tech than a true scientist, *Dr. Greene.* What was the last original idea you came up with anyway, huh? When was the last time you were brave enough to venture outside your secure little box? You can't take over the world with baby steps, pal. I tell you what—my new chemical will *save* humanity. You're either too dense to understand that or just plain chicken—"

The tirade stopped abruptly as Pendleton took out a notepad and began scribbling furiously. He mumbled a few chemical names to himself, as if working out an equation, and flipped from one page to the next, scribbling and scribbling.

Ethan clenched his teeth at the effrontery, shoved his hands into his smock pockets, and walked away without comment. If he had lingered, his fists may have made a comment on his behalf.

* * *

Dr. Ethan Greene worked late that evening, but no more than usual. He was dedicated to his work, and, being recently widowed, he had nowhere else to go. Exiting the building around ten-thirty, he went to a Mexican restaurant he liked to frequent. Pancho Villa's was a late-night mom-and-pop dive tucked away between a furniture outlet and a dollar store in a strip mall in downtown Henderson. The bland exterior and gaudy interior stopped most unknowing patrons at the door, but the quality and authenticity of the food was beyond compare. And at this late hour, Ethan was likely to be their only customer. That was good. He felt like being alone.

While working his way through his third sweet-pork tamale, Ethan's mind replayed the lambasting he'd received earlier. Stevie had really popped a cork this time. His bipolar swing had not only exceeded normal parameters but had found its way clean off the charts. It seemed clear that the erratic man needed to increase his personal dose of whatever med he was on; or better yet, find a new chemical with which to—

With a forkful of black beans poised halfway to his mouth, Ethan froze.

My chemical . . . With my new chemical . . . What was it he had said? *With my new chemical I'll save humanity . . .*

What new chemical was he referring to? The question had only one answer, and it had nothing to do with Dr. Cole's appetite suppressant.

Ethan's fork dropped to the plate, scattering beans across the table.

His waiter quickly approached. "Is everything okay, Señor?"

"I hope so."

Ethan tossed a twenty on the table and left the restaurant. By the time he got back to Scandia Labs, it was just before midnight.

Using his universal electronic passkey, Ethan entered the glass front doors. A night watchman sat behind a reception counter reading a paperback. "Good evening, Dr. Greene. Is there something wrong?" the large man asked.

"No, Kort. I just forgot a couple things I wanted to take home to work on," Ethan said with an easy smile.

"You need any help?"

"Thanks anyway," Ethan said as he passed by the guard.

Hailing an elevator, Ethan went directly to Pendleton's office. His universal passkey unlocked the lab door with a soft beep and a green light.

Once the blinds were opened, the streetlights outside illuminated the large room enough to negate switching on the overhead fluorescents. Ethan moved directly to Stevie's desk. Having worked with Pendleton for over a year, he was familiar with the man's quirks, habits, and foibles. A small key dangled from a lanyard around the bust of some Egyptian king believed to be the father of numerology. To anyone else the key looked like an innocent part of the artwork, perhaps just an ankh or a cartouche. Ethan knew better.

The key opened a large custom file cabinet that stood to one side of the scientist's desk. It took only a few minutes to find the files dealing with the THIQ project—and Pendleton's deviations from that research.

Everything was printed out in black-and-white. SPAAM: the new chemical that enabled subliminal control. Tribe Dingo's Dance: the mechanism by which the chemical was distributed. Cache Valley: the field test location. Utah State University: the population on which the test was being conducted. Jacqueline X: code named Gypsy, the field agent who processed and recorded everything about the illegal test. The means of distributing subliminal commands, although the commands themselves were not listed. And all of the data collected to date.

Ethan cringed, not only at the haphazard design and shoddy construction of the project, but at the core immorality of the concept. The likelihood for successful control of such a design was nil. The probability for disaster had to be in the ninetieth percentile. That anyone would willingly be involved in such an experiment was beyond comprehension.

THIRTY-FIVE

Wednesday, October 28

Passing by Michael Duce's office, Homer glanced in to see if his friend was busy so he could discuss the conversation he'd had with Kirk Lamont. The doctor of science was not in, but sitting in a cleared spot on his small, cluttered sofa was a very pretty blond, fashionably dressed in a wool blazer and a short pencil skirt. About twenty-six years old, he guessed.

Upon seeing him, the young woman stood and extended her hand. "Homer Winegar, I believe?" A visitor pass dangled from a lanyard in front of a blouse unbuttoned way too low for a respectable office professional.

Momentarily befuddled, Homer shook her hand. Her grip was firm. "Guilty as charged."

"I'm so glad to finally meet you. I stopped by your office, but you were out. Dr. Duce said he'd go find you. I'm Jacqueline Steinbeck. No relation to the author; I don't like mice, and I'm very particular about men," she said with good-natured spryness.

"I'm sure there are a lot of men who'd be very sad to hear that, Ms. Steinbeck," Homer responded with equal humor.

"Please, call me Jacqueline."

The woman had a full-mouthed smile and deeply blue eyes. As he studied her evenly tanned face framed by well-coiffed blond hair, Homer guessed her to be a headhunter for some corporation wanting to steal Mike from Wasatch BioChemical. In the cutthroat world of molecular bioengineering and designer biochemistry, billion-dollar corporations worldwide thought nothing of filching the brightest minds from competitors. Using an attractive liaison like Jacqueline was becoming more of a norm than a novelty. But Homer wasn't so easily seduced. He knew all too well that visually impressive bombshells such as Ms. Steinbeck would have little success without an equally impressive amount of brains. Despite the stereotype she portrayed, Homer knew that this woman meant business.

"Jacqueline, then. You're meeting with Dr. Duce, I presume?"

"Actually, I came to inquire about you, Dr. Winegar."

"Homer. And I'm not a doctor, just a desk jockey."

The woman looked truly puzzled. She reached into a leather attaché and pulled out a plastic-bound dossier. Flipping it open she asked, "Homer Winegar, born December 6, 1975?"

"Yes," Homer confirmed hesitantly.

"Attended UCLA, graduated magna cum laude in organic chemistry, class of '96? Doctorate in molecular chemistry in '99?"

"I wish." Homer chuckled. "No, I went to a trade school in Wisconsin. I've never even been to California, though my wife was schooled there."

"We know. Ms. Marquis graduated from UC San Diego with a master's in psychology."

"That's right," Homer said, trying to hide the frown coalescing between his eyebrows. "Who's 'we'?"

"My employer, Synergistics, in Silicon Valley. But apparently we have some misinformation on you," the woman said, flipping through the pages of her file. "You attended Jackson Elementary in South Carolina, correct?"

"Yes . . ."

"And John Calhoun High?"

"That's right."

"Then you say you went to a trade school in Wisconsin?"

"Not right away. Look, what's this all about?" Homer asked, his suspicions rising by the second.

"Well, for some reason, we don't seem to have the correct data here," she said, ignoring his question. "Where did you go right after high school?"

This wasn't right. No headhunter came after a potential employee without foreknowledge and preparation enough to regurgitate their background, degrees, and accolades as the foundation of a tantalizing offer. If Jacqueline Steinbeck had asked a bunch of questions about Michael Duce, Homer could rationalize her presence in his office. But to want to speak to *him,* and in Duce's office, Homer knew something shady was afoot.

"I'm sorry, but what I did after high school is none of your business. Where is Dr. Duce?"

"He went to look for you," she said with amplified innocence. "He's been gone about ten minutes."

"Look, Ms. Steinbeck, whatever you're selling, I'm not buying. Whatever you're offering, I'm not interested. Those dates you rattled off are public record and therefore inconsequential. I'm not looking for a new job, so you obviously have the wrong man."

"Actually, I believe you're exactly the man we need to talk to. We could double your salary."

"Not interested."

Jacqueline knifed the dossier into her briefcase and, with the panache of a sleight-of-hand illusionist, removed a glossy treatise in one fluid movement. Stepping closer, she forced the shiny document into Homer's hand. "This is just one of the perks that come when working for Synergistics."

It was a Club Med executive brochure, platinum tier. Images of opulent decadence splashed across the cover—hot stone massages, lobster and shrimp lunches, master's level golf against a background of white-sand beaches and turquoise lagoons. A prominent close-up featured a shapely young woman in a gold lamé bikini made from barely enough fabric to cover an anorexic Chihuahua. The stare she offered the camera was one of pure wantonness.

"In case it slipped your notice, that's me in the bikini," Jacqueline pointed out. Stepping closer still, she placed a hand on his arm and tiptoed to his ear. Her lips were so close Homer could feel her breath as she whispered, "I come with the package as one of the perks."

Just then, Michael Duce walked back into his office and stopped cold. "Oh, excuse me. I see you two have met."

Jacqueline smiled coquettishly at Mike then gave Homer a quick peck on the cheek.

Homer quickly stepped away from the young woman, flinging her hand from his arm. "We've said hello and good-bye," he voiced, shoving the brochure back toward Jacqueline.

"Homer, wait," Jacqueline pleaded. Turning to Mike, she said, "Thanks for the use of your office, Dr. Duce. It was brief but well worth it." She allowed a coy blush to color her cheeks as she made a point of holding the visitor pass in her teeth so she could button up her blouse.

"Ah . . . yeah, sure," Mike stumbled.

Homer read the look in Mike's eyes as more than awkward embarrassment. It was a look of shock, of disappointment in him. The implication this woman presented was clear. Homer was certain it was a setup from the beginning.

"I have zero interest in your offer, Ms. Steinbeck," Homer snapped. "Leave now so I don't have to call security."

Jacqueline feigned shock and hurt. "I can't believe you would treat me like this in front of your friend."

"Treat you like what? We just met," Homer said.

The pretty blond quickly gathered her things and stepped to the door. "If that's what you want people to believe, fine." She left in a huff.

Michael watched her leave then turned to his friend. "Homer?"

Homer was incensed to the point of boiling over—and very frightened. Was this girl a spy from his former life? He wanted to explain everything but somehow felt it would come across as made up. Mike knew about his past—quite a bit, in fact—but not *every-thing*. That was a can of worms Homer felt he'd left behind, fully repented of and never to be reopened.

"Not now, Mike. Suffice it to say I've never seen that woman before."

"So . . . nothing happened?" Mike asked carefully.

"You know me better than that," he snapped, storming from the office.

Homer headed down the hall at a very quick pace. As he turned a corner, he glanced back in time to see the young woman enter an elevator at the opposite end of the corridor. He exhaled slowly and leaned against a wall. His knees were rigid enough to prevent him from hitting the floor, but he wasn't sure for how long.

THIRTY-SIX

"Professor Winegar?"

Morgan looked up to see a very attractive young woman at her office door. "Yes?"

"I need an awkward moment of your time. May I come in?"

Intrigued, Morgan said, "Of course. Take a seat."

The young woman looked like any USU student, only she was dressed more fashionably, particularly for this week's early dose of winter. If she had been on an Ivy League campus, she would have blended right in with her button-down blouse, argyle sweater vest, pleated chinos, and penny loafers. Plus, the woman had professionally polished looks, gorgeous blond hair in a gentle wave, and a personal trainer–molded physique. Morgan was instantly envious.

"What can I do for you, Miss . . . ?"

"Jacqueline," the woman answered as she closed the door behind her. "I hope you don't mind. What I need to say is very embarrassing for me and . . . and will probably be for you, too."

Morgan intuited it went deeper than that. "Does this have to do with the trances?"

Jacqueline sat on the chair in front of the desk and pulled a tissue from a small handbag. Her eyes glistened as she struggled to control emotions on the verge of spilling over. "Something much worse, I'm afraid."

"Okay . . ." Morgan said with reservation.

The pretty blond stifled a sob and repeatedly beat her fists against her knees as if wrestling with some inner demon tormenting her soul.

"Are you in some kind of trouble?" Morgan prompted.

Morgan had learned early on that many people—predominantly women—were unable to put into words a play-by-play account of disturbing history, especially when that history contained abuse of any kind. If she could talk this girl through the maze of self-ridicule, self-incrimination, and self-loathing, to a starting point at which a dialogue could be established, then Morgan could find out what was troubling her.

"Yes . . . and no," the young woman finally said.

"Jacqueline, as you already appear to know, I *am* a licensed psychologist, but I'm not a psychiatrist or mental health counselor. If you need that kind of intervention I would be more than happy to call someone more qualified. We have some excellent, caring doctors—"

Jacqueline shook her head forcefully. "No, it's nothing like that, Professor Winegar."

Morgan was baffled. "Something having to do with school, then?"

A groan of anguish burst from the young woman. "No. It has to do with . . . with your husband."

"Homer?"

In a rush, Jacqueline blurted out, "It started out all innocent at first. I thought he was just a sweet guy trying to be nice. I didn't mean for it to end up like it did, but he was so supportive, helping me through a nasty relationship with a guy at the lab. I really shouldn't have taken advantage of him, cornering him in his office after hours all those nights. He has such a gentle touch and really knows how to make a girl feel good about herself, in spite of what others are saying. I just want you to know how sorry I am about . . . well, about every-thing."

Morgan stared dumbfounded at the contrite girl across from her. Surely this woman could not be talking about *her* Homer—the only man she had fully allowed into her life after her divorce; the man who had adopted her son and loved him unconditionally; the man who shared her dreams, her successes and failures; the man who knew her hopes and fears and deepest secrets; the man she thought had proven that not all men were alike and that some could actually be trusted.

Finally, expelling a breath she was not aware she was holding, Morgan said, "Wait. Back up a moment. I'm not sure I follow you. You say you work at Wasatch BioChem with my husband?"

Jacqueline nodded, slowly reining in her runaway emotions.

"How long have you worked there? I mean, I don't remember seeing you there before."

The young woman reached into her handbag and withdrew a Wasatch BioChemical name badge with her picture laminated on it. "About a year now. I moved here from Reno when I got a job in the records department."

"I see. And who's the guy you had troubles with?"

"Julien Vennichi."

The office lothario. A self-proclaimed Italian stallion. Morgan knew of the man's disreputable reputation. She'd met him once and was shocked at the suggestive leers she had received from him. He *was* very attractive: dark hair, flawless olive skin, deep brown eyes, a chiseled face, and a seductive Italian accent. He drew women to him like moths to a flame—or flies to dung, depending on your point of view. "So he came onto you? Vennichi, I mean."

With a snort of derision, Jacqueline said, "He asked for my phone number before I even had my coat off. He moves very fast, and for someone all alone in a new town, I guess I was an easy target."

Morgan said nothing, but she could relate all too well with the pretty young woman. Despite her best efforts, images of Brad Marquis flashed in her mind.

"To make matters worse, Julien was spreading rumors that *I* was manipulating *him* simply to get a better-paying job. You know, using him as a rung on the corporate ladder. Then one day Homer saw me crying and asked if he could help. I started meeting him after work and . . ." Her voice trailed off in embarrassment and shame.

"And what?"

"I guess I let him finish what Julien started," she said just above a whisper.

Morgan stared down at her desk, unable to focus on any single item. "That's what you meant by an 'awkward moment of my time.'"

"I'm so sorry," Jacqueline whimpered.

"I never suspected a thing," Morgan mumbled.

"Of course you wouldn't. Neither did I. Your husband knows how to keep a secret, Mrs. Winegar. I was completely unaware he used to work for the government and is now living under an assumed name."

Morgan's eyes snapped up. "What?" she almost laughed.

Jacqueline nodded vigorously while keeping her eyes on her soggy tissue. "He told a lot of secrets when we were . . . um . . . when he . . . oh, never mind. I've—I've already said too much. I promise it's over between us. I'm moving back to Reno tomorrow morning. I just thought you ought to know."

"You had an affair with my husband?" Morgan mumbled, still unbelieving. "No. It can't be. There's no way. Not Homer."

"He's a very convincing man, Mrs. Winegar. I'm sorry to dump this on you, but I don't want him to ruin anyone else's life."

Steeling her resolve, Morgan said, "I don't believe you. He's not the kind to do this. He never worked for the government, and he is not living under an assumed name."

"I was afraid you wouldn't believe me." Jacqueline stood and collected herself. "Just try looking into his past, Mrs. Winegar. Do some Web searches on his schooling or his family. You'll be surprised at what you *don't* find."

Jacqueline stepped to the office door. "If you still don't believe me after that, just ask his friend Dr. Duce. He . . . he *caught* us the other day."

And with that, the gorgeous, skinny blond quickly exited Morgan's office, leaving the college professor feeling nauseous, confused, angry, frightened, and very much alone.

THIRTY-SEVEN

Morgan cancelled her last class of the day and spent the time hunched over her computer. She searched every Web site she could think of trying to unearth information on her husband. As much as she didn't want to believe the preppy girl who had all but admitted to having an affair with Homer, she was nonetheless compelled to prove her wrong. Because she didn't like to talk about her past, she accepted that he didn't comment very much on his.

When they were courting, Homer said he was an implant to Utah; that he was born in South Carolina in a backwater town called Thatcher Creek; that he was the accidental son of his mother and the principal of the school where she worked; and that he was born at home with the help of a midwife and a few shots of moonshine. Not really a model entry into the world. His mother had died of infection shortly after childbirth because the midwife didn't use sterile technique in removing the afterbirth. He had been raised by aunts and uncles and foster parents until he was fifteen. At that point he'd lit out on his own and ended up in Valencia, California, working as an orange picker. He got his GED from a community college and continued working various jobs, developing various skills until he was thirty. When he hit that magic number, he moved to Utah for a change of scenery, and to perhaps go to a university. He had a natural aptitude for numbers, and was hired on at Wasatch BioChemical first as a lab assistant, and then worked his way up as a company statistician.

Because Homer had no family in South Carolina with whom he wanted to associate, they never visited. Morgan understood that. She had no desire to travel to San Diego to visit Zachary's biologic father and grandparents.

Their lives consisted of each other. They made a perfect union, a relationship forged from adversity and tempered with trust. She felt that just as a lump of coal subjected to intense pressure and heat forms a precious substance, the intensity of their previous lives formed a bond between them as strong as a diamond and equally as priceless.

Morgan could not believe that their diamond now had a flaw. It simply could not be.

But the more she searched for birth records, school transcripts, tax files, and driver's license histories, the more barren the void in her stomach became. The "Homer Winegars" she found online (and there weren't a lot) did not match anything she had accepted as being part of his past.

Morgan heard a raspy sound echoing around her office, and only after focusing did she realize it was the sound of her own breathing. She didn't know where to turn next. A small voice inside her soul said to just ask him. She had no reason to doubt him. All this was the result of one girl's confession. One very pretty, very shapely, very vulnerable girl.

Your relationship is built on trust, she argued. *You shouldn't assume guilt. As a psychologist you know better than to base conclusion on one testimony. Call him.*

Morgan found herself nodding, as if agreeing with the pragmatic side of her psyche. She picked up the phone and hit the speed dial to his office. The phone rang several times before an answering machine picked up. Morgan slammed the phone into the cradle.

Stop it, Morgan. You know him better than that.

But did she? After coming up empty on her Web search, questions and doubts began to spread like a black fungus on her soul. She picked up the phone again and dialed the office of Michael Duce.

"Dr. Duce."

"Hey, Mike. It's Morgan."

"Sister Winegar, what a pleasant surprise. What can I do for you?" The man's voice was always friendly, open.

She had always liked Mike. As an employer, he had taken Homer under his wing and helped craft him into a top-notch statistician. As a bishop, he had helped Homer form a new life. He had given her husband confidence, dignity, and resolve. Homer had said on more than one occasion how indebted he was to Michael Duce.

At least, that's what their story was. Now she wasn't even sure if she could trust the former bishop.

"I need to ask a question, Mike, and I need a straight answer."

There was a pause on the line. She heard Mike clear his throat. "Okay. Sure."

"Is there a new girl at the lab?"

"What? A new girl?" He sounded truly mystified.

"Yeah. A very pretty blond." Morgan's tone was even, flat.

"Oh. Her." His tone had turned hollow, guilt-ridden. "Yeah, I saw one the other day . . . but I have no idea who she is."

"Does she work with Homer?"

"No. Homer works alone; you know that, Morgan."

"Do I?"

A heavy sigh crossed the line. "Listen, kiddo. I saw Homer talking with some gal I haven't seen before. They were in my office yesterday. I came in, and Homer started acting real strange, like he was angry with her or something."

"Did you talk with them?"

"No. Homer said he'd never seen her before either. They both took off right after I barged in on them."

"Barged in? In other words, you caught them in a compromising situation?"

A lengthy pause emptied the connection, but Morgan knew Mike was still there, thinking.

"I feel you should talk to Homer about this. I . . . I honestly don't know what went on. But we're talking about Homer, Morgan. He's as trustworthy as they come."

"Really." It was a rhetorical comment.

"Look, I can tell you what I *thought* I saw, but I'm not sure it'd paint a nice picture."

"A picture's worth a thousand words, Mike, and I've got a very artsy imagination," Morgan said, slamming down the phone a second time.

THIRTY-EIGHT

Homer sat in his house, unable to move. As efficiently as a leech siphons blood, fear and self-doubt drained Homer's resolve. It was unfathomable that his former associates would still be looking for him, and at the same time that some company was poisoning the students at USU.

The phone rang. Homer jumped. The caller ID read Wasatch BioChemical.

First catching his breath, Homer answered, "Winegar residence."

"Homer, it's Mike. You got a minute?" Before he could answer, the scientist continued. "Because if you don't, you're going to want to carve out a couple and come down here—now."

There was a pronounced level of anxiety in Mike's tone. Homer said, "Sure, Mike. Is there a problem?"

The Ph.D. paused. "This might sound paranoid, but . . . well, is there any chance this line isn't clean?"

Homer understood the implication immediately. Now that his less-than-honorable history loomed afresh, it was a definite probability. "You mean a wire tap?"

"Frankly, yes. A private firm perhaps? CIA? FBI?"

With his nerves on a razor's edge, Homer snapped, "Anything's possible, Mike. I mean, who's to say? I know the government thinks it can listen in on any citizen's private conversations under the guise of national security irrespective of the Fourth Amendment, but . . . are you being serious?"

"Well, like I said, it's probably just paranoia. Still, can you spare a minute to come down here? I've just finished the chromatography, but I don't want to tell you over the phone."

"Sure thing, Mike. I'll be there in about twenty."

An audible sigh crossed the phone line. "Thanks, Homer."

Morgan was not home yet. It was her turn to pick up Zach from the academy, but she was usually back by now. Homer wrote a quick note and left it on the kitchen counter.

Honey. I had to run back to the lab. I don't know how long I'll be gone. Give Zach a kiss good night for me. I love you. —Homer

THIRTY-NINE

The building was dark except for a yellow glow sluicing from under the door to Mike's lab. It was after seven o'clock, and the majority of the staff had gone home. Homer entered the lab and saw his friend disassembling his chromatography equipment.

"So what did you find?" Homer asked.

Dr. Duce flinched and dropped an Erlenmeyer flask. The empty container struck the floor with a loud pop, sending shards of glass skittering every which way.

"Sorry about that, Mike. I thought you heard me."

"Geez, you scared me to death," the scientist said, panting from fright.

"Sorry." Homer collected a whisk and dustpan from a wall mount and began sweeping up the mess. "So what did you find?"

"I've never seen this chemical before. After I isolated it from all the other ingredients in the drink, it turned out to be some kind of morphine derivative. It looks like a prodrug with some other constituents attached. Unless I miss my guess, this has all the markings of a highly addictive substance."

"How high?"

"Heroin high. Crystal meth high. One dose could hook you."

Homer gave a low whistle. "How can you tell?"

"Well, without going into too much detail, generally speaking, the more hormone-like a chemical is, the faster it will bind to receptors and the longer it will hang on. It's just the way our systems operate. This thing looks a lot like apomorphine, but there're some side-chain structures that apparently alter its effects. I found traces of adenosine, isoquinoline, and a bunch of organic acids."

Homer tilted his head to one side. "You just lost me."

Grabbing a slip of paper, Mike scratched out a drawing.

"This is the parent structure of apomorphine. The body of the chemical has a structure similar to morphine and other narcotics, but this one usually does not have opiate activity."

"Then what *does* it do?" Homer asked.

"Traditionally, it was used to treat Parkinson's disease. Still is, I believe. That's because it's a very strong dopamine agonist. That means it attacks and stimulates dopamine receptors in our brain and other parts of the body."

"Is that bad?"

"Depends. At normal levels, dopamine helps to regulate nearly every system in our bodies. Too little dopamine brings on symptoms of Parkinson's, ADHD, slurring of speech, and the like. Too much and you get paranoia, hallucinations, even schizophrenia. But in levels way above normal thresholds, you get extreme euphoria. The association it has with narcotics is not fully understood, but there seems to be massive surges of dopamine released when we do certain things."

"Like . . . ?" Homer prompted.

"Like smoking methamphetamine or shooting heroin. Heck, like I said before, you get the same dopamine surge when viewing graphic stimuli like violence and pornography."

"And you think this chemical is what—a supercharged version of apomorphine?"

"Well, I can't tell without running clinical tests on it. But I do know this: if someone is intentionally putting this chemical into energy drinks found only at USU, their intent has to be a control of some kind. I can't believe the manufacturer of Tribe is behind this. The isolation of samples is too specific. I ran the same tests on the cans you purchased from grocery stores and came up blank. Unless this is happening elsewhere in the world, it sounds like someone has picked our little valley for an experiment."

"An experiment? Isn't that assuming quite a lot?" Homer asked without revealing he had already come to the same conclusion.

"You're the analyst. Can you think of a better explanation for finding a unique form of apomorphine in an isolated sample of energy drink?" asked Mike.

Homer didn't answer. He stared blankly at the deconstructed gas chromatograph as a reconstruction of thoughts scrambled to line up in his head. A disturbing sequence of probabilities assembled into an unstable line of dominos. If someone was doing this intentionally, then logic would predicate that they had an observer—perhaps several—measuring the results. And if they were watching the afflicted students, they would also notice the interest Morgan had taken in solving the mystery.

"Homer?"

Homer looked up, but his stare was hollow.

"Homer, are you okay? You look white as a sheet," Mike said.

Homer muttered a wordless affirmation.

Mike nodded. "I guess you've put two and two together just like I did. Someone is doing this on purpose. And if they aren't afraid to run the risk of harming innocent students, then they probably will have no qualms about dissuading anyone from looking into their little field test. That includes you and me. That's why I want out of it. Tonight, okay?"

"Sure, Mike," Homer said in little more than a mumble.

"Homer? This means that Morgan may be in serious danger, too."

"My thoughts exactly," Homer said, already halfway to the door.

FORTY

The acrid taste of bile rose in Morgan's throat as she read the note on the kitchen counter.

Run back to the lab for what—work? Reports? Jacqueline? Morgan's denial turned to bitterness. Bitterness to anger. Anger to hate. All men were pigs; Morgan was now convinced of that. First Bradley, now Homer—if indeed that was his real name.

She clawed the note into a ball and crushed it between her palms. Dropping it to the countertop, she then pummeled it with her fist, once, twice, three times, as if inflicting pain and suffering to the inanimate slip of paper would somehow transfer over to her husband.

"Mommy's angry?" Zachary said at her side as he struggled with his winter coat.

"Very angry," she hissed.

Willing herself not to cry, she dragged Zachary back to the garage, buckled him in his booster seat, and nearly broke the key wrenching it in the ignition. Barely missing the still-retracting garage door, Morgan lurched into the street and sped into the night.

* * *

Morgan drove without any particular destination in mind until a little voice from the back seat announced, "I'm hungry."

She was so upset over the revelation about her husband that she had lost track of time and the fact that she had Zachary with her.

"I'm sorry, honey. How about an adventure meal?"

"Okay," he said.

As they were leaving the drive-thru, Morgan's cell phone vibrated while playing "Für Elise" in the hands-off dash mount.

"Beethoven," Zachary said while looking for the toy in his kid's meal.

The caller ID read Cynthia Weatherwax, the receptionist at Zachary's school. She had access to the parent's cell numbers for emergency purposes.

"Hello," Morgan said, not really in the mood for conversation but assuming it might be something important dealing with her son.

"Hi, Morgan. Sorry for calling you so late on your cell. No one answered your home phone. Is Homer still at work?"

"I suppose."

"I thought as much. Listen, will you please tell Homer thanks again? He was so sweet to listen to my boobing and babbling, and was so compassionate and encouraging. And the flowers he sent were lovely and totally unnecessary."

"Flowers?"

"Oh, yes. He's such a wonderful man, Morgan. You're one lucky girl."

"Am I?"

Cynthia laughed, as if Morgan's question was meant as a joke. Morgan wasn't sure how much luck she had anymore.

"Well, I've got to run. See you tomorrow."

Just as Morgan hit disconnect, the phone played Beethoven a second time.

The caller ID read Homer Winegar. She ignored it, letting it play through the melodic tune as if it were a CD.

"Who is it, Mommy?"

"Wrong number," she said in a hollow voice.

"Morons," the boy spat, mimicking the reply Homer often gave when encountering wrong numbers and telemarketers.

Morgan could almost hear Homer's voice coming from her son's mouth. Zachary had quickly picked up on the fact that he and Homer were both boys and that Mommy was a girl. That created a natural bond between them, in addition to the fact that Homer was a naturally good dad.

But was he?

Who was her husband, really? That Jacqueline woman had said to look into his past, as if there was something hideous and despicable to be found. The trouble was there was nothing *to* find—just as the woman had predicted. Morgan ground her teeth in frustration.

"Not going home?" Zachary asked.

"No, honey, not right away. I just want to drive around for a bit, okay?"

"Okay," he said, playing with a toy elephant he'd received. "Can I hear music, please?"

"Sure, little ma—" Morgan stopped herself when she realized she had used the chummy moniker Homer had given their son. Somehow it left a sour taste in her mouth.

She switched on the radio to KUSU for some classical music, but they had a sports show playing. Instead, she skipped over to the local pop station. After a spot touting a used-car dealer's prices and service as the best in the valley, a song began to warble through the speakers. Morgan recognized it immediately. So did Zachary. "Toad Stomp." Morgan immediately pushed the preset button to another frequency, but it was too late.

"Whispers song, Mommy. I want whispers song, please."

Morgan knew that arguing was futile. She tuned back to the song and ground her teeth even harder. The action sounded like stone against stone in her head.

Morgan soon heard her son begin to mumble and hum along with the melody even though there were no audible lyrics accompanying the Australian music. She wondered if Mike's friend had deciphered the words Zachary was hearing. She also wondered how they played into the Aggie Trance. Additionally, she wondered how her husband could have been so deceptive for so long. *Unless he truly was a secret government operative . . .*

Morgan scoffed, thinking of Homer starring in a secret agent spy movie, as if he were James Bond himself. No. It was too far-fetched to actually happen.

"Final test is coming. The final reward," Zachary sang along as if at a karaoke bar. "Ulimate reward. Happy, happy, happy. Ecsassy. Pleasure. Ulimate reward."

Morgan frowned at the tone of the words. She couldn't hear them, but assuming Zach got them right, it sounded like a brainwashing primer.

"Meet challenge, children. Meet the challenge."

She instantly recognized Utah State's motto: Meet the challenge. It was a motto meant to inspire, to prompt students to raise the bar, to do as poet Robert Browning had urged in saying a man's reach should exceed his grasp.

Suddenly Zachary stopped singing. Morgan tilted the rearview mirror to see what he was doing. She was shocked to see a worried, frightened look on her son's face. "Zachary? Are you okay?"

The boy did not respond. His eyes were fixed on the headrest in front of him. Morgan thought she noticed a slight tremble on his lower lip.

"Zachary, sweetheart. What's wrong?"

"Bad words," he whispered.

"What was that, honey?"

The boy looked like he was on the precipice of one of his regressions. It ate at her that she always felt so helpless at these times. Even with her extensive college training, Homer seemed naturally so much better at handling this. But she didn't trust him anymore, and wondered if she could ever trust him again.

"Zachary?"

"Bad words," he repeated. "Mean words this time. Very mean."

"This time? You mean these are different words?" Morgan quickly turned off the radio, but Zachary continued to have a look of terror etched in his stare. "It's gone now, little man." Strangely, the words did not have the same aftertaste they had a moment ago.

"Bad, bad, bad, bad!" Each time Zachary repeated the word his tone increased not only in volume but in intensity.

"Shh, Zach, honey. It's okay. The bad words are gone now. Shh, let's think of something nice now."

"Mean, mean, mean!"

"Zachary, how about we get some ice cream before going home?" Morgan wanted to distract him in any way she could.

"Kill, kill, *killll* . . ." Zachary's little voice faded into a barely audible whisper. It was almost as if he had stopped breathing.

Morgan had to remind herself to keep inhaling and exhaling too.

FORTY-ONE

Homer's ringtone was the sound of a rooster crowing. Zachary loved it. Morgan always covered her face in embarrassment. The caller ID simply said OUT OF AREA.

"Hello?"

"Homer, this here is Kirk Lamont. You near a fax machine, pard?"

"I'm in my car. What's up?"

"Somethin' from the twilight zone, my friend. I did the audio separation of the MP3 files ya'll sent. I'd read the transcript to you, but it'd take too long. There are tens of thousands of sentences in there; hundreds of thousands of words. None of it makes two bits of sense to me, but I guarantee it's not being used for humanitarian purposes. You got access to Wi-Fi anywhere close?"

"There's a Laundromat at the next corner. They're Wi-Fi enabled."

"I'll start the transmission now; it may take a while to load. I'd ask what it all means, but I don't really wanna know. See, I'm a pretty smart guy, Homer. Now I know I sound like I come from a family where you'd have to line three of us up to get a full set of teeth, but I got me a Ph.D. that says I got more'n cobwebs in my attic. I'll tell you flat out I'm no mind reader, and I don't cotton to those who think they are. When it comes to pickin' through someone's brainpan and cookin' up the findings—well, that's just never sat right with me. No offense to psychiatrists and all. I'm just quotin' the gospel of Lamont, second chapter, third verse. All I'm sayin' is that, when I'm done with this, I'm done with it—ya know what I mean?"

"Yeah, I know. Hey, thanks for your help, Kirk. Go ahead and scramble and erase everything once it's sent. I don't want your fingerprints on this either."

"Already done that, pard. Godspeed to ya."

"Yeah. You too, Kirk."

Homer entered the Laundromat with his laptop in hand and immediately located a quiet, vacant corner in the complex. With sudden recognition, he realized it was the same place he had met Morgan. A rush of nostalgia temporarily dampened the anxiety that had churned a witch's brew in his stomach.

Situating himself in the corner, he plugged in and logged on. Accessing his e-mail, he found the nondescript file. Wisely, Kirk Lamont had used a generic e-mail server and a single-use access name. The header read: CONGRATULATIONS FROM TEXAS! There was an attached file. 163MB. Homer opened the file and began to read:

Disc 1: Week Three: Toad Stomp Subliminals
Children. Children that I love. My love. Children that I love. Come children. Come. Pleasure awaits. Pure pleasure awaits. Happiness. Children that I love. Pure pleasure. It awaits. Happy. Happy. A reward. Your reward. The ultimate reward. For the children who obey. For the children that I love. Do it. Obey and it will come. Pure pleasure. The ultimate reward . . .

Homer read the transcript for almost half an hour. The phrases repeated themselves but not in any recognizable pattern. Every so often a new angle was inserted, like a set of instructions, a time stamp, or a specific location. He was shocked at the volume of words crammed into the song. It was just as Zachary had said: too many words, too fast.

At four o'clock. Friday the twenty-third of October. Four o'clock. You must go. Your reward awaits. You must go. Friday the twenty-third. Four o'clock. My children whom

I love. My children will receive their ultimate reward. Happiness. Given freely. You must go to receive. The statue Phra Apaimanee. *Four o'clock. You must go. Your reward will be great. Your reward will be full. Pure happiness. Others will come. Be as one. Breathe as one. Do it. Pure ecstasy. Your ultimate reward. The thrill of pure love. The surge. The power. Remove your winter wear. Remove your shoes. Sit. Do it. Pure love awaits at the statue of* Phra Apaimanee . . .

Scrolling to the last paragraph in week three, he read,

Your desires are close. So very close. You can feel them, taste them. You want your reward so bad. It almost hurts. It will come. If you obey, you will receive. Sitting without a coat. The cold is your friend. Pain is your ally. You await the surge. Your reward. Do this and you will be blessed. At five o'clock, when the carillon chimes, you must turn to the person next to you and punch them in the face. Punch hard and you will be rewarded. Draw blood and you will be sated, awash in pure joy. Your ultimate reward. After that, you will come to and remember only the feeling of happiness. You will not recall these instructions, only the satisfaction of obedience.

Do this, and you will be ready to receive subsequent instructions. Instructions for the reward beyond ultimate, beyond imagination, beyond your wildest dreams. In one week, your happiness and your fantasies will all be fulfilled. It will be so complete you will never want again. Do it. The final test; the final reward awaits. Do it!

What final test? Homer opened the fourth week file and began reading. It was more of the same, if not more intensified, more mesmerizing, more seductive. Again scrolling to the last page, Homer's eyes widened as the words seemed to reach from the screen and pierce his chest with claws of cold steel. He sucked in air that felt as thick as oil. Chills crept down his spine as fluidly as a spider crawls across the threads of its own web.

Homer closed his laptop and ran to his car. Dialing Morgan's cell phone, he prayed she was not too busy to answer. The phone rang twenty times with no response. He had to get home. He had to tell Morgan. Friday, the usual day for the Aggie Trance, was only two days away. Anyone susceptible to the trance was in grave danger. The last lines in the final transcript read,

> *Be not afraid. You are loved; your desires are good. They will all be met with such power, such strength, such ecstasy that you will never want again. They will be met on Friday, October thirtieth. At four o'clock. Come to* Meet the Challenge: *The statue of the bull, west of the Spectrum.* Meet the Challenge. *Do it. Four o'clock. Do it. And bring a gun. If you can't get a gun, bring a knife. A big knife.*
>
> *At five o'clock, October thirtieth, those with guns will shoot those without; those with knives will fatally stab your neighbor. Anyone left alive will kill themselves. Kill. Kill, for the good of my children. It is for your glory, your promised reward. Kill, kill, kill.*
>
> *At five o'clock. Your destiny will be fulfilled. Your ultimate reward; the ultimate surge. Five o'clock. Kill, kill, kill.*

FORTY-TWO

Dr. Ethan Greene couldn't believe how much his hands trembled as he dialed the long-distance number. He knew this could mean the end of his job at Scandia Labs. He knew all his ideas, breakthroughs, and years of research would be lost forever due to contractual clauses with Gunter Bjorkman's company. At first he didn't believe Stevie's research would bear fruit. It was simply too fantastical. But the more he thought about it, the more he became convinced that he needed to intervene, even if the experiment did fall flat. Ethan was a man of principle, particularly when it came to human lives. The cancer that had taken his wife had made him that way.

Glancing at his watch, he wondered if anyone would be at the university. It was almost ten o'clock at night.

"Social Science Building. Professor Winegar office."

"Yes, hello. I know it's late, but is the professor in?"

"No, she went home hours ago. I'm her TA, Lanh Tran. Can I take message?"

"I'm Dr. Greene with Scandia Labs in Henderson, Nevada. I called the main office earlier today about a concern. When I gave them a few specifics, they said to contact Professor Winegar. I really need to speak with her as soon as possible."

"Oh, is this about Aggie Trance?" Lanh asked, becoming very animated.

"Yes, I believe so, although I'm not sure," the doctor said cautiously. "You're calling it a trance?"

"Strangest thing you ever saw, Dr. Greene," Lanh said, as if telling a ghost story. "Creep me out just thinking 'bout it. Kid takes a sip of soda and *snap!* they go into trance for an hour. Professor calls it a 'mass fugue.' Some real freaky juju, you know? Stuff my gramma say use to happen in the old country."

"Got it. Which soda?"

"Can't tell you, doc. Professor is still trying to figure it out. She's keeping real tight lid on specifics."

"I'm glad to hear that. But I have some information she'd be interested in; something that may very well put together a lot of the puzzle pieces she probably hasn't located yet," Ethan said, trying to sound as somber as possible.

"Serious?"

"As a heart attack, son. This may be lifesaving, okay?"

"Sure, doc. What your number?"

Ethan was afraid the young man didn't fully believe him. If the message did not get to Morgan Winegar, it *could* mean someone's life. "This is extremely important, Tran. Can you be sure she gets this?"

"Trust me, doc, I'm top dog when it come to this stuff."

The confirmation didn't instill much confidence in Ethan. Then another thought came to mind: "Does Professor Winegar have a dedicated fax line?"

"Yes. You want to fax her info?"

Ethan paused. He considered the possibility that this young man was in league with Steven Pendleton's agent. The information he'd gathered did not mention anyone other than Gypsy/Jacqueline. But, as he had worried earlier, there was no way for one agent to cover every contingency in an open field trial, regardless of the controls they thought they had in place. Still, he really had no choice; he had to trust the young man.

"Okay. Why don't you give me your fax number, and I'll write my return number on it for Professor Winegar. Please be sure she gets this as soon as possible. If she could call me first thing in the morning, I'd appreciate it."

"Sure, no problem, Dr. Greene. Thanks for calling."

Ethan hung up the phone and stared at the paperwork in front of him. The information could mean not only the ruin of his career at Scandia but everyone else's too. It could also mean indictments, substantial fines, jail time, and the like.

As an afterthought, he wondered if Pendleton had gone to the extreme of having his lab phone tapped. Because of the new camera in his lab, Ethan knew his every move was monitored. Perhaps . . . perhaps it would be better to leave Scandia anyway . . . before it was too late.

FORTY-THREE

Sitting alone at home, Homer folded his arms across his soured belly and rocked back and forth on a kitchen stool. Other than the quiet hum of the refrigerator, the house remained morbidly silent. He stared blankly at the printouts he'd run off on their inkjet. He'd only run a dozen pages from each week. Had he printed the entire file, it would have exceeded one thousand pages. Although clearly legible, the sampling of words bled together in a miasma of pure evil.

Bring a gun . . . bring a knife . . . Kill, kill, kill.

His cell phone sat on the counter next to the paperwork. Every time he looked at it, a flash of anxious fear shot through his nerves, as if the slim black phone were a scorpion with its stinger poised to strike. Each time he reached for it the thing seemed to hiss and click a sharp, metallic warning, causing Homer to recoil.

He asked himself again and again why Morgan would not pick up. The answer was one he didn't want to hear, the one foremost in his mind. They—whoever *they* were—had gotten to Morgan. The very idea caused his stomach to cramp even further.

The note he had left Morgan was now a barely recognizable lump of litter. He had no idea what to make of it, but his intuition warned of devastation. At first he'd worried that they might have kidnapped her. But then they would have either left a ransom note, or the note he'd written would be exactly where he'd left it. Instead, his note had been read, mutilated, then left on the counter as a sign. His mind replayed the encounter with the mystery woman in Duce's office. More poignantly, he remembered the look of shock on Mike's face when he'd seen Jacqueline pawing him. And then the kiss. Why hadn't he explained to Mike what had just transpired? Why had he run away like he was guilty of something? What if Mike—or even worse, Jacqueline—had gotten to Morgan before he'd had a chance to explain?

Homer closed his eyes and shook his head in self-condemnation.

No matter how many times or how many ways he tried to convince himself that keeping the truth, the whole truth, from Morgan was the prudent thing to do, deep down he knew that the bedrock of their relationship was a foundation of mutual trust. Any crack in that foundation, any flaw in that trust, and their entire relationship would collapse into a pile of jagged regrets.

Homer had kept his secret locked away for too long now. The door it hid behind bulged and creaked, as if barely restraining a viscous monster bent on escape. Homer did not want to open that door, didn't want to even think about that door. He had left deceit, swindle, and malicious ruin behind in another life, and he was loath to visit that life again, in memory or reality.

And yet, in reality, he was still living a life of deception. Only this time he was deceiving someone he deeply loved. He had never lied to her, but he hadn't told the whole truth either. The hypocrisy of his life often caused Homer to boil in self-revulsion, self-detestation.

A low roar built in Homer's throat until it erupted in a violent scream. It wasn't right. Morgan had to know. He had to trust that she would understand. And he had to be prepared to accept the consequences if she didn't.

Offering a silent prayer, Homer picked up the cell phone and dialed again. This time, Morgan picked it up on the first ring.

"Homer, where are you?"

"I'm at home. Listen, we need to talk. I found out some things we need to discuss right away."

"So have I," Morgan said as if growling.

A serrated dagger pierced his heart. Homer felt smaller than he had in his entire life. He pushed on, knowing he had to. Sheepishly, he said, "I'm afraid I may have opened Pandora's box."

"I thought her name was Jacqueline."

The dagger twisted. "That's what I was afraid of. Listen, you've got to believe me. I don't know who she is; I've never seen her before or since; and I think she might be associated with whoever's behind the trances."

There was a gut-wrenching pause on the line.

He muscled on. "Do you have Zachary?"

"Of course."

"Thank goodness for that," Homer said with an unintentional nervous twinge in his voice.

"Why?"

Instead of answering, Homer said, "The last trance involved violence, right?"

He could clearly hear Morgan's intake of breath. She must have guessed what he would ask next. "You think someone's planning a mass attack?"

"I don't know, but I don't want to chance it. I got the transcripts from those songs. We were right; they're loaded with subliminals."

"Oh, my." Tremulous breathing filled a brief pause. "Homer. What are we going to do?"

"Go forward with faith, hon. We can't stop now—not with people's lives at stake."

Another long pause caused Homer's grip to tighten around his phone.

"Are—are you as scared as I am?"

"I am, Morgan. I think these trances go a lot deeper than either of us guessed. I got the chemical results from Mike, too, and frankly they scare me to death. There's an extremely addictive substance in that drink. I think someone big is behind all this. Someone really big."

"Someone who would take whatever measures necessary to stop us from looking into this?" Morgan asked.

"I'm afraid so. In fact, I think the next Aggie Trance will involve random—"

"Killing," Morgan finished for him.

Homer swallowed hard. "Yeah. How did you know?"

"That song, 'Toad Stomp,' played just a minute ago. Zach said the words were mean. He said they kept repeating 'kill, kill, kill.'" Her tone of voice had become less embittered, more concerned.

"Friday, at the bronze steer—the *Meet the Challenge* statue across the street from Romney Stadium."

"In front of the Spectrum."

"They'll meet at four, just like all the others have. Only this time, at five o'clock, they'll kill each other."

Morgan paused yet again. Homer could tell she was overwhelmed by thoughts of the trance, their personal safety, and trusting him, and that she was not fairing well in the battle. "Homer?"

"Yes?"

"How come you knew just what to look for? I mean, you seem to be familiar with this sort of . . . deception."

"Unfortunately, yes, I am."

"That's what she told me—that Jacqueline woman. She also said you two had an affair. Homer I need to know the truth. Maybe not the whole truth right now, but eventually I will. Right now I just need to know you have never been with that woman."

Homer could hear the desperation in her voice. It was as if she were sinking into a vast quagmire, grasping at anything that would keep her afloat, if only a few seconds longer. Choked with emotion, Homer said, "Morgan Winegar. You are my entire world. There has never been and never will be anyone else but you."

A barely restrained cry pulsed through the phone. Homer could hear his wife trying to stifle one snuffle after another. "Oh, Homer," she cried, desperately seeking affirmation, "I did some Web searches, just like she said to, and she was right. You're not who you say you are."

"That's true, too. But it doesn't change how I feel about you. You've got to believe that."

"I do. I mean . . . I *want* to. I am just so confused right now. It's like the sky is falling and I don't know how to get out from under it."

"I'll show you how. We'll do it together. But not over the phone. How soon before you get home?"

Another sob delayed her answer. "Not long."

"I love you, Morgan Winegar. That is no lie. I love you."

"I . . . I love you too, Homer." There was a final lengthy pause as she tried to build up enough breath—and possibly courage—to ask the next question. "But . . . is *Winegar* really my last name?"

FORTY-FOUR

Thursday, October 29

It was just past midnight when Morgan turned onto their street. The entire neighborhood was gripped in early morning stillness, deathly quiet. Homer was waiting in the garage as she pulled in. Zachary was in his car seat, fast asleep.

Homer moved to the driver's door as Morgan put the car in park and shut it off. He opened her door and whispered, "Morgan, I am so sorry about all of this. There are a few skeletons in my past, but none of them changes how I feel about you and Zach. You've got to believe that."

Morgan considered him briefly before her eyes misted over. She stepped out of the car and fell into his arms. Nothing felt so good as to have her body pressed tightly against his, to feel the beat of his heart against hers and the warmth of his breath against her cheek. She had felt that way from the beginning. Homer was steady, unwavering, as firm a foundation as the stones at the base of the Logan Temple. That's what Morgan loved about him. She knew a disorienting fog could hide a shoal of rocks. A blinding snow storm could mask a sharp turn in the road. A blistering heat wave could cause an immoveable horizon to shimmer and dance. But Homer was constant. He was a safe harbor in any weather, and considering the storm that was brewing, that's exactly what she needed.

"I'm sorry for doubting you. But I am so confused right now and so terribly frightened."

Homer placed a lingering kiss atop her head. "Come on. Let's get

Zach into bed, and then I'll show you what I've found. After that, I'll answer any questions you have."

She nodded against his chest, not wanting to move from the security of his arms.

* * *

Homer watched in silence as Morgan scanned the transcripts from Kirk Lamont and skimmed the chromatography printouts from Michael Duce's lab. She kept shaking her head as if in denial. But the facts were there in black-and-white, and no amount of repudiation could make them vanish.

"Why, Homer? Why would anyone want to do such a thing?" Morgan said in a dry, raspy voice.

"I don't know, hon. My guess is they wanted a widely diverse field test, yet one that was also fairly well contained."

"But to what end? What does any of this show—that this new chemical is extremely addictive?"

"No. I think it goes much deeper than that."

"You mean with the subliminal commands in that stupid song?"

"Exactly. It looks to me like a pretty clear attempt at total mind control, but I've never seen any real proof that subliminal messaging even works."

Morgan thought hard for a moment before her eyebrows raised. "Hang on. I remember reading about some experiments done back in the sixties at a movie theater in New Jersey. A guy named . . . Vikar? Vickas? No, Vicary, I think. He used a machine called a tachistoscope to flash a message very quickly—something like twelve times a second—on the screen during the movie. It was too fast to register consciously, but the subconscious took it in. The message was, 'Hungry? Eat popcorn.' And sure enough, popcorn sales rose by 60 percent. But . . ." her words trailed off into silence.

"But what?"

"Well, that was just popcorn. How can a subliminal message make people do things that would normally seem crazy, even abhorrent to them?"

"From what Mike told me, the subliminal command triggers a chemical response primed by the energy drink. The resulting addictive rush of dopamine leaves the brain wanting more and more. And through the repetitive promises in the subliminals, the brain's response is to do everything necessary to receive that rush again and again—even if it means doing something that makes no sense."

Morgan frowned at her husband, not in anger but in mystification. "That's makes sense. But—no offense—how do *you* know? I mean, I know you're a top-notch research analyst, but . . . I guess what I still need to know is where you *really* learned to analyze. I need to know . . . to know who you are, Homer Winegar."

Homer took her hand in his and gently squeezed. He began by looking into her eyes, then had to look away. His gaze followed his right thumb as it tenderly stroked the back of her left hand. "What I'm about to tell you is the complete truth. Do you believe me?"

"I do," Morgan said without reservation.

"That was a life long ago, in a different part of the country. It's not a life I'm proud of. And yet, strangely, if it weren't for that life, I never would have ended up in Logan, Utah, and I never would have found you and Zachary or the Church. I thank God every day for that. I have never done anything to deserve such a gift, such a blessing, but it came my way regardless. Our family is my life. *You* are my life. You are not just a smoke screen I'm hiding behind. The life I had before no longer exists for me. I left that life through a government protection program. Everything I owned, everything I knew, everything that made me, me, vanished overnight. For the longest time I felt so defenseless, so . . . lost. I was like a child with all the responsibilities of an adult, coupled with a paranoid need to constantly look over my shoulder.

"And then I met you. The more we got to know each other, the more I learned how much you had endured. And yet, through your adversity, you became a new person, a wonderful, amazing person. That was when I realized I could let go of my past and start fresh. You taught me that. I decided right then that I would no longer be a masquerade of the man I was; instead, I'd do all I could to become a new person, starting life with a clean slate and no baggage. I know it sounds cliché, but after we got to know each other and you introduced me to the Church, well, I was truly 'born again.'"

Homer looked up with a pleading in his eyes that was as intense as it was pitiable. "I see now that I still have that baggage and always will until I come clean with you. But I am afraid, Morgan. I'm afraid someone may still be after me. If you knew all the details, you'd be in as much danger as I am. Zachary too." He paused a second time, swallowing hard. "I'm also afraid that in knowing my past, you'll decide I am not the right man for you and Zach and—"

He stopped abruptly as a constricting sob lodged in his throat. Morgan opened her mouth, but Homer held up his hand, indicating he was not done. "Know this, Morgan. I would *never* do anything to destroy what we have. I love you. I love Zachary. And as far as I am concerned, your last name *is* Winegar, same as mine. The other man, the other name no longer exists. Not even on paper. Not even in my mind. Hopefully, not even in yours."

Morgan didn't respond right away as she stared at her husband. She looked deeply into his eyes, as if trying to read what went on behind them. "Okay," she whispered, yet not as confidently as Homer had wished. "But I need some time to think about all this."

Wiping his eyes on his sleeve, Homer said, "Fair enough." It hurt to accept that partial answer from his wife, but he recognized the fragility of their situation and knew he couldn't push for a definitive answer.

Homer cleared his throat and said, "For now, I think we need to focus on the problem at hand: the premeditated mass murder and suicide at Utah State this Friday. We know *when* it's going to happen and *where* it's going to happen, but who's going to believe us enough to help us stop it? We don't have enough corroborating evidence."

"What about all this?" she asked, holding up the reports.

"From an analytical standpoint, those are two separate documents with no link between them. The subliminal commands are straightforward and incriminating, but we're only guessing the chemical in the Tribe makes people act on them."

Morgan broke eye contact and stared at the papers in her hands. "I see. Still, we can't just sit and wait for it to happen."

"Agreed."

"Okay then. Tomorrow morning I'll tell the dean and contact the campus authorities and tell them what we know."

"I'll call the Logan police department and try not to sound totally off my nut explaining it to them. And we'll get as many of your students as possible to help us prepare for the event."

"Prepare how? Who's going to want to get involved if there's a risk of being shot or stabbed?"

Morgan had a point. Homer was at a loss for an answer. The fatigue in her voice tugged at his heartstrings.

Homer reached over and took the stack of papers from her hands. "Honey, you try and get some sleep. I'll have this figured out by morning." He stood and helped her up from her chair.

"I don't think I can fall asleep right now," she said. "And how're you planning on staying awake all night?"

"I've got a can of Tribe in the fridge."

Morgan slugged his shoulder. "That's not funny."

"No," he agreed, putting an arm around her, "that was stupid. But if I don't get a little silly right now, I just might go insane."

Morgan hugged his waist. Homer hugged her back and was pleasantly surprised that she held on longer than he expected. But he questioned what that meant. Was it a showing of forgiveness, or a farewell embrace?

FORTY-FIVE

Homer called Wasatch BioChemical from Morgan's office early the following morning. He told Mike he wouldn't be coming in that day or the next.

"I figured you wouldn't," Mike said. "You going to be okay?"

"I'm not sure. This may all lead to something bigger than I can handle."

"Any idea who's behind it?"

"None. But I think I know who might be connected in a way."

"The blond?"

"Yeah."

"Homer . . ." The scientist paused a moment. "If it comes down to you needing to disappear . . ."

"Enough said, my friend. Hopefully it won't come to that."

Homer hung up and turned to his wife. She had just finished talking with the dean. "What did he say?"

"He doesn't want to create a panic. But he also doesn't want a Virginia Tech incident on his hands. He says he'll help any way we need, but he insists we inform the authorities. This isn't something for the campus police alone."

"Agreed. My first concern is for the students affected by the drug. We know the subliminal command has already been implanted. We can't do anything about that. Even if we tell them to stay away, subconsciously, they'll find some way to come. My other concern is finding the person recording the event."

"You mean someone from the university?"

"No, I mean whoever is behind all this. They'll want to know if their commands are actually obeyed. Something like face-punching is one thing, but murder—especially murder committed by young LDS college students—is going to push the envelope of mind control. The dilemma is, if we have too many authorities on the scene, whoever is observing the experiment will disappear. And they may be our only link to the source of this insanity. We still don't know who made the drug, how they got it into the Tribe drink, how extensive the distribution was, or what they intend to do next. For all we know, there may very well be another set of gatherings scheduled."

Morgan rubbed her temples as if willing a headache not to form. "But if we don't intervene, someone—perhaps a lot of people—will be killed."

"I know, hon." Homer picked up the phone and dialed another number. "I'll call the radio station and try to get them to stop playing that song, too."

It was then that Lanh Tran staggered into the office mumbling, "I really hate mornings." He had an overstuffed backpack weighing down one shoulder and a stack of files in the crook of the opposite arm. Somehow, he had also managed to get a bagel in one hand and a trashcan-sized fountain drink in the other. "Did you get faxes?"

Morgan frowned. "What faxes?"

"From the doctor in Nevada. I left them in the office box."

"I haven't checked it yet," Morgan said, returning to her review of the transcripts from Kirk Lamont.

Holding the bagel in his teeth, Lanh performed a Houdini-like escape from his school-inflicted burdens. Removing the bagel, he said, "I didn't look them over, but it sounded important."

"So is this," Morgan grumbled without looking up.

"Yeah. Okay, thanks," Homer said into the phone just before hanging up. "That was the Logan police. They're sending a Detective Hopkins up here."

"What's he gonna do?" Lanh said through a mouthful of bagel.

"Decide if there's enough information to warrant a larger response to our concerns. We've got some pieces to the puzzle, but nothing that really ties them all together."

Lanh forcefully swallowed an underchewed lump of his breakfast. "That's what the Nevada doc said. He claim he got the puzzle pieces we are missing."

Morgan's eyes snapped up. "He knows about the fugues?"

"Yeah. He got 'lifesaving information' he say," Lanh commented casually, as if sharing an anecdotal quip.

Morgan leapt from her chair and bolted from the office.

"When did he call?" Homer asked.

"Last night. It was late. Maybe ten or so?" the TA guessed with a drinking straw poised in still-life at his lips.

Morgan returned with a stack of papers in hand. "You're not going to believe this," she said hoarsely.

When neither man responded with more than a stare, she said, "The chemical comes from Scandia Labs in Henderson, Nevada. It's a black-box test. It says right here it *is* a type of apomorphine, a chemical called S-Pentanoic-Adenosyl Apomorphine. Just like Mike said, it has astronomical dopamine effects."

Homer barely constrained the epithet of shock threatening to burst from his lips.

"Homer, this confirms everything we've discovered so far."

He stood slowly. "It also validates the reality of tomorrow's fugue. It's going to happen, Morgan, and if we don't do something, a lot of people will die."

"This guy's number is listed here."

"Oh, yeah," Lanh chimed in. "He want you to call as soon as you get in."

Morgan went to the phone and dialed.

Lanh polished off his bagel and washed it down with soda. "So, Mr. W., did a total babe named Jacqueline get with you?" he asked Homer.

Homer drew a sharp breath. "You know her?"

"Not as well as I like to," he said with raised eyebrows and a boyish smirk. "She follow me home last week and ask a bunch of question about Aggie Trance. She helped with the survey at last trance."

"Really?"

"Yeah. She volunteer. She also ask a lot of questions about you and the professor."

"Seriously? What did you tell her?"

"Nothing really. Maybe where you work, your name. That's about all. She want to know where you live, but I didn't tell her. It in phonebook anyway, right?"

"Yes. What'd she look like?" Homer asked, believing he already knew the answer.

A dreamy look filled the TA's eyes. "Kind of girl Vietnamese young man not supposed to involve with. Kind of girl my mother frown at and my father give me high-five for. Blond, blue-eye, and all extras."

Homer looked across the desk at Morgan. She had finished her phone call and was listening to the two men talk.

"I know who she is," Homer said with a bitter edge.

"So do I," Morgan added.

"You do?" Lanh asked, clearly surprised. "So you meet her? That's way cool. Maybe you can hook me up? I not see her again since we last talked."

"Sorry, Lanh," Homer said. "This time I agree with your mother. That girl is bad news for any man, not just Vietnamese."

The TA looked mystified and crestfallen. "But—but she unbelievable beautiful."

"So is a Venus flytrap to a fly."

"Oh."

"Exactly," Homer said. To Morgan he asked, "Did you get a hold of the guy from Nevada?"

"No. A lab tech said he hadn't come in yet. He also said that wasn't normal. He said Dr. Greene is usually the first in the building and the last to leave."

Homer nodded. "Okay. Keep trying. Lanh, can you give me any other info on this Jacqueline girl?"

"I wish. Sorry, Mr. W. I don't know her address or phone number or even her last name."

"Dang. Okay then, can you make me a copy of those faxes? I want to look them over in some detail before Detective Hopkins gets here."

"Sure thing," the TA said.

FORTY-SIX

Homer and Morgan took several turns reading each page of Ethan Greene's faxes. Much of it was disjointed and too technical for their expertise, but they understood enough, and none of it was good news.

"Ah-ha. There's a notation here that talks about a backdoor override to the subliminal programming," Homer said. "That'll help."

Lanh asked, "How?"

"If we can find the override and give it to as many affected people as possible, we may be able to stop the preloaded command," he explained.

"But there's close to a million words here," Morgan said. "What if it's a code within a code? We may never find it."

"Even if we do, can we get to everyone in time?" Lanh asked.

"Those we can't contact, we'll try to intercept at the gathering."

"That going to be some tricky timing," the TA predicted.

"Yes, it is," Morgan agreed, "particularly since we don't know the backdoor code." Morgan paused as she reached for the stack of transcripts from Kirk Lamont. "Lahn, I want you to go through these subliminals word for word to see if you can decipher the override."

"All of this?" he moaned, reluctantly accepting the intimidating file.

"You do this and I'll sign off on your master's thesis, sight unseen."

In way of encouragement, Homer said, "I'm sure it's a sequence of words or phrases. On the few pages I've read, the author—a Dr.

Steven Pendleton—has listed three consonants several times, but they don't mean anything to me. There's an F, a D, and an R, but there's no 'stop command' I can find afterwards."

"Start digging," Morgan told her TA. "You've got just over twenty-four hours."

* * *

It was near two o'clock before Detective Les Hopkins showed up. He was a lot younger than Homer had expected. The timbre of his voice over the phone had led Homer to believe the man was in his fifties. In reality the detective looked to be no more than twenty-five to thirty.

Introductions were made. The detective shook hands with everyone in the room and moved to a proffered chair. "So what makes you think there's going to be a shooting?"

Homer said, "Before we show you what we have, I'd like to ask how much you know about subliminal messaging and biochemistry?"

Hopkins looked from Homer to Morgan and back again with a confused expression. "I guess about as much as you know about law enforcement and crime scene investigation." The man's words were flat but with a hint of antagonism.

Homer smiled awkwardly. "Sorry. I didn't mean it like that, detective. What I meant was in order to explain why we feel a crisis is imminent we need to get into quite a bit of science. I didn't mean to imply that you don't have the ability to understand it; I was just wondering how deep we'll need to explain everything."

Hopkins took out a small notepad and clicked open a pen. At first, he didn't say anything as he stared back at Homer. Then he pursed his lips and scribbled some notes. "Ready when you are."

Morgan gave a brief synopsis of events over the past four weeks and her reaction to them. She produced her notes on each gathering and highlighted the level of preprogrammed response necessary in each event. She introduced the Tribe Dingo's Dance factor and then turned it over to Homer.

"I work as an analyst at Wasatch BioChemical with some very smart guys. One of them broke down the chemicals in a sample of the contaminated energy drink. We were both shocked at what he found."

Homer briefly explained the chemistry of addictions and the potential harm the new chemical could cause. During this time, the detective would write one or two words, seemingly without removing his eyes from the speaker. Homer was quite sure he'd have to repeat it all a second time due to the man's lack of focus. Then, quite unexpectedly, the officer asked, "How's the program inputted?"

"There's a song being played on a local station. I checked it out, and they told me they had a special contract with a recording company to give the song airtime for market analysis. The thing is that the song is laced to the teeth with subliminal messages, programming whoever hears it to do exactly as the music instructs."

Detective Hopkins scribbled about three or four words, then hesitated. His mouth was set in a firm line across his face, neither frowning nor smiling.

Homer continued. "The average person can't hear the subliminals. In fact, I'd say that less than one one-hundredth of a percent of any population could tell something was out of place—hence the designation, *subliminal*. We discovered it when my son heard the hidden words. He's autistic, you see, and has a gift with music. Anyway, I sent the recordings off to a specialist in audio effects, and he was able to isolate and transcribe the messages. Here's a copy of them," Homer said, handing the officer the thick stack of printed pages.

Homer and Morgan waited for a response, but none came. The man scanned the pages for a moment, clicked his pen and jotted a word or two, scratched his head, then glanced up, as if waiting for more.

"We suspected that the chemical and the subliminal messages were connected, but we didn't have anything to tie them together until this came," Morgan explained, handing the man Ethan's disclosure. "Dr. Greene is a scientist at the company where the chemical—or drug, as he calls it—was made. He has become disenchanted with the company but doesn't want to leave them until this illegal testing gets cleared up."

Hopkins shuffled through the stack of papers now in his hands, often clicking his pen and writing something in his notepad, then turning back to the beginning of the stack and starting all over. Twenty minutes passed before he looked up again.

"Excellent work, Winegars. If this is all legit, then you do have a situation on your hands."

"So what should we do next?" Morgan asked.

"Nothing. I can take it from here. I'll have SWAT and ambulances on the scene first thing in morning. Do you have any clue what this 'backdoor code' is?"

"No," Homer said, wishing he had a different answer. "There were three letters referencing the code, but that's all. We have no idea what they mean."

"Where are they?" Hopkins asked, flipping through the pages.

Morgan rounded her desk and helped the lawman find the notation.

"Ah," was all he said.

"One more thing," Homer said. "It's obvious someone came here to set everything up. We think there may still be one cohort, maybe more, in the area observing the outcome."

"*Gypsy*, it says here," Detective Hopkins confirmed. "Any idea who she is?"

"Sort of," Homer said with a tilt of his head. "I've actually met her. She goes by Jacqueline. I don't know if that's her real name, and unfortunately, we don't know where to find her."

"You think she'll be at *Meet the Challenge* tomorrow evening?" Hopkins asked.

"I'd bet on it," Homer affirmed.

"That puts a halt on the SWAT and ambulances. She'll know we're on to her and she'll bolt."

Homer tapped his wristwatch. "You can see our concern, detective. Something's got to be done soon. Time's slipping by awfully quick."

Detective Hopkins stood and handed the stack of papers to Morgan. "Professor Winegar. I want you to call everyone on your list who has experienced a . . . what did you call it?"

"A fugue."

"Yeah, that. Call them and tell them not to go anywhere near the *Meet the Challenge* statue at four."

"I don't believe that'll do any good," Morgan said. "When a person has been subliminally programmed, and that programming is augmented with drugs, then nothing said to them during consciousness will work."

Hopkins nodded. "Maybe. Maybe not. Correct me if I'm wrong, but even when someone is under hypnosis, they are aware of their surroundings and can only be hypnotized if they let themselves?"

"Yes, but we're talking about drug-induced subconscious control, detective. I don't believe you can override such a system," Morgan said.

"Try it anyway. You never know. Maybe one or two of the kids didn't hear the entire message or only had a sip of Tribe. It's worth a try, even if it saves only one student."

"I'll give you a hand," Homer said to his wife.

"No, I need you to come with me," Hopkins said. "You said you've seen this woman, 'Gypsy'?"

"Yes."

"Up close?"

Homer noticed Morgan's knuckles blanch as her hands formed fists.

"Only once. But that was enough."

"Come out to my car. I've got a computer link to HQ. You can look at some file photos while I arrange emergency services. You can also search for anything we've got on this Dr. Pendleton. It's a shot in the dark, but you never know."

"Okay, but I don't think either of them is from around here," Homer argued.

"No sweat. We can download files from all over the country, Vegas included, and even from INTERPOL, in case they've had any foreign altercations. I've got a few other ideas we can discuss while you're looking. I'll search the Web for different combinations of these three letters to see what comes up. With any luck, we may just be able to prevent this thing from reaching completion."

FORTY-SEVEN

Friday, October 30

Jacqueline leaned against the cement wall lining the incline to the Dee Glen Smith Spectrum, USU's immense basketball arena. From this position she had an elevated view of the parking area adjacent to the bronze image of the university's mascot: the very muscular, alarmingly fearsome bull. The sculpture was entitled *Meet the Challenge.* Smiling, Jacqueline felt she already had. This was the last test. After reporting the results, she could head back to Vegas, pack her things, then skip off to Belize to work on her tan and try to figure out how best to invest and capitalize on close to three million dollars.

The past week had been unseasonably cool, the locals all said, even for Cache Valley. Being used to Las Vegas weather, Jacqueline found it downright frigid. Accordingly, she wore a heavy jacket over a thick cashmere sweater.

Jacqueline drew the jacket lapels across her neck as a brisk breeze nipped at her from the north. Her shimmering blond hair danced on the chilled currents of air. In spite of the cold, she never wore a hat. She didn't look good in them.

To the west, blue-black clouds perched atop the Wellsvilles like giant vultures poised to swoop down on a valley full of fresh death. Over the USU campus, a few wispy, striated clouds created a silky meshwork across the brassy sky.

Glancing at her watch, Jacqueline noted the time as two minutes to four. Even with school in session, the parking lot was only about half full. A small group of students lingered around the bull. Others were casually walking toward the statue.

Plugged into one ear, a miniature sports radio was tuned to the local pop station. "Toad Stomp" had just finished airing, as per the contract. A three-second jingle now played in her ear, followed by the weather forecast for Cache Valley: increasing clouds, rain turning to snow, highs only in the lower thirties. Following that depressing news, a new tune from Sarah McLachlan began.

Precisely at four o'clock, the USU carillon chimed its Westminster tune followed by four bongs. Jacqueline saw a group of young men walking along the sidewalk paralleling Romney Stadium suddenly change course and cross the street toward the bronze cast of the university's mascot. Another young man was coming down the incline toward her. A couple of girls walking up the incline abruptly turned around and headed toward the bull.

Jacqueline had a digital camcorder in hand. From her position halfway up the Spectrum hillside, she had a safe view of the imminent gathering and forthcoming hysteria. Most of the summer foliage on the hillside was now bare, leaving a relatively clear view of all avenues leading to the bovine statuary. Steven "Don Juan" Pendleton wanted an extra-inclusive report on the final event that night. He'd seemed more excited than usual about the results. Or was it nerves?

Whatever. She'd give him coverage worthy of an MSNBC senior field reporter. But not before Jacqueline made her own copy to sell to the reality media slimes who loved to profit from exploiting human suffering. She wasn't sure what the final subliminal command was, but she could guess. It was going to be shocking.

The crowd began to form quickly. Nearly all wore winter coats and hats.

Jacqueline had begun filming a few seconds before four o'clock to record the carillon in the background. Her hard drive held four hours of high-quality video. This event would only take an hour, with maybe a few minutes of very profitable after-event copy. There were a number of students she didn't recognize, but that wasn't unusual. She also noticed a number of older people, perhaps university staff or those who had inadvertently drunk some spiked Dingo's Dance and subsequently heard a broadcast of "Toad Stomp."

The wind began to pick up, shifting randomly, tousling her hair to one side or the other.

"Hello, Gypsy."

The male voice came from directly behind her. Jacqueline spun around, ready to strike. She gasped when she recognized the face.

"Stevie! What are you doing here?"

The Scandia scientist was dressed like everyone else on campus, allowing him to look like just another grad student. "I couldn't wait. I had to see this for myself."

"But . . ." Jacqueline wasn't sure what to say. "Isn't this a bit risky?"

"Why? If no one mistrusts you, why would I be any more suspect?"

Jacqueline thought about his reply. Although she couldn't argue with the simplicity of his logic, she still didn't like him being there. "When'd you get here?"

"About three hours ago. I took a private commuter to the Logan airport. I've been wandering the campus checking out the gathering points to better assess your reports."

"You found my reports lacking?" she asked, somewhat perturbed.

"No, they're satisfactory. I was just checking out the parameters of the field. It's difficult to grasp that from one simple account."

Simple?

"So, how's everything going here?"

"You heard the carillon. Just watch."

The crowd was already upwards of seventy people and growing. Because some individuals had gathered before the carillon chime, Jacqueline wondered if there had been a subliminal *anticipation* of the event that drew them to the appointed place before the chosen time. She was about to ask Stevie but decided against it. She wasn't in the mood for one of his ultra-technical explanations. He'd probably just discount it anyway, still assuming she was all body and no brains. *Well, let him think that.*

Ten minutes passed.

Twenty minutes and the crowd had more than doubled. The group formed an even quarter-circle in the corner of the parking lot by the bull. To a person, they stared at the sculpture, not moving, not talking, oblivious to the buffeting wind and encroaching storm.

The dark clouds had taken flight from their perch on the Wellsville Mountains and glided over the valley toward Utah State. The churning, boiling mass intensified as it neared the gathering, as if gaining nourishment from the wispy, lesser clouds in its path.

Thirty minutes.

"Does it usually take this long to assemble?" Stevie asked.

"Yes. Remember, not everyone is close to the gathering point when the carillon chimes. Some may not even be on campus when it rings, but eventually they all come."

"Just one more fascinating aspect of my chemical creation," Pendleton said as if equating SPAAM to Frankenstein's monster.

The gathering soon reached over two hundred in number. Jacqueline wondered how so many people could be affected when there were only 192 chemically laced cans of Tribe to begin with. Perhaps a few students had shared with classmates. Maybe one or two cans found their way into a frat party punch bowl along with who-knew-what-else thrown into that societal, alchemist's brew.

At forty-five minutes the crowd seemed to have reached its maximum volume. True to form, a second crowd coalesced around those in the trance. Cameras clicked and camera phones beeped, but few words were uttered. A dozen campus police officers showed up and began organizing a perimeter for crowd control. As ineffectual as it was, that was to be expected. It was well-known that Professor Winegar had issued specific instructions in the event of another Aggie Trance. Apparently she had asked that observers remain quiet. A ghostly hush blanketed the scene with only an occasional cough or the clicking of a camera lens to compete with the icy wind.

Having never stopped filming, Jacqueline used her zoom lens to capture close-ups of several of those entranced. She recognized many faces from previous gatherings, including Peter Stokes, her original contact. She blinked in surprise when she identified Lanh Tran in the crowd. *Poor kid,* she thought sincerely. He'd been a lot of fun, if somewhat naïve. For the most part, Lanh looked like everyone else in the gathering—except for his head. Seeing only his profile from her vantage point, she had no idea what his eyes were doing. If subliminally programmed, he'd be fixated on *Meet the Challenge,* becoming a statue himself. But Lanh's head slowly turned from side to side, as if clandestinely observing the crowd from its interior.

Jacqueline's grin grew into a smile. The kid was a true researcher after all, mixing with the crowd to gather the purest data. Without a doubt, he'd be the volunteer to don an alligator costume and swim among the man-eating reptiles to better examine their habits. Crazy kid.

A stiff gust of glacial air staggered Stevie against Jacqueline.

"Sorry," he said. "It's so awesome seeing this with you, Jacqueline. It's like a date to a 'Gladiators vs. Christians' spectacle."

She swore under her breath, repositioned herself, and continued filming, capturing both telephoto and wide shots of the trance. The viewfinder on her camcorder had an internal clock: 4:50 PM.

Ten more minutes and the excitement would begin. There were so many more people than expected. This *was* going to be a massacre.

FORTY-EIGHT

The mystical silence of the gathering was shattered by a blaring announcement issued through a set of loudspeakers attached to the roof of a large van in the parking lot.

"I think we consider too much the good luck of the early bird and not enough the bad luck of the early worm."

There was a crackle over the loudspeakers as the person on the microphone ended his statement. A number of people observing the gathering turned toward the van, questioning its purpose. Even Jacqueline couldn't figure out its intent, nor did she remember seeing it arrive. It must have been there from the beginning. No one in the trance moved an eyelash.

"What was that?" Stevie asked.

Jacqueline didn't answer. Why should she know anyway? The viewfinder of her camcorder registered 4:52 PM.

"It is common sense to take a method and try it. If it fails, admit it frankly and try another. But above all, try another."

Jacqueline didn't recognize the second statement either.

A low murmur came from the outer crowd.

"Uh-oh," Stevie muttered. "Someone's got three ambulances in the stadium parking lot across the street. Do you think they know?"

Jacqueline didn't answer. The emergency services must have come when she was concentrating on filming the event. She felt sure she would have noticed them otherwise.

4:53 PM.

"The test of our progress is not whether we add to the abundance of those who have much. It is whether we provide enough to those who have little."

Some people began to gravitate toward the van. Jacqueline turned her camera from the gathering to the van. It was a nondescript old-model panel van to which someone had jerry-rigged two massive speakers.

"There are many ways of going forward, but only one way of standing still."

4:55 PM.

Jacqueline knew this was an attempt to thwart the gathering. But how?

Suddenly Pendleton let fly a string of vulgarity. "They've found the backdoor!"

"When you get to the end of your rope, tie a knot and hang on."

The clock was still ticking.

4:56 PM.

"A reactionary is a somnambulist walking backwards."

Jacqueline abruptly realized what Pendleton was cursing about. The loudspeakers were blaring quotes from Franklin Delano Roosevelt. FDR.

"Never before have we had so little time in which to do so much."

4:57 PM.

Stevie's entire body began to tremble. Jacqueline could not determine if it was from anxiety or anger or the weather.

"The only thing we have to fear—"

"—is fear itself," the crowd said along with the loudspeakers.

A communal intake of breath showed the astonishment of everyone present.

"That's the one!" Stevie screamed. *They've found the backdoor to SPAAM!"*

The speakers crackled again. "Children. You will forget all previous commands. You will not go through with your assigned task."

4:58 PM.

"You will receive your reward without finishing your final task. You are to stop immediately. Drop all weapons, now!"

A number of coats opened up. Handguns, a few rifles, and butcher knives appeared.

"Gun!" a few voices yelled in unison.

In a blur of action, nearly 20 percent of those in the gathering jumped on those who had produced the weapons. Those watching from the sidelines moved back as a single body.

4:59 PM.

"My children. You are to stop all actions previously promised to bring your reward. To experience the surge, all you need do is sit down where you are. Do so now!"

The entranced crowd obeyed without hesitation. Both Stevie and Jacqueline gawked openly.

His brainchild, his cerebral offspring, was dying right in front of him.

Her hopes, her dreams were vanishing before her eyes.

The ambulances moved to the Spectrum parking lot and began setting up triage to treat any possible injuries or those suffering any aftereffects of the trance.

5:00 PM.

The carillon rang out its classic Westminster tune.

No one moved.

No violent acts were committed.

Instead, everyone sitting sighed and cheered and laughed and cried.

"Thank you, my children. You have fulfilled your obligations. You no longer need obey these commands."

Although Jacqueline had never heard the exact wording of the subliminal messages, she knew the specifics: where the gatherings would take place, the time of onset. She knew there were backdoor code words, but how could *they* know? Stevie had told her no one knew other than the two of them. They were programmed into the subliminals of each recording . . . but those went by so quickly. No one could hear a sentence transmitted in a nanosecond; a paragraph in a millisecond.

"How did they find out?" Jacqueline spat at Pendleton.

The scientist was without words. He leaned against the cement wall and stared at the dormant groundcover on the other side.

"Sound familiar?" a voice asked directly behind the two Nevada natives.

Jacqueline spun around, almost dropping her camcorder. She yanked the earbud from her ear and, with a feigned, innocent smile stammered, "H—ho—holy cow. You scared me."

Dr. Steven Pendleton froze, refusing or unable to turn around.

Homer and Morgan Winegar glared at Jacqueline with somber, stone faces. Two uniformed law officers with firearms in hand flanked them on either side. None of the four smiled back.

FORTY-NINE

Jacqueline's mind grappled to gain quick purchase of her predicament. Obviously, the Winegars knew her part in the trances. But there was no proof. There couldn't be. It'd all been organized and executed so perfectly. She'd made sure of that. The only one who could point a speculative finger at her was that radio station manager, Dwight Hampton. But they'd only met once. And none of that paperwork had her name on it. She'd interacted with both Winegars but only as a shy, abused girl. She'd said nothing about the trances while in their company.

Stevie held perfectly still, as if thinking no one would see him that way. Would he come to her rescue? Doubtful. *The jerk.* Jacqueline noticed Morgan's glare was especially hateful. *That might work.*

"So, Morgan, did you confront your slimeball husband?" she asked, hoping for some instinctive, feminine, anti-male bonding.

"I sure did," Morgan replied in a monotone.

"Did he fess up to everything?"

"Pretty much."

Crossing her arms defensively across her chest, she spat, "Homer, I still cannot believe the things you made me do. I'm still embarrassed just thinking about them. You took advantage of me, and you took advantage of Morgan. I'm surprised your poor wife is still speaking to you."

"Yeah. Me too," Homer said without emotion.

Jacqueline moved a step closer to Morgan. "If you haven't filed for divorce yet, sweetheart, I recommend you call *my* lawyer," she said with an overabundance of emotion spilling from her sympathetic expression. "He can squeeze water from granite."

"Super. I'd recommend *you* call him immediately," Morgan said with barely restrained bitterness. "You're going to need a good one."

Feigned shock was Jacqueline's best well-rehearsed expression. "What—what are you talking about?"

"Scandia Labs, Tribe's Dingo's Dance energy drink, 'Toad Stomp.' Any of these sound familiar to you?" Homer asked. "If they don't, just ask Dr. Pendleton. He's standing right behind you."

"What?" she replied, looking truly surprised.

Keep playing the chameleon, she told herself. *Admit to nothing. Keep them guessing.*

Steven Pendleton turned around. The look on his face was as good as any recorded confession.

"We'll take that camcorder, if you please," one of the police officers said without a hint of negotiation in his tone.

Jacqueline bit her lip as if straining to quell a torrent of swear words. She held out the palm-sized recorder. The officer had her drop it in a plastic baggie.

"Hello, Dr. Pendleton," Homer said. "I recognize you from your Scandia Labs personnel photo. I wish I could say it's good to meet you."

"You've got nothing on me," the young scientist hissed, trying hard—and failing miserably—to sound fierce.

"Or me," Jacqueline added.

"Really? I've got a stack of evidence from Dr. Ethan Greene in my office that says otherwise," Morgan said calmly. "And we've been behind you long enough to know we've got your voice discussing everything on this camcorder."

In spite of the growing chill, the looming snow clouds, and the crystallizing, turbulent air, Jacqueline's practiced, polished façade melted. She swallowed a choking lump of dread past her suddenly dry throat and turned to face Stevie. "*You* got me into this. You made me drink your toxic elixir and brainwashed me into doing these despicable tasks."

Stevie just brayed a laugh. Her act was good . . . but not very convincing. "You really think they're going to believe that?"

Jacqueline looked into the eyes of her accusers. The nerd who'd promised her millions was right. She glanced at the gathering down below. Even though the tragedy had been averted, there was still a buzz of excitement rising from the crowd. In addition to the emergency services, several people continued to offer aid to those still stunned, bewildered, or frightened.

Jacqueline berated herself for not seeing it sooner. The reason the crowd seemed so large was that not everyone was under the trance. Someone—undoubtedly the Winegars—had positioned people—including Lanh Tran—to try to thwart the final task. If they had not found the disarming code, those stationed throughout the gathering would have done their best to stop any attempted violence.

"Disappointed, Jacqueline? Or do you prefer 'Gypsy'?" Morgan asked.

Jacqueline cursed under her breath then decided it didn't matter and cursed out loud. Screaming each word, frost plumes ejected forcefully past her lips, as if velocity and volume would amplify their offensiveness.

"Is that a confession?" Homer asked.

"You'll get nothing from me," she hissed, still facing the gathering.

One of the officers stepped forward. "Please put your hands behind you back, ma'am. You too, sir," he said to the two.

Both complied without a struggle. The lawman began to read Jacqueline and Stevie their Miranda rights as he fitted both with handcuffs.

As one officer led Jacqueline past Morgan, she stopped and scowled. "I was serious about your husband. He's not who he says he is."

"Why should that concern you?" Morgan asked.

Jacqueline glanced over at Homer. His expression was deadpan, yet challenging. "If I'm going down, so is he."

Morgan turned toward her husband. For Jacqueline's benefit, she said, "It's a good thing I trust you with my life."

* * *

The aftereffects of the final gathering were negligible. No shots had been fired and no stab wounds inflicted. Although the majority of weapons gathered were knives, the number of guns the students had been able to acquire was disturbing. All of those entranced gave their names—most of which were repeat participants—and all checked in with the paramedics for a quick but thorough once-over. A couple of girls still had bruises from the previous week; the rest had nothing more than a few shaken nerves.

Homer and Morgan accompanied the police to the station to testify against Jacqueline and Stevie. Detective Hopkins had all the necessary paperwork filled out in advance. He'd also been able to procure a copy of the airtime contract from Dwight Hampton at the radio station, along with the promise of an affidavit when he picked her out of a lineup.

Hopkins also contacted the Henderson police department and asked them to pick up Ethan Greene as soon as possible. The Winegars promised to keep trying to reach the scientist.

Heading back to Morgan's office, Homer confided, "If Scandia is anything like Pendleton, Dr. Greene may already be dead."

FIFTY

Morgan dialed Dr. Ethan Greene's cell number, praying that he would answer; not only so she could ask him some questions but to confirm that the man was still alive. The phone rang two times before the line connected.

"Dr. Greene."

"Dr. Greene, this is Morgan Winegar from USU. Are you okay?"

"Am I okay?" The man sounded mildly amused. "Why, yes, I'm fine."

Morgan breathed a huge sigh of relief. "Thank goodness. We thought for sure Scandia Labs would put a price on your head for exposing their wrongdoings."

"Hardly," he chuckled. "I'm too well-known around here. Besides, I'm not the one in the limelight. That'd be Gunter Bjorkman, our CEO."

"Same goes for Steven Pendleton. He's up here, behind bars."

"That's good news indeed. So you got my faxes then. I was a bit concerned. Your TA seemed to be . . . distracted. No offense."

"Lanh Tran is a natural multi-tasker, although he doesn't always come across that way. It's so good to hear you're okay. I've been trying to reach you all night."

"Really? That's flattering to say the least. I've been downtown testifying against Bjorkman and his part in this mess. I left my cell phone in the office. Sorry."

"So where's Bjorkman?" she asked.

"He's with the FBI. We were both with them all night, and when we opened his office this morning, we uncovered some pretty interesting stuff, including Bjorkman's approval on the SPAAM project."

"And you?"

"I'm trying to hold things together at the lab. I'm on an exceedingly tight leash with the Feds, but they've pretty much figured out who was masterminding the experiment up there in Utah, and my name's nowhere near it."

"But . . . Dr. Pendleton claims you were involved too."

"Nah. The entire company will be shaken up for some time. The board is looking for a new CEO as we speak. But I have a lot of friends here who've all backed me up on my innocence in this matter. It appears the only ones who had any inkling of the mess were Bjorkman and Pendleton. A few others were associated but with pretty thick blinders on."

"Oh, good. I can't tell you how relieved I am to hear that. And I can't thank you enough for sending the information on Pendleton's experiment when you did. You may have saved over a hundred lives."

"That many?" Ethan exclaimed.

Morgan gave the scientist a brief rundown of everything that had transpired over the past few weeks, including using the backdoor to shut down the last task, and the capture of Stevie and Jacqueline. Ethan listened in silence right up to the end.

"Professor Winegar, I assure you I had no clue what Pendleton was up to until I saw his files. That's why I immediately forwarded them to you. I guess I was just turning a blind eye to his experiments. I suspected they were unethical—perhaps even illegal—but I still can't believe he'd stoop to something like mass murder."

"He's pretty much fessed up to everything already. It's almost as if he still wants credit for his amazing discovery. You know, for all his scientific bluster, he turned out to be a pretty dumb kid. No doubt the man's brilliant, just very misguided."

"You're being too kind."

"Perhaps." Morgan paused before asking her next question, dreading the answer the Scandia researcher might give. "Dr. Greene, I need to ask you a scientific question for the benefit of everyone up here."

"Go ahead."

"How long will the effects of Pendleton's drug last?"

"I don't know. I spent hours poring over Stevie's notes last night. What he uncovered is amazing stuff. I've already applied for permission to study it further—through the proper channels, that is, with FDA approval and all that. It may well lead to significant inroads on addictive behavior in humans.

"As for your question, I'm almost positive a naturally based chemical like SPAAM will eventually break down and be eliminated from the body."

"Almost positive?"

"Yeah. Sorry I can't be more reassuring. That's the nature of biochemical research; most times you can only guess at the end result. Still, you can be certain there will be withdrawal symptoms among those who drank the stuff."

Morgan pondered his answer for a moment before responding. "I'm going to take that as a positive answer."

"Good. That's the way it was meant."

FIFTY-ONE

The Winegars decided to endure a brief jaunt of very cold trick-or-treating to get their minds off the events of the past few days. At home they watched Zachary place his candy in meticulous rows and columns, first according to size, then color, then flavor. Had Homer not intervened, the boy could have gone on for hours.

"Let's pack it up now, son."

"Aw, Daddy."

Watching Homer help Zachary put his sugary plunder into several categorized plastic baggies, Morgan asked, "Do you think the authorities will want to completely shut down Scandia Labs?"

"With the information Dr. Greene gave and his willingness to comply with the investigation, I hope not."

"Any idea what will become of him?"

"Greene? With any luck, just a slap on the wrist. From what he told the FBI, he was only involved with THIQ, not SPAAM."

Morgan scoffed. "Scientists and their silly acronyms."

"Yeah, well, it's better than writing a chemical name that's a paragraph long."

"All done, Mommy," Zachary announced. "See?"

"Very good, sweetheart. You did a great job. Now be sure to brush your teeth extra good, okay?"

"Aw, Mommy," the boy whined.

"No, she's right, little man. If you don't brush your teeth then nasty, ugly bacteria will chew them down to nothing, and you'll be forced to eat nothing but Malt-O-Meal the rest of your life."

Zachary ran to the bathroom howling, "Yucky! Yucky! I'll brush right now."

Morgan snickered. "I'm not so sure that'll help his OCD. He could be in there all night now."

Homer shrugged. "Could be worse."

After a vigorous session with the toothbrush, a potty stop, and evening prayers, Zachary was nestled into bed.

Snuggling next to Homer on the couch, with a fire crackling in the hearth and the lights extinguished, Morgan spoke in hushed tones. "Homer, I . . . I've been thinking a lot about your past. I really don't need to know anything more. I fell in love with who you are now, not who you were back then. And I know you're not supposed to tell anyone anything—"

"Stop," Homer interrupted as he took her hands in his. "I've been thinking about it, too. In fact, it's something that's plagued me ever since we met, and . . . well, it's time I come fully clean."

"Is this going to make me hate you?"

"I hope not. The thing I want you to remember—no, the thing I *need* you to remember—is that you were not part of my . . . my disguise. A vital element of the protection program is being able to move to a new location and start over *completely;* not only with a brand new identity, but with a brand new life, one with zero connections to the past. That's exactly what I did. I had no intention of seeking out a wife. I just got lucky. Blessed. Blessed beyond anything I could have dreamed or imagined."

"Now you're just sucking up," she teased.

"No, I'm not. I'm coming clean. I won't get into details. They're not important. Suffice it to say I worked for a billion-dollar investment firm. They had their hands in so many entities it was hard to keep them straight. That's why they hired me. I've always had a talent with numbers, and they paid me good money to become a laundryman. I could take a million-dollar profit and work it into an infrastructure loss for one of their above-board subsidiaries. The paper trails took so many bumps and turns, including several to and from the Caribbean and South America, that it was nearly impossible to put two and two together. It was fine for a while. I mean, I was never concerned about being a moral pillar of the community, and it *was* only money. But as I looked deeper into the comings and goings of their assets, I realized not all of it was harmless.

"See, I was far enough up the line to access the kind of information that could shut down the company. I mean shut them down hard. Well, one day I did some money laundering for a clandestine research lab in the mountains of Northern California. It was considered a 'speculative' venture, but I learned it involved illegal human drug testing of the creepiest kind. That's when I figured I'd had enough. Just in time, too. A few weeks later the top blew off their operation, and a lot of people went to prison."

"You're kind of a magnet for that stuff," Morgan said in a humorless voice.

"Yeah, apparently. Anyway, I went to the FBI with a four-gig jump drive bulging with incriminating evidence, which they exchanged for a clean slate. The very next day I came up missing. They circulated rumors that my old employer had dumped me somewhere in the Bermuda Triangle, or some such nonsense. I honestly don't know, although I'm sure I could research it out. The thing is, I don't want to. My break from the past is 100 percent complete. I am not that guy anymore. I am Homer Winegar. I have a birth certificate to prove it. My life started over when I moved to Utah, and it truly *began* when I met you in that Laundromat."

Morgan could not stop a tear from coursing down her cheek. Homer wondered if the tear was from sorrow or anger or gratitude. He squeezed her hand and stared plaintively at the fire, but the dancing flames offered no answers in their pop and hiss and flicker.

Morgan wiped her eyes on her sleeve. "Thank you," she whispered in a thick voice.

"Are . . . are we okay then?" he asked with equal emotion.

She nodded vigorously. "I was dreading that you'd feel our meeting was just a convenient coincidence."

"Maybe," Homer admitted after a pause. Then, somewhat philosophically, he continued. "See, having met you, I realize that some things are *meant* to happen. I used to think coincidence was just that: coincidence. I now realize that, in *my* life, coincidence is just

Heavenly Father's way of remaining anonymous. Were you a convenience? Okay, yes—one that was *meant* to be; one that I would not exchange for all the money or fame or power in the world; one that I thank God for every day of my life. That's God's honest truth."

Morgan smiled and snuggled tighter against her husband. "Thank you, Homer. That's just what I needed to hear."

He kissed the top of her head. "Do you still love me then?"

She brought his hand to her lips and kissed it. "Even more than ice cream."

AUTHOR'S NOTES

In writing this novel I wanted to accomplish three things: explain the chemical nature of addiction; explain how the subconscious can influence our actions; and demonstrate the bonding power trust can bring to a marriage.

While the scientific concepts in this novel are all real, they are presented in the extreme purely for entertainment value. Below is a list of some questions that may come up while reading *Altered State*.

Is THIQ a real substance?
Yes. It is an actual byproduct of acetaldehyde found in the brains of alcoholics. THIQ latches onto the body's opiate receptors in much the same way that heroin does and causes a breakdown of opiate receptors. A medical examiner in Texas discovered it by accident. It's a fascinating story that is too cumbersome to include here.

Is SPAAM a real chemical?
No. However, even though SPAAM is a fictional drug created for this novel, it is based on actual chemical and hormonal entities. Apomorphine is a real chemical with many beneficial uses. But, like nearly all medications, it has the potential for abuse. I took brazen artistic license and blended the characteristics of a few known chemicals into SPAAM, including those that affect GABA. (The fact that the name sounds like Spam, a suspicious blend of random pork products, is somewhat coincidental.)

Is grehlin a real appetite-boosting hormone?

Yes. It is currently a hot topic of research. Grehlin is secreted when our stomach is empty, essentially telling us that we are hungry. For reasons we don't understand, in some people grehlin never shuts off, even after a huge meal. That's why many people never feel sated and overeat to an extreme.

Is there such a thing as Asperger's syndrome?

Yes. It is a form of passive developmental disorder that mimics classic autism—with some important differences. Children with AS are typically higher-functioning than those with traditional autism. Additionally, they often have near-normal intelligence and language development, and better social interaction skills. Occasionally, children with AS will exhibit prodigy-like talents in areas such as auditory perception, math, and music.

Is subliminal mind control possible?

Yes . . . to a point. But this area of research remains controversial. The varying aspects of mind control discussed in the novel are accurate, but only as supported by specific studies. There are an equal number of studies that show it is not possible. That is why I chose to combine it with a chemical primer that would facilitate such control. The experiment in which a tachistoscope was used was real, as were the results.

Are energy drinks bad for you?

Possibly. Too much of any substance can be harmful, especially artificial stimulants such as caffeine. The candle nut herb used in Tribe is real and is used by the aborigines as described.

Is "Toad Stomp" a real song?

No. There was a group called Ayers Rock back in the '70s, however; they played a unique blend of jazz/rock fusion mixed with a little R&B. The closest I could find to modern aboriginal music is a group called Nomad.

Were the FDR quotes real?
Yes. Being a great orator, FDR actually has many more citations attributed to him. I chose the ones most applicable to this story.

Are the statues mentioned on the USU campus real?
Yes. There are actually several more. I wish I could have used them all.

Can addiction be overcome?
YES. That's the best message of all. Through alternate chemical intervention and counseling, even the deepest addictions can be conquered. It's never easy, and rarely can it be done on your own—but it *is* worth the effort. If you feel you have any addiction, be it alcohol, drugs (prescription and/or illicit), pornography, gambling, violence—basically anything—I admonish you to seek help from a physician and/or a certified addiction counselor. There are several excellent centers from which to choose. Your doctor or church authority can recommend one if you have questions. A second source (which actually should be your primary source) is your Heavenly Father. Even if you feel you have totally blown your life due to an addiction, I testify that God still loves you and has prepared a way for you to conquer your addiction *and* be forgiven through the Atonement of His Son, Jesus Christ.

—Gregg Luke, R.Ph.

ABOUT THE AUTHOR

 Gregg Luke was born in Bakersfield, California, but spent the majority of his childhood and young adult life in Santa Barbara, California. He served an LDS mission in Wisconsin, then pursued his education in natural sciences at SBCC, UCSB, and BYU. He completed his schooling at the University of Utah, College of Pharmacy. His biggest loves are his family, the gospel, reading, writing, music, singing, science, and nature.

Visit Gregg at www.greggluke.com